In Another World With My Smartphone

Patora Fuyuhara
Illustration·Eiji Usatsuka

IN ANOTHER WORLD WITH MY SMARTPHONE: VOLUME 2
by Patora Fuyuhara

Translated by Andrew Hodgson
Edited by DxS

Original Japanese edition published in 2015 by Hobby Japan
This English edition is published by arrangement with Hobby Japan, Tokyo

Find more books like this one at www.j-novel.club!

President and Publisher: Samuel Pinansky
Managing Editor: Aimee Zink

ISBN: 978-1-7183-5001-4
Printed in Korea
First Printing: February 2019
10 9 8 7 6 5 4 3 2 1

PERPLEXED BY THE SUDDEN VOICE, I STARTED LOOKING AROUND. MOMENTS LATER, I NOTICED A GIRL SITTING ON A RED CHAIR IN FRONT OF THE WINDOW.

"OH? YOU BROUGHT OVER QUITE THE STRANGE GUEST THIS TIME, PAULA."

In Another World With My Smartphone 2

Four beautiful flowers decorated the party hall.

Kokonoe Yae
A SAMURAI GIRL WHO LEFT THE FAR EAST COUNTRY OF EASHEN TO WANDER THE LANDS AND HONE HER SKILLS. SHE BOASTS A SERIOUS, STOIC PERSONALITY, AND TENDS TO POUR HER HEART AND SOUL INTO HER TRAINING. ALSO, SHE EATS A LOT.

Linze Silhoueska
TOUYA SAVED LINZE AND HER SISTER FROM BEING SWINDLED. THOUGH GENERALLY A RESERVED GIRL, SHE CAN SHOW TRUE STRENGTH OF HEART EVERY ONCE IN A WHILE. THE YOUNGER TWIN.

**Yumina
Urnea Belfast**
THE CROWN PRINCESS OF THE
KINGDOM OF BELFAST. POLITE AND
CAREFUL AS SHE IS, YUMINA IS AN
EXEMPLARY MEMBER OF ROYALTY.
THAT BEING SAID, HER ACTIONS CAN
BE SURPRISINGLY BOLD AT TIMES.
SHE'S CURRENTLY ACCOMPANYING
TOUYA ON HIS ADVENTURES
AS HIS FIANCÉE.

Elze Silhoueska

AN ADVENTURER
WHO FIGHTS WITH DUAL
GAUNTLETS. SHE'S THE TYPE
TO PUNCH FIRST, AND ASK
QUESTIONS LATER. THE
OLDER TWIN.

Contents

Area Near the Kingdom of Belfast

The Kingdom
of Lihnea

The Refreese
Imperium

Bern, ◎
The Imperial City

The Regulus
Empire

Melicia
Mountain Range

Gallaria, ◎
Heart of the Empire

The Kingdom
of Belfast

Lake Palette

Alephis, ◎
The Royal Capital

Reflet
◎

The Great
Gau River

The Kingdom
of Mismede

Berge, ◎
Capital of Beasts

N

The Sea of
Trees

A few days had passed, and once Kohaku had finally been freed from cuddle-hell, the tiger suddenly said it wanted to explore the town a little. I decided to tag along, too.

We left the inn and walked down the main street. Once we got out in the open, we decided to head for the marketplace, since there were always loads of different kinds of people around there.

The marketplace always had a bunch of stalls and mats out selling all kinds of things, from food and sundries to clothes or antiques. We walked in among that crowd as I let my eyes wander from stall to stall, idly searching for any good bargains.

«It really is quite crowded here.»

«Well, we *are* in the town center. When you're looking to get something for cheap, this is typically the place everyone comes to.» Kohaku and I were able to converse without other people hearing. A summoner was mentally connected to their contracted beast, and as such, we could communicate our thoughts through something akin to telepathy. I was really glad to learn this, since if people caught me talking to a tiger in the middle of the street they'd probably think I'd lost my mind.

Although Kohaku had taken a cub's form, a tiger was still a tiger, and tigers typically stood out when taken around in public. That said, the most that would ever really happen was people looking on from a distance as though they'd just passed some people filming a scene for a movie or something. Nobody ever overreacted to the sight at all, and every now and then some kids or girls would come up and pat Kohaku on the head.

We had decided that Kohaku should take on the form of a cub when other people were around. Because of that, Kohaku would sometimes make purring noises when being petted, to the great delight of any girls present, leading to further cuddly torture. Just when I'd finally freed my tiger from our own party's female captors, poor Kohaku had to put up with yet more attacks from all directions. Watching the sight made even *me* feel bad…

That said, there really were a lot of people around. I had to make sure I wouldn't get separated from Kohaku. Though we could've just used our telepathy to find each other in no time, it'd still be better if it didn't have to come to that.

While we probably wouldn't have gotten separated anyway, I decided to pick Kohaku up and carry the little fuzzball around. Didn't want the poor thing accidentally getting kicked while weaving in and out of the huge crowd. Kohaku tried to resist at first, but eventually calmed down and rested in my arms.

As we were walking, Kohaku suddenly looked up and to the right, as if catching notice of someone.

«My lord, is that not Yae over there?»

«Hm?» I lined my sight up with Kohaku's, and sure enough, I found Yae crouching down, trying to cheer up a 4-year-old girl who was sobbing away in front of her. They were at the end of the street, out of the way from the hustle and bustle of the crowd.

"Hey Yae, what's up?"

"Touya-dono? And Kohaku, too?" Yae seemed relieved to see us. It was rare to see her make an expression like that. *What's wrong here, I wonder…*

"Who's this girl?"

"I'm not quite sure, but it seems as though she's lost, it does." *A lost kid, huh...* I wasn't surprised considering the size of the crowd. I scanned the crowd from left to right, and suddenly felt that finding this girl's parents could prove to be quite the challenge.

"Excuse me, what's your name?"

"Waah... mommy... I want my mommy... aaah..." No good. She was so upset she couldn't even tell me her name. I had to calm her down if I wanted to find out anything from her.

"I have tried to ask her for her name and personal details, but my attempts have borne no fruit, none at all." Yae frowned as she spoke. *Hmm... gotta make her talk somehow.*

I lifted up Kohaku in my hands and held the tiger cub in front of the crying little girl. The girl was startled into silence for a moment, but her expression quickly twisted into one on the verge of tears once more. I transmitted a mental order to Kohaku.

"What is your name, child?" Kohaku began talking to the young girl. The girl, who had until that point been doing nothing but crying, suddenly stopped at the sight of a talking tiger cub. She blinked and rubbed her eyes several times as if she was trying to make sure she wasn't dreaming.

"What might be your name?"

"...L-Lim..."

"I see. So your name is Lim." The little girl gulped and nodded in response. Alright, the Kohaku distraction plan was a success. Pretty much anyone would be completely taken aback if a white tiger cub started talking right in front of them. Next up, the search begins.

"[Search]: Lim's Family." I cast [Search], which was easily one of my most useful Null spells. It was capable of finding anything I specified, but only within a radius of fifty meters... and this was one

11

of the times it failed me. That meant that the girl's parents weren't anywhere close.

"Did you find anything, then?"

"Nope. Not a trace. All I learned was that they're not anywhere within fifty meters of here." *Hm, what to do... I could always walk around with* [Search] *activated and hope they come within 50 meters of me... Man, the short range on this thing is super inconvenient...*

Oh... there's a thought. I wouldn't be able to tell if someone was a member of Lim's family at a glance. That may have been why my [Search] spell wasn't reacting. The fact that I couldn't tell whether something just wasn't there or if the spell was simply failing to react to it was another one of the spell's shortcomings. I simply couldn't grasp what sort of standards it operated by.

That time I found the poison using my [Search] spell, I don't think I would've been able to identify it as poison at a glance, but had I ingested any of it, I would've been able to tell immediately that I had been poisoned. Why did that cause it to react? That time I went looking for vanilla, too, I could tell that it was what I was looking for because it smelled like vanilla... I simply couldn't detect any pattern to it.

Thinking about it in a very rough sense like that, I could ask the person in question if they were the one I was trying to locate with [Search], and they could lie to me, meaning I wouldn't recognize them. Maybe that was why it wasn't working...

I decided I needed more information, so I motioned to Kohaku once more.

"With whom did you come here?"

"...My mommy."

"What color clothing was your mother... er, your mommy wearing?"

"Umm… they were green." Thanks to Kohaku, we got a lot of information from the girl. Lim's mother had long, light brown hair, was wearing green clothes and a silver bracelet, had blue eyes, and was fairly thin. I had enough information to form a vague image of her in my mind. Now if I saw anyone matching the description, I would probably think "This person could be Lim's mother," or something along those lines. I tried casting the spell once more.

"**[Search]: Lim's Mother.**" …But there were no hits. My efforts were in vain.

"Did it work this time, perhaps?" I shook my head in response. It seemed like the problem really was the hopelessly short range of the spell. It would've been extremely useful if it was the size of, say, the map app as it appeared on my smartphone's screen. Was there anyone who could create a **[Search]** app for me?

…Wait a minute.

My map app, and my **[Search]** *spell… Should I try? Well… it's worth a shot at least.* I pulled my smartphone out of my pocket.

"**[Enchant]: [Search].**" I attempted to infuse the **[Search]** spell into my phone using **[Enchant]**. A tiny light left my fingertip and flowed into my smartphone's screen. Only one way to find out if it worked… I fired up my map app and focused it on the area nearby with myself at the center. I zoomed out so that the map covered not only the marketplace, but all of Reflet, then entered the words "Lim's mother" into the search bar. A single arrow appeared on the screen indicating that my target was located there.

"Wow, it actually worked!" Lim, who had been cuddling Kohaku, jumped back a little at my sudden outburst, but it didn't seem like I'd frightened her to tears, which was good.

I stood up and lightly patted Lim on the head.

"Let's go get you back to your mommy, yeah?" Off we went to the place the map pointed to.

"Mommyyy!"

"Lim!" I felt an indescribable sense of relief at seeing the little girl reunited with her mother after several hours of being lost. We found Lim's mother at the town guard's station. It was something like a police box, I figured. Which, honestly… meant the whole thing would've been over if we'd just made the sensible decision to take the girl to one of the town's guards and explain that she was lost. It had taken longer than it should have to sort the ordeal out, but I managed to gain quite the useful little thing from it.

Yae and I bowed our heads slightly as we saw off the mother and daughter, Lim happily waving her hand as they walked away.

"Hey Yae, there's something I wanna test out. Could you play along with me for a bit?"

"Hm…? I do not mind, not at all, but what might it be…?" I took Yae to Aer's cafe, Parent, and then asked her a number of questions while we placed our orders.

The questions were about Yae's home. I asked her to describe to me everything about its appearance from the outside, the layout of the rooms, how the family dojo was set up, all as detailed as possible. I also learned that they had a pet dog, that there were sakura trees in their garden, and even of the scratches on a wooden post where Yae would compare her height with her older brother.

Having derived what I figured would be enough information, I fired up my map app and input the [Search] spell, trained fully on Yae's house. In response, a small arrow showed up pointing to the far east of the continent, at a specific location in Eashen.

I zoomed in on where the arrow was pointing. Oedo, in Eashen. Somewhere in the east of that area… A place called Hashiba.

"Okay, Yae, tell me if I'm right or not. Is your house in a place called Hashiba, in the east of Oedo? Somewhere with a shrine nearby."

"That's absolutely correct, it is, but... how could you possibly know this much, I must ask?" Yae gave me a startled look, and I learned that the experiment was a success. I had gained a search engine that functioned with a global range. Finally, a more useful application of that spell.

I had never been able to locate people or animals or the like on my map before, but my map app had been upgraded with a brand new function. Still, I needed to know quite a lot about what I was searching for in order to narrow the results down with any degree of precision.

When I explained all of those facts to Yae, she asked me if I could test it out by searching for her brother. I asked several questions about her brother and learned that he had a peculiar scar on his cheek, which made narrowing the results down pretty easy.

"Looks like he's in the dojo. He's moving around a lot in there, so he might be in the middle of a match."

"That very much sounds like brother, indeed." I handed over the smartphone to Yae so she could see the screen better, and she smiled as she gazed at the little arrow that was her brother.

"My brother is a rather gentle person by nature, you see, but he becomes completely different when holding a sword, he does. He gets so entranced with his swordplay that he has, on occasion, completely forgotten to eat anything at all, he has." Yae talked away quite happily about her brother. All the while, she continued to gaze at his little arrow on the screen with a look that said she wanted to see him again.

"Sounds like you're really close to your big brother, huh?"

"...Indeed, that may be so. I do love my strong, kind, good-natured older brother, I do." I could tell even from how she spoke that Yae must've been very close to him.

"Come to think of it, you somewhat resemble my older brother, you do, Touya-dono. For instance, your gentle attitude and kind-hearted nature."

"Well, it's quite the honor to be compared to the big brother you love so much." I shrugged and drank my water. There was no way my swordsmanship was on the level of Yae's big brother, so she must have just meant that I had a similar personality to him.

"That's correct. You are very much like the older brother I love so... much...?" Yae drifted off mid-sentence. She raised her face from the smartphone's screen and met my eyes with her own. Her face turned beet-red in an instant and she suddenly grew all flustered.

"I-It is not like that, yes?! I meant only to say that Touya-dono resembles my older brother, not that I love you as I do my older brother, b-but that does not mean I dislike you, it does not, only that, umm... yes, right! My older brother is family, and I love him like family! It's a familial kind of love... Love?! N-Not in that sense, of course, not at all! You understand, of course, yes?!" Yae suddenly spewed forth something resembling human language, but I couldn't make heads or tails of what she was saying. I simply thought that it was nice that she loved her big brother like that.

"Thanks for waiting. I've brought your order!" Someone brought out a large tray covered in a great amount of light foodstuffs, most of which Yae had ordered, and set it down before us. Yae, her face still bright red, began wordlessly munching away at the snacks in front of us. She really did go through food at an astonishing pace...

I figured she was probably just embarrassed to have found herself admitting to someone else that she loved her big brother dearly.

I decided to keep my stirring suspicions of her brother complex to myself, though, in order to save her further embarrassment.

I returned to the Silver Moon Inn and went straight back to my room. There was something I wanted to try out.

I had learned that I could enchant specific spells into the apps on my phone, so it was likely that I could do more with that.

For example, the spell **[Long Sense]**, which allowed me to project all five of my senses across great distances. What if I were to enchant that into my phone's camera app?

"[Enchant]: [Long Sense]." I tried testing it out. When I fired it up, what filled the camera was not what was on the other end of its lens, but instead a perfect capture of what I was seeing with my own field of vision. I tried manipulating the field of vision it reflected by moving my own "sight" into the room next door. I sent my vision further yet until it reached Linze's room. Linze herself wasn't there. The room appeared to be vacant. Just then I remembered her saying that she was going shopping with Elze.

Gazing down at the smartphone's screen with my physical body, I could see Linze's room on the camera. It was a weird feeling, having two sets of eyes trained on the same place. It was like looking at something in a game displayed on both an upper and lower screen. My real eyes and my projected eyesight.

I pressed the button on my phone to take a picture... and it worked. Didn't expect that. The photo that the camera had taken was of the inside of Linze's room.

I could now take clear photos of things from great distances away. I could even sneak my vision in and take photos of the inside of a perfectly locked room. In fact, it was highly likely that I could record videos using this method, too.

Right on that note, I heard a door opening and focused my vision toward it. Linze had returned. That probably meant that Elze was back, too.

While my thoughts idly drifted in that direction, Linze began taking her clothes off. She removed her top and started unbuttoning her blouse. Her beautiful, pale skin suddenly filled the whole of my vision.

W-Whoa there, hold on a sec?! Not good, very not good! I should've noticed sooner, but all I've done with this spell is turn myself into a peeping tom! I shut off my [**Long Sense**] as quickly as I could react.

That was a close one... Any longer and I would've been able to see... everything...? Darn, it really was so close, too... No! No no no, no! If anyone ever found out about that incident, I'd lose everyone's trust right away. I had to avoid that at all costs. Trust was hard enough to gain the first time around, but losing it once would only make it even harder to gain back. I made the right decision...! At least, I liked to believe so. *No, wait a minute... Even if I'd just kept watching like that, it's not like anybody would have found out... Right...? Hmm...*

"...Touya, are you in?"

"Y-Yes?! Wh-Whatever could be the matter?!" My internal conflict was interrupted by Linze's voice and a couple of knocks from the other side of my room's door. I hurriedly shoved my smartphone back into my pocket, then opened the door slowly and Linze's face came peeking through. She was wearing different clothes now.

"Ah...? Is something the matter?"

"N-Not at all! Why, whatever might have given you that idea?! N-Now that's cleared up, can I help you with shomeshing?" I bit my tongue. I *really* needed to calm myself down.

"Today, at an antique store, I found this and bought it, and umm..." Linze presented a rolled up object to me. It was some kind of wrapped wooden tube containing a parchment. I looked it over, and it was written in a language I'd never seen before.

"So, what is it?"

"I believe it's a magic scroll, but it's written in Ancient Magic Script, so I can only read a small part of it..." Ah... that explained why she brought it to me.

First, I took an empty glass from atop a table and some silver coins from my wallet. Next, I cast [**Modeling**] on the items and transformed them into a pair of glasses. I used my magic to enchant the glasses with the ability to read Ancient Magic Script. Thus, I completed the process of creating my Perfect Translation Glasses.

The glasses that I had made for Charlotte before were made to read Ancient Spirit Script, meanwhile the pair I had made for Linze were to read Ancient Magic Script. I had no idea what the difference was, but I was just the guy casting the spells, so I didn't have to know what they were for.

Anyway, I handed the translation glasses over to Linze. She put them on, and they suited her so well that I pictured her as some kind of scholarly student. She looked really cute wearing glasses. Now fully equipped, the young scholar turned her sights to the magic scroll.

"Ah...! This is... incredible! I'd heard about it before, but seeing it myself is completely different!" Linze spoke with great surprise as she devoured every last letter on the scroll in front of her.

"What's it say?"

"It appears to be the record of a spell of ancient magic. A Water type spell... called [**Bubble Bomb**]... an offensive spell, it seems...?" Linze let out a few puzzled groans as she continued to read through the scroll. Seemed I'd come to her rescue. I still felt a little guilty about having peeked in on her while she was changing, but this was probably a good step toward making up for that.

Having gone over the scroll, Linze insisted that she try out the spell as soon as possible, but it was already quite late, so I told her I'd tag along the next day and got her to give up on it for the night. The minute Linze left, I whipped out my smartphone and deleted the photo I'd taken of her room. Better to dispose of the evidence while I still could. I definitely didn't need the title of Peeping Tom on my head.

Now that I think about it... [**Apport**] *for theft,* [**Long Sense**] *for peeping,* [**Gate**] *for housebreaking, and now an enchanted camera app for voyeuristic photography... I seem to be accumulating a lot of Crime-Elemental magic as of late...*

I decided that from then on, I would practice my dubious skills in moderation.

The next day, I went with Linze to the eastern forest. I was able to use [**Gate**] since it was somewhere we'd already been before. I recalled that there was a wide open area inside the woods, so we set that as our destination. That place was perfect for magic training, so long as it wasn't Fire magic since we didn't want to risk starting any forest fires.

We made our way through the woods and came out into the clearing. Linze took out the scroll and read it over carefully a number of times with the translation glasses, before preparing her silver wand and concentrating her magic.

"Come forth, Water! Ballistic Bubbles: [Bubble Bomb]!" Several small balls of water appeared around the end of Linze's wand, but they all fell lifelessly to the ground. Seemed like her attempt had failed.

She prepared her wand once more and tried chanting the spell again.

"Come forth, Water! Ballistic Bubbles: [Bubble Bomb]!" Again, little balls of water gathered around the end of her wand, and again they simply fell to the ground. Another failure. Well, it *was* ancient magic we were talking about. I had a feeling it probably wasn't so easy to get the hang of.

Linze read through the scroll again before making another attempt at it, but it only led to yet more failure.

She tried the same thing over and over, and each time little balls of water would form in the air, move ever so slightly, and then fall to the ground. A string of failed attempts.

After ten attempts, Linze became unsteady on her feet, falling down on one knee shortly after. I rushed over to her to help support her upright.

"Linze, you okay?!"

"...I-I'm fine, I'm only... running low on magic... I'll be... better after... a little... rest..." Linze was spacing out as she explained the situation to me. So this was what having zero MP was like. There was no way I could just leave her in that condition.

"...Umm, T-Touya...?!" I picked up the dizzy Linze and carried her under my arm while I opened up a [Gate]. It looked like she was hurt somewhere, since her body stiffened up and her face burned bright red. I just had to have her bear with it for a little while.

We returned to the back garden of the Silver Moon, and I carried Linze upstairs to her room. I set her down in her bed and noticed that her face was still bright red, so I put my hand to her head to make sure she hadn't come down with a fever. *I sure hope she's okay.*

"...Ha, hahh...!"

"Looks like you don't have a fever, at least. Just stay right there, I'm gonna go get Elze." I called Elze in from the room next door and had her remove Linze's armor for her. There was no way I could've touched all over Linze's body myself, even if it was with good intentions.

I left Linze in Elze's care after that. Having seen her practice until her magic ran completely dry, I couldn't decide whether she was simply taking her magic very seriously or whether she was struggling for dear life just to get by. There was that time I first met Charlotte, too. Was that just how mages were in this world? At the very least, there appeared to be a fair few among their ranks with such straightforward dispositions. Saying they gave it their all was just another way of putting it.

The next day, Linze was back to normal. I learned then that once someone had run out of magic, they'd usually fully recover after a day's rest.

"...S-Sorry for causing you trouble yesterday!" Linze apologized to me, but I didn't feel she'd done anything that warranted an apology. Just like the previous day, we headed out into the forest so that Linze could practice trying to learn her new spell.

Linze tried and she failed, and she tried and she failed. I kept watch on her from a distance, and made her stop after her ninth failure. Any more and she'd end up in the same state as last time.

"Let's take a break for a bit."

"...Okay." I handed a flask of cold tea over to Linze.

"Feel like you're getting the hang of it?"

"...Not in the slightest. When casting a spell, the end result is greatly influenced by your knowledge of it, which makes it a challenge to learn spells I've never seen in action before..." In other words, she couldn't form a clear picture of the spell in her mind because she didn't know how it was supposed to look.

We rested there for an hour, but her magic didn't recover much and Linze was down again after two more failed attempts at the spell. Following that, we called it quits for the day.

Linze kept practicing and practicing in the same manner for the next few days. Every single day until her magic was on the brink of exhaustion. It took about an hour of non-stop casting for Linze's magic to reach its limits, leaving us taking breaks for the rest of the time. Things weren't proceeding very smoothly at all.

"You're really giving it your best, huh, Linze? Even after all those failed attempts, you haven't even thought about throwing in the towel."

"I'm... clumsy when it comes to things... like this... Only by doing the same thing... over and over... can I finally acquire any new spells. It's always been this way, so you don't have to worry about me." Linze spoke with a smile. She was a strong girl. Whatever didn't kill her only made her stronger. She understood fully well that it was important not to give up if you ever wanted to make any real progress with anything.

Even so, there had to be a more efficient way of going about things. Like, a way to let Linze make more attempts at the spell before she ran out of energy, or something along those lines... Hrmmm... I decided to consult Charlotte about it, since she was apparently the best mage in the country.

I stopped Linze right before her magic ran out for the day and took her back to the inn. Once there, I asked Yumina to tag along while I opened up a new [Gate] and went off to the castle to meet Charlotte. Without Yumina by my side, it was hard to even walk around inside the castle… Apparently they took me for a suspicious individual…

We found Charlotte in the castle's research tower, but for some reason she had bags under her eyes. She told us she hadn't been sleeping much recently. Even so, she heard me out and even came up with a solution to our problems. In exchange, however, she made me promise to help out with her research when I next had the time…

The next day, I went to the eastern forest with Linze yet again. And once more, Linze tried and failed to cast her new spell. Recognizing that her magic was about to reach its limit, Linze decided herself that it was time to call it a day. That was my cue.

"Linze, come here for a second."

"Hm…? What is it?" Linze stood in front of me, and I grasped both of her hands in mine.

"H-H-Huh?! Wh-What's going on…?"

"Calm down. Just chill out."

"Ch-Chill myself?!"

"Umm… it's a figure of speech. It means relax a little." I calmed down the panicking Linze and focused my magic, casting the incantation for the non-elemental spell I had learned about from Charlotte the other day. My hands began glowing with a warm light.

"[Transfer]."

"H-Huh?!" The light left my hands and sunk into Linze's, to which she reacted with a start. I took that as a sign that it had worked properly.

"My magic… has completely recovered. But, in an instant…? How…?" All thanks to my new Null spell, [**Transfer**]. It allowed me to share my own magic reserves with other people. There were apparently a few people who could use this one, with one such person being Charlotte's old mentor.

From what Charlotte had told me, she would be made to practice her spells until her magic ran out completely, only to have it recovered, and then made to practice to the brink of collapse once more. That mentor of hers had to have been a monster in disguise.

I wasn't one to talk, though, since I was about to put Linze through the same. Though unlike Charlotte's old mentor, I wouldn't be forcing her into it.

I only just then recalled the magical toll I'd been paying to keep Kohaku materialized in this world, but I was able to fully recover Linze's magic for even less than that. Basically, what this meant was that even doing both things at once was well within the range of my magic's natural recovery rate. Though that didn't mean Linze had a particularly small capacity for magic, but was rather an indication that my own magic was so monstrous.

All in all, it was a good thing that Linze was now able to practice her magic without fear of collapsing anytime soon.

"Come forth, Water! Ballistic Bubbles: [Bubble Bomb]!" Linze spent the next several hours after that trying to master the spell. I was amazed at her perseverance. Still, while we had covered the problem of magical exhaustion, there was nothing I could do for physical fatigue.

I made her take a break for her own well-being.

"It really is, difficult… I just can't seem to grasp the nature of this spell…"

"That so…" Ancient magic was turning out to be as difficult as I'd expected. Since there were hardly any people who still used it, there were no real examples to follow. All Linze could do was try to solidify her own mental image of the spell until it worked.

"…If only I at least knew what [**Bubble Bomb**] meant…"

"…Come again?" I sounded like a total idiot, but Linze's words threw me for a loop for a second. *Huh? She doesn't know what the spell's name means?*

"You want to know what [**Bubble Bomb**] means?"

"Eh? Well, yes. There is a meaning to the name of every spell. For example, the [**Fire**] part from **Fire Storm** means to create flames, and…"

"Whoa whoa whoa, no, hold up a sec." What did that mean? The spell's name was being translated… too literally? The words themselves were being used without regard for whether the person reading it knew what they even meant? I borrowed the scroll from Linze for a moment and cast [**Reading**] on it… I saw the words for "Bubble Bomb"… but it was written in katakana… Well, that sure explained a lot.

So they'd see a spell name like [**Fireball**], but… they had no idea what it actually meant. Similarly you would have to understand the meaning behind the different shapes among the spells. [**Fire Arrow**], [**Fireball**], and [**Fire Storm**] all shared the word [**Fire**], so it was safe to say they could group the spells and guess the effect based on that even without understanding the words. But even if you could tell from the names that they were all fire related, that didn't help with picturing the shapes of each individual spell.

So what did that mean? That there were a bunch of people running around yelling the names of spells that they'd just sort of learned without really understanding how they worked? It all seemed just… a bit too strange for me. People would talk about these spells all the time, but to them they were just using words and phrases that were completely alien? When Elze used [**Boost**] she didn't know the spell name was about increasing her own strength? They all seemed to have roughly figured it out, at least, but only through sheer brute force methods. *Well, I guess it is English, after all... Dear God, please fix your translations to convey meaning as well, rather than just directly converting the words.*

...Was the image of a bubble bomb just that hard to grasp over here? I mean, sure, they weren't exactly common daily words back home, but still, it shouldn't be that hard to picture...

"What's the matter...?"

"Ah, nothing... er, about that spell... **[Bubble]** means like a watery kind of foam, and **[Bomb]** means well uh... bomb, yeah? You know, kaboom and stuff."

"...What's a bomb, exactly?"

"Eesh, well, uh, it's an object that blows up. You know, like that **[Explosion]** spell you can cast." Linze sat and thought over my words in silence. After a while, she raised her head and readied her wand to take another shot at it.

"Come forth, Water! Ballistic Bubbles: [Bubble Bomb]!" A single lump of water... or rather, a round ball like a soap bubble appeared floating just in front of Linze's wand.

The bubble had a diameter of about twenty centimeters. It looked like Linze could control the bubble by concentrating on it. She let it drift around in mid-air for a while before pointing it at a single tree which she bumped it into.

The next instant, the tree burst into splinters with a deafening roar. I could only sit and watch in dumbfounded amazement.

Linze just seemed pleased to have gotten it to work.

"...I did it..." **[Bubble Bomb]**, *huh... one hell of an ancient spell.* It packed a serious punch.

Linze tried it out again. This time five bubbles appeared, then a sixth. She sent all of the bubbles flying toward different trees. The moment the bubbles made contact with the trees, it triggered a series of violent explosions mowing down a chunk of the forest before our very eyes.

This spell was beginning to terrify me already... Meanwhile, Linze dashed over to me and bowed her head.

"I was only able to master this spell thanks to your help, Touya. Thank you very much!"

"Nah, I'd say it was your own efforts that led up to this. I only helped out a little right at the end." I really wasn't used to being thanked by people for every little thing. I was more impressed with how Linze refused to give up on learning the spell no matter how much the experience drained her in the process. She struck me as the hardworking type who took things one step at a time, starting with what she knew and building on that with her own efforts.

I was happy to have learned something new about Linze. Feeling that our efforts had been duly rewarded, I opened up a [Gate] to take us back to the Silver Moon.

"Hmm... what am I gonna do about this...?" Elze seemed troubled. She sat at a table in the dining room, looking at her favorite metallic gauntlets. Those gauntlets were heavily damaged from a fight the day prior.

It was all thanks to a particular encounter we had gone through the day before. We'd ended up having to fight a bunch of Gargoyles: monsters with stone bodies.

We had gone to apprehend a group of thieves for a guild quest, and among them was someone proficient in Dark-type magic.

The Gargoyles were this person's contracted familiars. It became a tough fight for us when those devil-shaped stone monsters surrounded us from all sides. They were extremely hard, so swords didn't work against them at all. They also resisted magic, and arrows bounced right off them. Elze was the only one of us capable of dealing any significant damage against them.

Once we had some breathing room, Linze was able to start shooting off her larger-scale destructive spells like [**Explosion**] and [**Bubble Bomb**], which I used as cover to charge in and cast [**Paralyze**] on the summoner. Once we'd made it out safely, we took the thieves and their mage friend and turned them in to the royal knights.

We cleared the quest, but Elze's gauntlets were badly damaged in the process.

"Guess I'll just have to buy a new pair…"

"You probably should, yeah. I could restore the shape of those ones by casting [**Modeling**] on them, but I don't think they'd hold out very long with a quick patch-up job like that."

"This sucks… These were the best gauntlets I've ever used…" Elze seemed really down about it. *It's always sad when something you like breaks, regardless of the reason.*

"Gonna go look for new ones at the Eight Bears Weapon Shop?"

"I took a look earlier. Barral said they won't have anything like that in stock for at least another five days." That was a fairly long time to be without weapons for an adventurer. You might think that gauntlets shouldn't be that hard to come across when there were whole suits of armor available for purchase, but gauntlets made as weapons required strengthening in different parts. There wasn't really much demand for those types, so fewer places stocked them.

People like Elze, whose primary weapons were their own two hands and martial arts knowledge applied by way of extreme close range weapons like battle gauntlets, were collectively referred to as brawlers. There weren't many fistfighters in Belfast. The demi-human Kingdom of Mismede was a different story, however. Since their population was primarily beastmen, whose physical prowess was generally well above that of humans from birth, it made a lot of sense.

"Touya, take me to the capital. I can't wait five days for new weapons!" She really didn't need to rush herself, but I didn't particularly mind. Elze was the type to move almost reflexively when she came up with an idea. On the other hand, Linze was the type to knock on a strong stone bridge before crossing it just to make sure. Given the same situation, Elze would sooner dash across it faster than it got the chance to collapse. That was just how those sisters were.

"If we're going to the capital anyway, there was this store called Berkut... I remember seeing an enchanted 'Gauntlet of Demi-God Strength' there." Berkut was the name of the shop I'd bought my enchanted white coat from. This coat was enchanted to offer resistance to all elemental magic that the wearer was proficient in — which, in my case, meant all of them. The catch was that it reduced the wearer's resistance to any elements that they weren't proficient in — in my case, none of them. It was a real steal.

"What's this about a Demi-God gauntlet?"

"I dunno, something about a muscle-enhancing enchantment on it, I think."

"Well, now you've got my attention!" Elze looked at me with new life in her eyes, grabbed me by the hand, and dragged me out to the inn's back garden.

"Okay, let's go! C'mon, no time like the present!"

"Hold your horses! Do you even have any money on you?!"

"I withdrew some from the guild earlier. Now let's go!" This girl really did take action the moment something sprang to mind!

I remember thinking to myself that it wouldn't hurt for her to slow down a little sometimes...

"Hello, and welcome to Berkut." We were greeted by the same girl who had served me the last time I came to this shop. Unlike last time, though, she didn't ask for any form of ID. If she really remembered me from that one time we met, then that was pretty incredible customer service.

She must have judged at a glance that Elze was with me, because Elze wasn't asked for any ID, either. Elze herself cast her gaze all around the store, evidently surprised by how high-class the place was. *Come on, it's not exactly amazing enough to drop your jaw at...*

"What can I help you with today?"

"Right, er, the last time I was here I saw a gauntlet on display, something about Demi-God strength? You wouldn't happen to still have that, would you?"

"I'm very sorry, I'm afraid we sold that item some time ago..." That was a shame. Elze let out a dissatisfied groan when she heard the news. Just went to show that enchanted items could only warm shelves for so long unless there was some kind of odd quirk or two about them like with my coat.

"Are you searching for arm guards?"

"Sort of. We're actually looking for attack-oriented gauntlets." Since they were a type primarily designed for punching rather than guarding, they were technically weapons, but at the end of the day gauntlets were still primarily classified as defensive equipment. It wouldn't be strange for an armor shop to stock them. If anything, it would make more sense than looking for them in a weapon shop.

"Attack-oriented gauntlets, correct? We do have some other available pairs of enchanted gauntlets, if you would like to see them."

"Oh, you have other enchanted gauntlets? Yes, please let us see them."

"Understood. Right this way, please." The lady said that and then led us toward the back of the store. Right around the place where I'd found my coat, actually.

She took two pairs of gauntlets down and placed them on the countertop.

One pair was a beautiful pair of streamlined, metallic green gauntlets.

The other was a set of angular, red-and-gold colored gauntlets.

"These gauntlets here are enchanted with a type of wind magic. They will blow away any incoming arrows or other ranged attacks. Unfortunately, they do not block magic attacks, but still offer fairly high magical resistance." The employee explained the pair of metallic green gauntlets to us. Physical attack-blocking enchantments sounded pretty useful. It was a shame they wouldn't block magic attacks, but high magic resistance was still pretty good.

"This pair here, on the other hand, is capable of storing up the wielder's magic before unleashing it in one extremely powerful attack. It takes time for the magic to accumulate within the gauntlets, but they're also enchanted with a hardening spell, so they're unlikely to break even with heavy use." Next up she explained the red-and-gold gauntlets. Unlike the metallic green ones, these ones seemed to place much more emphasis on raw strength. By the sound of things, they also let you use something like a "Focus Punch" move you might see in video games.

Basically, the choice came down to one of attack or defense. It was a difficult decision. I preferred to tighten my defenses and keep myself safe long enough to come up with a strategy to defeat the enemy, so I'd have gone with the metallic green pair, but knowing

Elze, she seemed more likely to go for the red-and-gold pair that emphasized pure offensive power.

"I'll take both sets."

"Huh?!" I couldn't hold back my surprise when, in contrast to my trying to weigh the merits and demerits of each pair, Elze simply skipped having to make that choice altogether.

"You're really buying both pairs?"

"Well, they both seem useful. If I mix and match, I can get the best of both worlds."

"Sure, I guess, but then what happens to the leftover mismatched pair?"

"I'll keep them as spare, duh. There's always a chance I could break one of them like what happened with my old pair." Elze made a good point. As long as they were being used as weapons and not just armor, there was no telling when they might get damaged or broken. I was concerned about the spare pair being on opposite hands, what with people generally being more comfortable throwing punches with their dominant hand, but Elze told me not to worry about that.

To begin with, her fighting style didn't place preference on one hand over the other. In boxing terms, she would've been what was known as a switch-hitter.

"Very well, please equip each pair and let me know if anything feels out of place. I'll make any necessary adjustments for you."

"Thanks, but they feel fine to me as-is." Elze tried on each pair of gauntlets and confirmed that both sets were comfortable enough on her hands.

"Well then, this green pair is fourteen gold coins, and this red-and-gold pair is seventeen gold coins." Thirty one gold in total. Three million, one hundred thousand yen, huh. They were pretty expensive… Or, wait, was that cheap for two pairs of enchanted weapons…? This shop never failed to toss my sense of monetary value right out the window.

"…Touya."

"What's up?"

"…Could you lend me one gold? I came up a little short."

"This is why I told you to make sure you had enough money before we came here…" I took one gold coin out of my wallet and gave it to Elze.

She paid for the gauntlets with three platinum coins and one gold coin. She got the gauntlets placed in bags, but they were huge and bulky so I ended up carrying them for her. Seemed that the man was naturally expected to carry the lady's bags in this world, too…

"Thank you for your patronage, we hope to see you again." The employee lady saw us off as we left Berkut behind us.

"Guess I should've expected the capital to have a good selection of equipment, even though it did turn out a teeny tiny bit more expensive than I'd planned for." Elze seemed pleased with her purchase as she walked alongside me. I sort of understood the feeling of having found exactly what you went looking for at the shops.

Unsurprisingly, though, the four gauntlets really were heavy. I looked around for an alley so that I could open up a [Gate] to take us back to the inn.

"Elze, let's find an alley somewhere so I can—" I turned my head to talk to Elze, but she was gone.

"Elze?" I turned around to look for Elze and saw her standing in front of a shop a fair ways back. She was looking at something in the window. *What could've hooked her attention like that?* I walked back up to Elze and peeked over her shoulder to see what it was. Hoho, so that was it.

A black top adorned with white frills, and a large ribbon on the chest. Plus, a black mini-skirt with three frilled layers.

It reminded me of a goth-loli style dress, with slight differences.

Elze simply stood there, completely entranced by it.

"...You want it?"

"Huh? Whawah?! T-Touya?!" She drew away from me with a bright red face like I'd just given her the fright of her life. What was with that reaction?

"Err, uhm, th-this is... yeah! For Linze! I thought that Linze would look really good in it! She seems like she'd like these types of clothes, doesn't she?! Unlike me, of course! Hahaha!" The moment Elze opened her mouth, she started rambling. Seemed like she was always thinking of her little sister.

"I think it'd suit you just as well as it would Linze, though."

"Wha...?!" Elze's face turned even redder, and she started flapping her lips like a fish out of water. *Seriously, calm down.* Why was she acting so weird, anyway?

"What are you talking about? It'd look way better on Linze than it would on me..."

"Y'think so? You're both cute enough to pull it off. You *are* twins."

"C-C-Cute...?! What are you saying all of a sudden?!" Elze's fist crashed into my side with a painful thud. *Augh! That really hurt, you know!*

"I was only saying... that you'd look good... in these clothes, too..."

I explained myself to Elze while clutching my aching side. Looking closely, I noticed that she had broken out in a cold sweat.

"There's no way an outfit like this would suit me..."

"I'm telling you, it'd look great on you."

"You don't need to flatter me. I know fully well what kind of outfits I could or couldn't pull off."

"Now see here, you…" Why was she trying so hard to deny it? I felt like she didn't think I was being sincere with her, even though I honestly did think she'd look great in that outfit. The fact that she was putting up so much resistance to the idea started to annoy me, even.

"For one thing, I'm not the type of person to wear clothes like that in the first place, and…"

"If you won't believe me, then fine! We'll just have to go in and get them to let you try it on!"

"Huh?! Wait…! Touya?!" I grabbed her by the hand and half-dragged her into the shop. I got the lady at the counter to bring the clothes over from their display in the window, and then forced them into Elze's hands and led her to the changing rooms.

"Hang on a second! What are you thinking?!"

"Look, we've already come this far. Just get in there and try those clothes on. Trust me." I drew the curtain closed from outside and went to take a look around the rest of the shop. I killed some time browsing through the belts and accessories they had. Before too long, Elze timidly drew the curtain open.

"Very nice." Elze looked fairly different from usual in those clothes.

She actually looked pretty great in that goth-loli style outfit, especially with her long silver hair. *See? I knew I was right. Not just anyone can pull that kind of look off.*

"See…? I told you! I-I told you it doesn't suit me at all…"

"*Huuuh?!* How can you even still *say* that?!" By that point, I was at my wits' end trying to convince her, so my voice rose in pitch a bit. Her self-confidence was remarkably low. How hard was she squinting to think that she looked anything but amazing dressed like that? *Now that I've come this far... I'm not gonna back down until you give up and see some sense!*

"Like I said, it looks great on you. Don't you think so, ma'am?!"

I turned to the lady at the counter.

"I agree. I think it looks lovely on you, miss." This time I even got the shop employee to chime in along with me. Hell, the changing room even had a mirror in it. Had Elze completely overlooked that fact before stepping out, or what?

"Y-You really think so...?" Elze blushed, pinched the front of the skirt in her fingers, and did a little twirl. It really did look great on her. She was adorable.

Right then... I went to talk with the employee.

"Excuse me, we'll take these clothes."

"What?!" I paid for the clothes without giving Elze a chance to resist. Three silver, pretty expensive for regular day-to-day clothes.

"Touya, wait a minute! I wasn't planning on actually buying these!"

"You're not buying them, *I* am. And I'm giving them to you as a present." I wasn't about to let Elze leave without buying those clothes when she looked so great in them. Plus I wanted everyone else to see how cute she looked, too. I got a paper bag from the counter, and gave it to Elze for her to put her old clothes in.

We left the shop, and Elze bashfully raised her head to thank me.

"Thanks..."

"No problem. Now let's get back so we can show off your new clothes to everyone else!"

"Huh?! No, wait, that's maybe a bit too embarrassing for me...!" I grabbed the now-dressed-up Elze by the hand and set off running.

The other girls all complimented Elze when they saw her wearing her new outfit. *See? I knew I wasn't wrong. Everyone else agrees, too.*

There was only one issue. When the girls learned that I had bought the clothes for Elze as a gift, they suddenly displayed slightly more mixed feelings on the matter. In the end, it was decided that I was to buy new clothes for each of the girls in the name of fairness.

...Seriously, why do these things keep happening to me?

A while later...

"It's a letter from my father. He says to read this and head over to the royal palace immediately." A letter arrived at the Silver Moon, delivered by a horse-drawn carriage. Yumina explained what it was after looking it over. *Something's giving me a bad feeling here... but I guess I can't just ignore it.*

"What does it say, then?"

"In gratitude and recognition of how Touya Mochizuki handled the incident some time ago, I would like to bestow a noble title upon him."

"A title?!" Elze and the others raised their voices in surprise. *Oh, so it's that, then... Well, I'm not entirely surprised it came to this.*

It makes sense that the one engaged to Princess Yumina should be one of noble lineage. Given that her engagement hadn't yet been announced to the public, they were likely arranging things behind the scenes in order to project the proper image for me when I was finally revealed to the population.

"Hey, uh, can I refuse the title?"

"Yes, you can refuse if you truly wish. I merely ask that you formally refuse it in person."

"Refuse?!" The girls raised their voices in alarm once again. *Sheesh, you girls sure make a racket.*

"Marriage aside, you shouldn't refuse the title! It's a total waste!" Elze spouted her opinion, honest as always. But honestly... taking that title would make me head of a noble house, right? That didn't really suit me at all...

"If you join the ranks of nobility, it means you'd be serving the country... You'd have duties and responsibilities to attend to, like governing a plot of land." Linze quietly mumbled while running her hands through Kohaku's fur. *As I thought, it's a total drag... Definitely gonna refuse it.*

"Touya-dono, what reason will you give when you refuse?"

"Uh... I'll probably say that the adventurer life suits me better."

Putting it like that even made me think I was lying about it. Still, I wanted to avoid the wrath of Yumina's parents, so this was probably the best way to go about it.

"That will be fine, don't worry. My father won't want to force your hand, either."

"Alright, let's get going." Seems he wanted Elze and the others to come to the palace as well. Not as formal attendants to the title ceremony or anything; it seemed more like he wanted to meet and thank the girls who were so diligently looking after his daughter. The three of them were too terrified by the prospect to accept at first, but after thinking it over they realized the benefits of meeting the king himself.

"Oh, Kohaku. You wanna stay behind this time?"

"If you command it, I will stay—"

"Nope."

Oh. Unanimous rejection by the girls.

"We can't leave Kohaku behind, moron!"

"Yes, it'd be too sad…"

"Kohaku is our valued companion as well, Kohaku is!"

"Don't worry Touya, Kohaku can come with us. I'll keep an eye out." *Geez, Kohaku sure is popular.* I was a little bit jealous, but in truth, even I understood that Kohaku's fluffiness had no equal in terms of appeal.

I opened up a [Gate] right away, and we were at the royal palace in a flash. Yumina's room to be exact.

Well, I said Yumina's room, but it wasn't a bedroom or sitting room. It was a room made to welcome guests. The king had given me permission to use this room for my [Gate] spell whenever I brought Yumina to visit.

As we left the room, the guardsman outside looked puzzled for a second, then his expression shifted to one of suspicion, but he quickly grew calm after he saw Yumina.

We walked for a while, then Yumina opened a door at the end of a hallway. Through the door we saw the king, General Leon, and Olga the Mismede Ambassador all enjoying tea together.

"Father!"

"Oh, Yumina!" Upon seeing his daughter, the king rose up from his chair and rushed over to embrace her.

"You seem happy and healthy, I'm pleased."

"I'm by Touya's side, Father. There's no way I could be unhappy." *Agh… you're embarrassing me…!* My cheeks flushed red as Yumina spoke, then the king turned to me.

"It's been some time, young Touya."

"It has."

"Are the people with you your companions? You needn't worry about formalities here, friends. Raise your heads." I turned around to see what the king was talking about, and saw that the girls behind me were all bowing profusely, heads on the floor. *Geez… it's worse than the time you guys met Sue.* I noted that they hadn't bowed for Yumina, however. But that was probably because they were so shocked she'd willingly come back to the inn with me.

"Touya." Olga walked over to me. Her foxy ears and tail combo were alluring as ever. Inappropriate thoughts danced around in my mind… *I need to touch the fluffy tail… Which is softer, her fur or Kohaku?*

"I need you to know that you have my deepest gratitude. Not only did you save His Majesty, you also saved the Kingdom of Mismede. Should you ever visit our fair kingdom, I assure you that you will receive a warm welcome."

Olga bowed her head to me. *No, darn it. I don't want to impose any more! I don't want to stand out, either…*

"How's Arma? She holding up well?"

"She's doing very well, thank you. If I'd known you were coming here today, I'd have brought her with me, actually." Olga laughed wryly, but she suddenly froze up and stared at something behind me. Puzzled at what was wrong, I turned and saw that she was staring right at Kohaku.

"…Touya, what is that?"

"Oh, this is Kohaku, a little tiger cub that I'm looking after. Wanna say hi to the lady, Kohaku?"

"Rawr!" We had decided that for the sake of simplicity, Kohaku should just pretend to be a regular tiger cub. Having a talking tiger walking around with us would be way too much of a spectacle. Also, explaining it to everyone all the time would get old super fast.

Olga continued to stare suspiciously at Kohaku, narrowing her eyes and tilting her head slightly.

"Is there something wrong?"

"Ah, it's nothing. It's just that in Mismede, the White Tiger is seen as a heavenly messenger from God. They say that the White Monarch itself is a member of the White Tiger species." *Forget the species, Kohaku's the real deal... Come to think of it, Yumina did mention something about Kohaku being the King of Beasts...* I wondered whether or not it'd be a good idea to take that tiger to Mismede.

Suddenly, a shock ran through my body. Someone had smacked me hard on the back. It was General Leon. *Can this guy only communicate through hitting people or something?!*

"It's been a while, Touya my boy! Bwaha, I never expected you to get married to the little princess! You really are an interesting man, aren't you?! I thought perhaps we could spar together sometime!"

"I'm not her husband yet, so I'll refuse, thanks." I felt like if I trained with that guy my body would splinter into pieces before it got any stronger. After all, he was the kind of guy who smacked you around as a way of saying hello. That being said, he was definitely not a bad person...

Wait a second... I noticed a pair of copper-brown gauntlets hanging from the general's waist. They didn't seem particularly flashy or ornamental, but for some reason they emanated the feeling of courage and bravery.

"General, what're those?"

"Hm? Ah, I have these on me because there's a military exercise going on today. I'm a fighter! Gauntlet fighter, to be precise. Haven't you heard of me...? They call me Fire Fist Leon!"

Sadly, I hadn't heard of him at all. I hadn't heard anyone talk about him, either. However, in stark contrast to my stunned silence, someone behind me suddenly spoke up in an excited voice.

"Whoa!!! I've heard about you! You're that flaming fist guy who wiped out a whole bandit camp all on his own in the Melicia

Mountains, right?! I've heard all kinds of stuff… Is it true you had a duel to the death with a Stone Golem?!"

"Ohoho, you sure know your stuff, don't you? Are you a fighter too? It's rare to see a girl take up the art of fisticuffs!"

The general smiled broadly as he looked over at the excited Elze, noting the mismatched gauntlets hanging from her waist.

"How about it, would you like to take part in today's military training?"

"Wh-What, can I?!" Elze nodded her head over and over, a beaming smile plastered on her face. It'd be good for her to learn more techniques from him, I supposed. As I looked at Elze and Leon, the king beckoned me over to him.

"By the way, Touya… In regards to the noble title I wanted to grant…"

"Ahh, listen… I appreciate the offer and all, but…" I felt bad for the king, but I still had to refuse him. I really didn't feel like being a nobleman, at least not for the time being.

"In truth, I fully expected you to decline. It's just that it would've reflected poorly upon me if I, the king, had not offered a most generous reward to the man who saved my life. So in this case I just needed to create the known situation of 'he tried to grant a title to his savior, but the boy graciously refused.' That being said, if you had accepted the title it would have been yours to take." Well, that's royalty for you. You really had to keep an eye on everything you were doing, down to the smallest detail… Looked like for the king, appearance was king. Just as I was feeling sorry for the king, someone suddenly burst through the door into the room.

"I HEARD TOUYA WAS HERE, WHERE IS HE?!" It was Charlotte, the court magician. I almost didn't recognize her for a moment. Honestly, she looked totally different this time around. She had heavy bags under her eyes, and her hair was all frizzed out and disheveled. As she suddenly started marching toward me, I noticed that the eyes behind her glasses were bloodshot. *Agh! What the heck is going on? She's scaring me!* As if to prevent my escape, she seized me by the coat with one hand, and held out several silver coins and drinking glasses with her other hand.

"H-Hey! These glasses, I need more! Th-Three pairs more of them, yes! I taught you [**Transfer**] the other day, so help me out, okay?!"

"H-Huh? I mean, you *did* help me the other day, but what's this about glasses?!" Despite being terrified of Charlotte's looks, I managed to sputter out what I wanted to ask.

"What do you *mean* by that?! I can't decipher fast enough…! I'm at my limit, right?! I can't do it all alone! It's impossible, impossible I tell you! I figure out what one thing says but there's always more to decipher. It's never-ending! Do you even *know* how much work I have to do?! Do you even *know* how much work I have to do?!" *Why the repetition? Is she a broken record?!* She didn't have to scream at me like that while she was trying to ask for help… Still, I was way too freaked out to try and refuse, so I went ahead and cast both [**Modeling**] and [**Enchant**] in quick succession, turning those coins and drinking glasses into translation glasses in no time at all.

"Thank you so very much!" Charlotte quickly snatched up the glasses I made and, her business concluded, looked about ready to shoot out of the room as quickly as she had entered.

"Just be sure to keep things composed and well-handled, Charlotte. We don't want word of this spreading to the Empire, do we?"

"Understood, Your Highness!" Charlotte answered the king almost immediately and shot out of the room like a bullet. *What just happened?*

"Charlotte has been acting somewhat troubling, lately. Ever since she got that peculiar instrument, she's been holed up in her quarters doing nothing but work. She's going to end up wearing herself out at this rate! We may end up needing you to use [**Recovery**] on her soon enough, Touya."

Oh dear lord, I've accidentally invented the shut-in character trait. The "gets obsessed with something and retreats from the world like a hermit" kind of person... Whoops.

"Just now... was that really Lady Charlotte, the court magician...?" Linze murmured quietly, staring at the door. Well, I'm not surprised by her reaction to that display. Charlotte certainly didn't *look* like the greatest mage in the kingdom.

"Aww... I wanted to talk about magic with her..."

"Ooh, I wouldn't do that if I were you! If you speak to Charlotte while she's in this state, she'll have you spend half the day aiding her wild experiments, and the other half of the day listening to her lecture on Ancient Spirit Magic! Better to wait until she's calmed down a bit." The general shook his head side to side as he spoke. *Yeah, I doubt she'd be receptive to anything said by anyone while she's in this state...*

"Well then, it's time to prepare for the ceremony! You'll need to slip into a more appropriate set of clothes, Touya my boy!" The king clapped his hands and, as if on command, two maids appeared. *Darn it... what a drag.*

"Linze, Yae. What're you two gonna do? Wait here for me?"

"I think I'll go and watch Elze spar..."

"I will do that too, I will!" *Guess everyone except Yumina's going to the training session, then... Looks like Yumina's looking after Kohaku, too. Well, guess I'll just get changed as fast as I can.*

A maid escorted me to a private room, where I changed into a fresh set of clothes.

…Somehow, I got a house…

Before I knew it, I'd accepted a property and that was that, I guess. You might be wondering who in their right mind gave me a house. Well, it was the king.

On the day of my nobility ceremony, things were going exactly as planned.

"Oh great adventurer who saved my very life, allow me to bestow upon you a noble title."

"I'm unworthy, Your Majesty. I was merely doing what an adventurer should."

"Very well, I won't force this upon you if you truly wish to decline." Up until that point, everything was going as planned.

"That said, allowing the one who saved my life to return empty-handed would be a great discourtesy. Therefore, in place of entering you into the ranks of nobility, I have prepared a reward sum in addition to a mansion that I might hope should serve as your base of operations amidst your many adventures."

"What." As the king spoke, an elderly man stepped forward. He was holding a silver platter with a bag of money and a set of keys upon it. Distracted by the king's words, I absentmindedly accepted the items without even thinking.

I snapped to my senses when I felt the weight of the bag in my hands, but the elderly fellow had already backed off! *Drat… missed my chance to give them back.*

"This was but a display to keep up appearances. I wait with eager anticipation to see what you might accomplish in the days to come." I couldn't help but give up at this point…

"Western district... Palaran Avenue, 2A... Even the outer ring of the district is gaudy..." Yumina murmured as she checked over the documentation.

The capital was divided into two rings, one outer and one inner, both of which circled the castle. Royalty, aristocrats, important merchants, and people of high status tended to live in the inner circle around the castle, and then the outer circle was across the river.

Many people from different walks of life lived in the outer circle, and it was further divided into eastern, western, and southern wards. There was no northern ward, as Lake Palette took up the space in that area. It seemed that the western sector of the outer district was where many affluent people lived. It was in this western sector that my new property was waiting for me.

"So, now what?" After washing off the sweat she had worked up from the day's training with the general, Elze asked me that with apparent curiosity in her eyes. Honestly, it was all a bit too much for someone of my stature.

"I guess giving it back isn't even an option."

"Returning something you've already accepted is very, very rude. It hurts the honor of the one that gave you it." True enough. No decent person would ever take a gift and then go "nah, I don't like it, keep it." Linze was completely right. I had no choice but to accept it.

I laid myself out on the grass in the corner of the castle's training grounds. White clouds were gently flowing through the clear blue sky. It was reminiscent of the sky I saw when I first came to this world.

"It's not just the property, either. I also got a lot of money... I actually have no idea what to do with it all."

"How much did you receive, Touya-dono?" Yae looked down at me as I continued to relax.

"…Twenty royal coins."

"Twenty royal coins?!" Elze, Linze, and Yae's voices spectacularly rang out and resonated. Their surprise was completely reasonable.

Royal coins were a currency with more value than platinum. Ten times more, to be exact. I heard they were too big of a currency to see much use in standard marketplaces.

By the standards of the world I once inhabited, a royal coin would be approximately ten million yen. So, the amount I got was about two hundred million. Basically, that money, plus the house, was the value of the king's life. I couldn't even tell if that was a lot. Apparently, this was merely the king's pocket change. Should've asked why he was saving it…

Wait, what if it was all just betrothal money? What if taking all this meant that I was locked into marrying Yumina? Though, shouldn't betrothal money go from the groom to the bride, and not the other way around? Maybe this was a dowry and… Man, it was a pain to think about.

Whatever the case, keeping the money on my person was scary, so I let the duke hold onto it.

"Anyway, I got a house now, so maybe I should just retire?"

"Doing that would turn you into a failure of a person in no time…" Elze sighed, and instead of giving a reply, I raised my upper body. Having money meant not having to work? There was something off about that. Not like having money would ever be a problem, though…

"How about we go and take a look at it? It's only about thirty minutes away." We had no reason to refuse Yumina's proposal, so we gathered ourselves and went to take a look at the place.

"Hm? It's here…?" I couldn't hold myself back from saying that.

The residence stood on elevated ground in the western ward of the outer district, looking like it had a great view of the horizon. Walls painted white and a red roof… A refined, three story western-style building… That was all fine and dandy. I had nothing negative to say about the design, and I quite liked that it was in a quiet place, away from the residential areas. Still…

"This is way too huge…" Well, it was smaller than Duke Ortlinde's or Viscount Swordrick's homes. However, it was still more than large enough to fit people of such high stature.

I used my key to open the gates and entered the grounds. What came into view before my eyes was a large lawn, a flower bed with all kinds of vivid flora, and a pond with a small fountain inside it. Farther off in the distance, I even saw a stable.

We opened the double door and walked into the entrance hall. What greeted us was a crimson carpet and a stairway leading to the second floor.

"This is quite a nice house. I like it." With Kohaku in her arms, Yumina — the only one of us who was used to such environments — calmly walked into the hall. After catching up to her, I couldn't help but let my honest thoughts turn to voice.

"A house this large will be a pain to clean… even with the five of us living here."

"What?!" Elze, Linze and Yae looked at me, completely flabbergasted. I had no idea why.

"Uhm… Touya-dono. Five? Are we to live here as well? Are we?"

"Huh? Why would you even have to ask? It's only natural, right?" Why did we even have to talk about it, anyway? With a house this large, taking in as many reliable people as possible was only natural. As that thought ran through my mind, Elze timidly spoke up.

"B-But this house was given to you by the king. Isn't it for you to share with Yumina?" Well, I suddenly understood everything. This house was the king's way of helping Yumina out on her endeavor. Seems I accepted quite the troublesome gift…

I didn't hate Yumina or anything, but I couldn't see her as someone I'd marry. So far, she felt more like a little sister to me than anything.

Linze quietly spoke to me next.

"I-If it's a house meant for two people who like each other, I don't think we should be living here…"

"Like each other? I like each of you as much as the other. You're all family to me, so there's absolutely nothing wrong with you living he—" Hm? Linze's face was kind of red. Why? Actually, Elze and Yae were looking a bit pink, too.

"I-I'll look around the second floor!"

"M-Me too! I-I'll look at the attic!"

"I-I-I'm interested in the kitchen, I am!" The three of them scattered in all directions. Why?

"I see… So you like the four us about the same and see us as family. I'd say I got one step closer." Seeing them off, Yumina smiled.

"I want to become your wife and spend my life with you, Touya. However, I don't intend to monopolize you, so I don't mind this arrangement at all. I'm going to have a talk with them. You just wait in the living room." *Huh? What? Excuse me?* Leaving me with Kohaku, Yumina began walking up the stairs.

I didn't really get the situation, but I decided to do as I was told and walked toward the living room. On the way, I looked at the bathroom, parlor, granary, and the wine cellar, and they were all completely empty. Not a single shelf…

I opened the second to last door on the first floor and finally found the living room. As obvious as it might've been — it was huge. Though, it probably felt bigger than it was because it had nothing but the fireplace and the curtains. *I'll have to buy lots of furniture and other stuff.* The king probably considered that when he gave me the money.

The window on one of the walls had an entrance to a terrace that gave a great view of the estate's territory and the rest of the western ward.

I walked out into the garden, where I was greeted by a comfortable wind.

"It's a nice garden. Naptime here would feel great." Kohaku spread out on the grass.

"Do you like it?"

"Yes. Very much so." All the more reason to consider living here, I figured. Settling in would be quite troublesome, but...

"Touya." Hearing my name called out, I turned around to see Yumina standing there with all the others. However, the other three were avoiding my gaze. *What's with them? Their faces are still kinda red, too...*

"U-Uhm, Touya... can we really live here with you?" Linze muttered.

"Hm? Sure you can."

"...You won't tell us to get out later on, right?" Elze said, clearly full of doubt.

"Don't be stupid!"

"You'll, um... treat us exactly like you'd treat Yumina-dono, will you?"

"Sure!" Why was she even asking me that? I had no family in this world, so they were the closest thing. That much was obvious.

…Why did they all look so flustered? Sure, living in such a mansion might be overwhelming, but it was already mine, so they had no reason to hold themselves back.

Ah, I got it. They were embarrassed about living without paying any expenses, essentially becoming freeloaders. I didn't mind at all, really.

"Well, there you have it. We'll all be living here from now on. There's no rush. Feel free to decide when you have your feelings in order," Yumina proclaimed to the blushing trio.

"Alrighty…"

"Y-Yes…"

"I understand, I do." In response to Yumina's words, the other three nodded, their faces still red. Feelings in order? I didn't really get it.

"What're you guys talking about?"

"It's a secret." There was that unison again… Alrighty, then. Wait, was I actually the one with the lowest position in the household?!

"Well then, shall we go and choose our rooms?" Yumina suggested.

"I want the one on the corner of the second floor."

"I-I'd be happy to take the one next to the library on the third floor," Linze nervously stated.

"I would like a first floor room that faces the garden, I would." The girls got all cheery and started talking among themselves. Boy, did I feel like an outsider. Well, with all the rooms we had, I was perfectly fine with them picking the ones they wanted. After all, we'd still have a load of empty ones regardless…

"Hmm, I'm not entirely sure if the five of us will be able to look after the place…"

"It's impossible."

"Well, you're straightforward…" There was no hesitation in Yumina's response. Even cleaning would be too much for us. We had our guild work, so there was no way we could ever do something like gardening.

"We're going to have to hire help. Fortunately, I already have some people in mind." Seemed like I could leave it all to her, then… We really needed more help around, that was true. A royal like Yumina likely had some good methods of acquiring quality human resources.

Anyway, it was time to prepare to move. Though, that only involved bringing our stuff here through a [Gate]. Then, all we had left was furniture and similar things. The house had absolutely nothing in it, after all.

We should also tell our friends back in Reflet.

With the search for servants and other business we had, we decided to move in three days later. I felt like things were going to take a turn for the hectic.

Finally, the day of the big move came around. We said our goodbyes to the people who looked after us while we stayed in the town. Micah and Dolan of the "Silver Moon Inn," Aer of the "Parent Cafe," Mr. Barral from the "Eight Bears Weapon Shop"… Zanac of "Fashion King Zanac," too. With that, we said goodbye to Reflet itself.

The first place I called home in this new world. I had a lot of feelings about the matter. Even though I could come back any time I wanted through the [Gate] spell, it was still an emotional farewell.

Dolan said something or other about putting Reflet on the map for being the original "shogi town." The king was surprisingly enthusiastic about shogi, so the plan didn't seem too far-fetched in the grand scheme of things.

As a farewell gift to Zanac, I printed off some papers with various uniform designs on them. Who knows, maybe he'd officially develop a sexy nurse outfit or the sailor school uniform as a result. …I wasn't formally suggesting them, but I had a feeling Zanac might take the bait.

To Aer, I gave a book consisting of some new recipes, along with cooking tools I had formed with my [**Modeling**] spell. Just little things like an ice cream scoop, a round cake cutter, and assorted small template cutters in the shapes of a heart, a star, and a circle. I resolved to come back for a bite to eat once she figured them all out.

Similarly, I gave Micah a kitchen knife, a peeler, a manual fruit juicer, a grater, and a few recipes on the side as well. With that, I was sure the Silver Moon would see its culinary power grow both exponentially and ferociously.

After we said our goodbyes, we returned to the royal capital. Several carriages were stationed outside the house. It seemed they were already moving our furniture in. Yumina was outside, directing the workers as they carried odds and ends into the house. When she noticed we were back, she ran over to greet us.

"Touya, you're right on time. There's a man here seeking employment as housekeeping staff, can you come and meet him?"

"Huh? Right now?" An older man clad in a formal black suit walked in my direction. He had white hair, and a sturdy mustache. *Hm… don't I know him from somewhere? Oh, right, he's the guy who presented me with the key on a platter back when I was being granted my house.*

"Pleasure to meet you, though we have met once already. My name is Laim. The pleasure is mine." The man calling himself Laim bowed his head to me. *This guy's gotta be, what... in his sixties? Despite his looks, his mannerisms were surprisingly spry.*

"Old Laim has served my father personally for many years. He'd make a fine butler, don't you think?"

"What?!" *This guy looked after the king himself?! We've reeled in an absurdly high-class person!*

"How'd we even get someone like him?"

"Ah, I've since passed on that old role to my son. As it happens, the princess extended an invitation to me shortly afterward. I thought it would be something of an honor to serve the man that saved my younger brother's life."

"Younger brother?"

"Yes, he goes by Leim. He serves the venerable Duke Ortlinde and his family."

"Oh! Leim, the butler who was with Sue!" No wonder I thought he looked familiar, they looked almost the same. So the two brothers served the king and the duke, who also happened to be brothers. *A butler brother duo, eh...?*

"Well, how about it? Shall we hire him?"

"Well, it's not that I dislike the idea or anything, but... is it really okay? Aren't there better places for him to work?"

"Not at all. I'll be working here from now on. Thank you very much for understanding." Laim bowed his head slightly. Well, there was no reason to decline his kind offer. We decided to put him in charge of other employees and household management. Basically, we pushed all of the managerial responsibilities onto him.

"Well then, I would like to make a request, sir."

"There's no need to call me sir!"

"On the contrary. I am now an employee here, so it's very important that we establish who the master of the house is, and who the humble servant is. So, with that said and done, sir, there are a few capable workers I would like to see put to work here. Would you care to meet them?" I wanted that "sir" stuff to end already, but it seemed to be futile. He was steadfast, so there was no fighting it. That's a professional butler for you.

Laim left the mansion as quick as the breeze. Seemed like he was going to gather the prospective workers for me. He sure worked fast...

"We've hired a wonderful butler." Elze carried her bags into the mansion. Linze and Yae followed shortly afterward, and Yumina went back to dictating what furniture was placed where.

I went up to my own room to drop off my luggage, and then returned downstairs to help the others.

My room was the most spacious room on the second floor, for the moment at least. It was honestly largely on account of the fact that it only had a closet and a bed in it. I didn't even have any bedding on that bed of mine. Still, furniture was due that day, so my room would soon have a chest of drawers, a desk, some chairs, and shelving for books on display. Naturally, I'd have some bedding included in all of that too.

Come to think of it, couldn't I just make my own chairs and stuff with my [**Modeling**] spell? It would probably save me a ton of expenses, too... Wait, no, if I did that, everyone would want me to make furniture for them. I definitely didn't want the extra hassle. It'd be a real pain... I decided that things were fine as they were.

Hm... which spell would be best for unloading furniture? I had a feeling I'd be carrying the heavy stuff. I was the only man in the house, after all. I definitely had to show off my reliable side at least once in a while.

While I was deep in thought, Elze walked by, having already cast [**Boost**] on herself. The girl was shifting furniture at an amazing speed. *H-Huh? Do you guys even need my help? Hmph, I won't let myself be beaten!* This had suddenly become a matter of male pride. I cast [**Boost**] upon myself and began to carry furniture just as fast as Elze.

After all the furniture was carried inside, we gathered together on the terrace for a tea break.

We'd successfully finished putting our furniture in our bedrooms, and we'd furnished all the other major rooms like the kitchen, living room, and guest suite. All that was left was organizing my clothing and various books.

Elze and I competed a little bit to see who could carry the most using the [**Boost**] spell, but the victory went to Elze. [**Boost**] *itself is a Null spell that amplifies one's physical abilities, but it uses the caster's physical strength as a base.*

…It was pretty embarrassing to lose in a contest of physical strength to a girl, so I thought I should probably train harder. *That's it, starting tomorrow, I'll go running outside.*

I can't match Elze in physical strength, I can't match Linze in magical knowledge and patience, I can't hold a candle to Yae's swordplay, and Yumina's archery abilities along with her general mannerisms completely outshine mine… It's actually depressing.

"Things are finally settling down…"

"There are still various little household items left to buy, there are."

"We can just buy those as we come to need them and they'll appear naturally enough."

"Right. Let's finish here for today, then," Yumina said. It was true that we were short on general household goods, though. Daily necessities like tableware and cleaning supplies. A bathtub as well, come to think of it. *Do we have any personal cleaning products at the moment? I don't think so...* Oh, we'd need a trash can too. We had more left to buy than I initially thought.

Everyone brought up what they thought the house needed, and we compiled a list. We all decided that we'd go out and buy them later. After everyone finished giving their opinion, Laim came from the front gates with a group of men and women in tow.

"Greetings, sir. These are the individuals that I mentioned earlier. They all have my personal approval, and have been investigated thoroughly. They're the best hires you could possibly get." ...I just couldn't get used to that "sir" thing. I wish he'd call me something else already. When he uses a term like "sir," it makes me feel old. I felt like it would maybe suit me after ten more years or so, but definitely not right now.

"Greetings, I'm from the Maid's Guild. My name is Lapis. It's a pleasure to meet you."

"Heyyy there, I've aaalso come from the Maid's Guild. My name is Cecile. It'll be a pleaaaasure to work with you." Two girls stood in front of me and bowed their heads. They were wearing stereotypical maid uniforms. Lapis had a dignified air about her and held her dark black hair in a bob curl cut. Cecile, on the other hand, had light brown hair and a sweet smile painted on her face. They both looked to be about twenty years old. The two girls were wearing stereotypical French maid outfits, complete with the frilly headpieces.

Wait, there's a Maid's Guild? Then again, it'd be pretty easy to commit a crime as a maid. Stealing would probably be simple in that line of work. Having a formal system where all maids are subject to tough background checks and proper education made a lot of sense to me. Plus, registered maids would be a matter of public record, too.

Laim informed me that the two girls would be charged with cleaning the house, and also help him with household administration when needed.

"I'm Julio, your gardener! Ah, this is Crea, she's my wife."

"I'm Crea. I'll be taking care of the cooking." Next up to introduce themselves was a married couple that I think were in their late twenties.

The duo was made up of a relaxed young man with golden-blond hair, and an equally calm looking young woman with reddish hair. The two of them looked to be quite similar in personality. They both seemed fairly laid back.

Julio was apparently the son of one of Leim's friends. He was to be put in charge of flower arranging, vegetable growing, and general gardening duties. Crea, his wife, was to be our personal cook.

Seems she'd been working for quite some time as an apprentice cook for the aristocratic elite of the kingdom. I decided I'd show her the recipes that I'd printed out for Micah when I had the time.

"The name's Thomas. Until recently, I was a Heavy Infantryman."

"You can call me Huck. Spent most of my life serving in the Light Cavalry." *A heavy guardsman and a light guardsman, huh...*

Their figures matched their titles, too. Both of them seemed to be in their fifties. Laim reached out to them because they recently retired from the kingdom's military. Seemed that they'd be alternating between gatekeeping duty and general mansion security. The gate had to be manned at night as well. Were they going to rotate shifts or something?

Would two guys be enough? I thought maybe I should hire a couple of others as well. I figured that was an area for Laim's expertise.

That aside, Thomas and Huck... they were seriously called *Tom and Huck*? I'd be willing to bet they got up to a ton of mischief in their childhood.

They seemed fine to me, so I took Laim's suggestion and hired them.

"Thomas and Huck live in the capital, so they need no special arrangements... However, the others and I would prefer to live on the grounds. Is that fair to you, sir?" I accepted Laim's terms, since they seemed fine to me. We had a lot of rooms anyway, so it wasn't an issue.

I felt that Julio and Crea deserved some space of their own, being a married couple and all, so I requested that their room be further away from everyone else so they could spend some time together. That said, us all being in the same building and all, I felt that they weren't really being given much "alone time" to begin with. I'd prefer to let the happy couple enjoy their quality time together.

I gave each of the new employees some money and told them to go out and buy some necessary goods. I gave a separate sum to Lapis and Crea, and instructed them specifically. Lapis was to purchase the general goods from the earlier list, and Crea was to purchase food and utensils for the kitchen.

Everyone ended up going shopping, with the exception of Laim, who said he wanted to give the mansion a thorough inspection. He said that he wanted to know his new workplace down to the very last crevice. Honestly, I'd tip my hat to him if I was wearing one.

"Things finally seem to be dying down..." I still wasn't used to my new home, and we already had seven servants added to the roster. *The money I got from the king should be enough for the time being...* I was starting to worry about my financial situation, just a bit. But to be honest, there'd be no point in worrying about it either way.

"It'll be fine if we leave everything in good old Laim's hands. There's a good reason my father has kept him employed since he was young."

"I still can't believe we ended up hiring the king's old butler."

"I'm sure he expects great things from you." Yumina sipped her tea as she spoke, matter-of-factly. *Don't make me feel any more pressure...*

"...I don't believe we'd be able to handle it all on our own, so I'm very thankful we have such a capable butler in our service." Linze mumbled as she plucked a cookie from the table and fed it to Kohaku, who was stretched out over her lap. She wasn't wrong. He'd certainly be helping us a lot in the future.

Hm? Did I just hear the sound of a carriage rolling up to the front gate? Have Lapis and the others returned already? Were there really so many bags that they needed a carriage?

As I thought about it, Laim suddenly came out from the inside of the mansion.

"Sir, we have visitors. It is the good Duke Ortlinde, and his daughter, young Lady Sue."

"Huh? Sue and the duke are here?!" *Ah, my mansion has its first visitors already...* I wondered what brought them here.

Right after Laim announced the arrival of our visitors, Sue and her father appeared on the terrace.

"Howdy neighbor. Nice to see your face around these parts." Duke Ortlinde chuckled heartily as he spoke. Well, he says "neighbor," but he lives in a district within the inner ring, and my place was way out on the outer ring. But, to be fair, it was definitely a lot closer than Reflet.

"It's been a while, Sue."

"Indeed it has, Yumi." Yumina and Sue greeted each other quite politely. Oh yeah, I kind of forgot those two were cousins. But seeing them so close together, I noticed they looked pretty similar with their blonde hair. That being said, they were definitely far apart in terms of personality...

"I must say, I was very surprised when I learned of your engagement to Touya, Yumi."

"Pretty sure the most surprised one was me..." In all honesty, I didn't get it. I still had no idea how to process the situation. When they made it to the table on the terrace, Laim brought us all tea. Truly a butler of the highest caliber.

"To be honest, I had intended to have Sue and Touya marry each other. Alas, it seems you beat me to it. You and my older brother, on the ball as usual!"

"Oh, you planned such a thing for me, Father? Well, if it's Touya, I don't think I'd mind an arranged marriage at all. Spending my days with him would certainly be fun..."

"Aha, I see. Well then, how about it, Touya? Would you like to marry my Sue along with Yumina?"

"Hey now, let's not get carried away. I'd appreciate it if you didn't bully me so much." Duke Ortlinde might just be joking, but I could see an unmistakably worrying sparkle in Sue's eyes as she looked at me. I'd prefer not to let anything lead her to a misunderstanding...

"Well, I'll refrain from pressing the issue for today, at least. I actually have a favor to ask of you." *What do you mean by "for today"?!* Ignoring my narrowed gaze, the duke continued talking.

"We've actually decided to pursue a formal alliance with the Kingdom of Mismede. My intention is for the two kings to sit in conference together to hash out the details." *Ah, Mismede. The southern kingdom populated by beastmen. The country that the fox sisters, Olga and Arma, hail from. So they decided to form an alliance, after all...* I was relieved.

"Ideally, one of the kings would come to visit the other for the negotiations, but as you'd expect it's a very dangerous task. There's no guarantee either party would be safe from harm. Monsters could attack them on the road, or opportunists could stand in their way."

"...You need Touya's **[Gate]**, right?"

"Correct you are. Cutting straight to the point as always, Linze." The duke gave a little chuckle as he sipped at his tea. *Well, it is true that you can move safely through use of the* **[Gate]** *spell, but still...*

"I can only travel to places I've been to before. Wait, don't tell me..." I had a bad feeling all of a sudden. Quite a strong one, too.

"That's right. I need you to go to Mismede."

...Yep, that makes sense. I get it. I totally get it. It's an extremely convenient spell. If not for the limitation of only being able to go to places I've personally been to before, I could have easily started up a massively successful express delivery service.

"How long will it take to get to Mismede, anyway?"

"Hm, about six days by carriage." *Huh, that's actually shorter than I thought.*

"Well, six days to reach the Great Gau River, at least. From there it'd be another four days to reach the Kingdom of Mismede. Provided it all goes to plan, that is..." *Ten days, then. That's kind of a pain, actually... Give me a house and then send me off on a trip so I can't even live in it?! I swear, these people...*

"I'm going to forward this quest to the guild, with the stipulation that your party be the ones to take the job. That way, you'll be rewarded formally for your efforts and your Guild Rank will increase, too. I think you'll find that agreeable, no?"

Sly dog... you've already worked all this out. Well, to be fair, it's a simple enough job. And hell, a little trip to another country might be nice. He has a point, too. It's definitely convenient for us. To be honest, I'm interested in finding out what kind of place Mismede is, as well.

"Well, it seems fair to me. I'll take the job! What about you guys?" Everyone else nodded in approval. Seems like it was a no-brainer.

"You have my thanks. The ambassador from Mismede will be returning home, so she'll be escorting you around their capital."

"Oh, Olga's returning home? What about her little sister, Arma?"

"Ah, about that. The ambassador and her younger sister will be joining you on the trip, so you will also receive an armed cavalry escort." Made sense to me. That was a little calming to hear, honestly. As I understood it, Mismede had more nature to it than Belfast. A dense jungle full of monsters, something like that... I wondered if it was going to be similar in climate to South America or Southeast Asia.

I hope it's an interesting place... Mismede, the little-explored kingdom of beastmen... Well, it was our destination, so we'd find out about it soon enough.

"But... will going there be fine, will it?"

"Hm? What's wrong, Yae?"

"If it's known that you can use [**Gate**] over there, Touya-dono... Well, it's a dangerous spell, is it not? You could go anywhere, any time, without having to tell anyone about it... What if they mark you for assassination as a dangerous person of interest...?" *No need to say something so scary, Yae.*

That being said, I've been using it pretty much without reserve until now. You might tell me that, but nothing's really about to change.

But really, was such a thing possible? Well, even if it was, there was no way I could prevent people getting suspicious of me.

"No, no. Don't worry about such a thing. I confirmed it with Charlotte, you can't use the **[Gate]** spell to go everywhere. Magical barriers can be erected to restrict travel via that kind of magic. They'll surely know that as well, and thus all they have to do is take the necessary precautions." The duke did his best to dispel Yae's anxieties.

"Is that right, Touya?"

"...First I've heard of it." Elze seemed exasperated at my reaction. *I mean, when I first learned the* **[Gate]** *spell, all I knew about it was from what I'd read in that book! It's not like I knew that it could transport me to a specific place with only the right details, you know?!*

"Even a small magical barrier should be enough to prevent it. For example, a weak barrier could be erected around the royal capital. With that in place, you'd be able to freely warp out of town, but warping back in would be an impossibility. Actually, Charlotte already erected a barrier around the castle. The only exception being the entry room Yumina selected." *Huh, she already took such a precaution?* Well, despite her... unconventional appearance, she still was the court magician after all. Seemed she was less disorderly than I had initially thought.

Well, if we really wanted we could still easily invade the castle through Yumina's room. I wondered why they trusted me so much... Oh, it was probably because of Yumina's Mystic Eyes.

"...But if Touya entered the barrier, he could still open a **[Gate]** and allow troops to pour in through it, couldn't he...? I think it would be better for all of us if they don't know what Touya is capable of."

"Hmph… that's a fair point. It's better not to arouse suspicion if it can be avoided. Could you not infuse the [Gate] spell into an object like you did for Charlotte's spectacles?" Oh, there was a thought. If I just used something like an enchanted mirror to act as a portal to facilitate the meeting, and then smashed it up afterward, they probably wouldn't get suspicious of me.

If I presented it as a case of "mirror A is connected to mirror B," then it might be enough to avoid any worry. I'd have to create the second mirror by enchanting it once I reached Mismede, though.

If I did something like that, they might not suspect that I could personally teleport myself.

"Well then, now that that's settled…"

"Oh uh, let's think… How about three days from now?"

"Very well, then." *Hm, things are about to get even more hectic around here. We'll have to prepare for the long road ahead.*

"Aww… I want to visit Mismede as well!" Sue enviously nibbled on her finger. Part of me hoped she wouldn't ask to come with us. I felt bad for feeling that way, but I really didn't want any more complications.

"Since I'll be able to warp back after my trip, I'll bring you with me next time, Sue."

"Seriously?! Yay! You're as amazing as always, Touya!" Sue leaned over the table, directing a big beaming smile right at me. That smile warmed my heart. I knew I had to be sure to keep my promise.

We decided to discuss the finer details of the Mismede expedition. Our talk with the duke carried on long into the evening…

All I could hear was the rattling of our shaking carriage. We were following the road as we rode a chain of three wide wagons, each drawn by two horses.

The one at the front contained five knights from Belfast, while the one at the back had the same amount of Mismedian soldiers. They were guarding the carriage in the middle, which had my party, Mismede Ambassador Olga, and her little sister Arma in it.

Linze and Elze sat up front, while the rest of us were in the midst of a heated battle inside the passenger car.

"Grr... there, it is!" Yae flipped over one of the many face-down cards. And, sad as it might've been, it had a number different to the revealed one.

"How unfortunate. The correct answer was here and here." It was Yumina's turn. Without hesitation, she turned over two of the cards... which were the two of spades and hearts. She took both of them off the table.

As Yumina, Yae, and Arma played a game of memory match using the cards, Olga and I were facing each other in shogi.

Doing nothing but letting the carriage shake us was boring, so we had taken out the shogi set. Then, I used [**Drawing**] to print out some paper and combined it with [**Modeling**] to synthesize thin wooden boards to create a set of cards.

It would've taken too long to teach them the scoring hands for poker and the like, so instead I just brought up a simple game of memory. However, Yae was quite inept when it came to recalling things, so she had lost every single round.

"I was defeated again, I was…"

"Seems like it's not your game, Yae." With a wry smile, I moved one of my pieces.

"And that's checkmate."

"Agh…!" Olga glared at the board. It was hopeless. There was nothing she could do.

"So I was defeated, too… You are far better at this than me, Touya." Olga complained, clearly looking sour. Truth be told, as far as shogi players went, I was among the weaker ones. Still, I'd taught her how to play mere moments ago, so of course she lost. Honestly, I was afraid of just how much better than me she'd become after a few more games. Therefore, I took the liberty of ending it and taking the victory with me before that happened.

"Yae, let's switch. Try playing against Olga."

"Very well. Dolan-dono taught me how to play shogi back at the Silver Moon, so I might have better luck here, I might…" *Taught? Looked more like he just forced you to play with him to me…*

"Alright, how about we try something other than memory now?" After switching with Yae, I shuffled my handmade cards, added one joker, and began explaining the rules of another game to Yumina and Arma. It was a game where tactics were the key to victory — the extremely advanced game of old maid.

"Fgahh…" Kohaku was sleeping peacefully in a corner of the carriage.

Upon learning the rules, the two quickly grew enthralled with old maid, while Yae and Olga, who were evenly matched in skill, glared at the shogi board with great intensity. That was how we spent our shaky journey to Mismede.

"And so, the cat beastman in boots became a noble and lived happily ever after." The end of my campfire story was greeted by roaring applause from everyone listening. I couldn't help but blush a bit. It started off as a little tale to tell before we slept, but I got caught in the moment and made it into something grand.

"That was so nice, Touya!" Arma excitedly spoke up as the ears above her head twitched excitedly. I could also see that bushy tail of hers pleasantly sway side-to-side.

"It was a wonderful tale, Touya. I have to ask, though. Where did you learn it?"

"Ah, I got it from a bard who once visited the place where I used to live." I answered Olga's query with a simple white lie. The Mismedian soldiers gathered around the fire seemed to enjoy it, too. A story of a cat beastman in boots who saved his master and did lots of great deeds. A creature skilled with a blade, and sharp of mind.

With the discrimination beastmen faced, I'd assumed such feel-good stories where they met prosperity were few and far between. Though, I did hope they excused the extra dramatization I added.

"Touya knows many other stories."

"Really?! Please tell more of them, Touya!" Yumina's words made Arma's eyes light up. The little foxgirl excitedly bent toward me. *I'm glad the two of them get along so well. Guess it must be easy to talk with someone around your own age.*

"That's it for today. Wait for more tomorrow." With a smile, I gently rejected Arma's request.

Suddenly, one of the smaller Mismedian soldiers stood up and placed his finger near his mouth, signaling everyone to be quiet. The ears on his head were twitching. *They look like… rabbit ears? Guess he's a bunny beastman.*

"We have several people approaching our position. They're stealthily closing in… We're their target, no doubt about it." His words made the other soldiers silently unsheathe their blades, and sharpen their senses. They were about to do their job, basically. They entered a defensive formation meant to protect Olga and Arma. The Belfast knights also left their carriage and began observing their surroundings.

"Who are they?" I inquired.

"Probably just bandits. No threat on their own, but trouble in great numbers." The one who answered was the captain of the Mismedian military escort group. He was a wolf beastman who specialized in dual-wielding blades.

«Master, there are definitely people in the vicinity searching for us. I don't believe they're friendly, either. As the wolf said, they're likely bandits.» Kohaku spoke in a voice that only I could hear.

Bandits, eh? Guess it's time to investigate.

I took out my smartphone and ran the map app. It displayed the surrounding area. *Alright… a simple search for "bandits" got a bunch of pins to drop on the map. Whoa, there's quite a lot of them.*

"Eight to the north, five to the east, eight to the south, and seven to the west. There are twenty-eight in total."

"You can sense them too?!" The captain turned to me in surprise. We were outnumbered. Not like we couldn't win, but we probably wouldn't come out unscathed.

"…Guess I can try it now." It was a chance for me to test a specific application of one of my spells. *By all accounts, it should work, but…*

"**[Enchant]: [Multiple].**" I buffed the map app with a Null spell that allowed the continuous abbreviation of chants and simultaneous activation. One by one, I tapped the bandit markers on the screen, setting them as my targets. It was kind of a pain, but I was done in no time, really.

"[Paralyze]." With that, I unleashed the spell on everyone my app had highlighted. A moment later, I could hear several groans and thuds from the surrounding woods.

"Ugh!"

"Ngh!"

"Gyah!"

"Hhgh!"

"Ahgh!" A vivid array of voices rang out, and then came the sounds of collapsing men. Apparently, it worked.

"Wh-What did you do?"

"Used a paralysis spell. They should all be immobilized now, I think…"

"What, all of them?!"

"If there aren't more than twenty-eight, then yeah." Due to the way my [Search] spell worked, my targets were only people I'd personally judge as "bandits." In other words, if there were normal people who merely looked like bandits to me, they'd be caught by the spell, too. But that was quite unlikely, given where we were. I still decided to use [Paralyze] though, just in case. Didn't want to hurt any bystanders.

The soldiers and knights entered the woods and dragged out the collapsed bandits. Twenty-eight of them in total, as I expected. Each had a lizard-shaped tattoo on the back of their hands, which was likely a symbol of their gang. They were all partners in crime, no doubt about it.

"Amazing! You took out so many in a mere moment…" Olga muttered, clearly dumbfounded.

"Good thing none of them had any magic-warding talismans on them. Spells like [**Paralyze**] get blocked by even the slightest amount of magic resistance." I was glad they weren't prepared for something like that.

Even if they were, there were several other problems with this method of mine. For one, I was lucky they weren't moving much, because it was way harder to lock on to a moving target. Also, the targeting process itself was pretty darn tedious.

"Well, that worked out. I didn't expect anything like that to happen, though," the guard captain lightly muttered.

"Honestly, it's all because of that guy who heard them coming. He was definitely impressive."

"Oh, you mean Lain? He's a rabbit beastman. You won't find a better pair of ears." The captain laughed as he dragged a bandit off and looked over at the rabbit-eared boy. He was a small and meek guy with silky red hair. Looked about my age. *Ah, so he's called Lain.* Oh, by the way, the wolfish captain's name was Garm.

"Paralysis should last about an hour for humans. What do we do with them?"

"Well, were we in Mismede, we could take the simple approach of killing them before things get messy, but I guess that's not how things go here." Garm called over to the captain of the Belfast knights. The one who came over was a blond youth in clattering full plate armor. *Dang, that guy's handsome...*

Lyon Blitz, a knight belonging to the kingdom's first order. Twenty-one years old. He was the son of Leon Blitz, and I still had trouble believing he and that general were related. Though he definitely was the second son of the general, the earnest and diligent Lyon was completely unlike his eccentric father.

After listening to Garm's explanation of the situation, Lyon took a moment to ponder before proposing his solution.

"For now, let's tie them all up and send a mounted messenger to the next town to bring some guards over. They should come by morning, so we can just hand the bandits over to them and resume our journey. What say you?" Garm didn't seem to have any objections, so our course of action was decided. We bound and gagged the bandits. Just to be on the safe side, I also used earth magic to dig some holes and bury them, leaving only their heads exposed. With the paralyzing magic still active, it looked like a small field of limp heads. *This looks kinda surreal...*

"We shall take care of the ruffians, while Mismedian soldiers will watch out for any outside threats. I leave the princess to you, Sir Touya." Lyon whispered those words into my ear.

It just so happened that, aside from my group and Olga, he was the only one who knew that Yumina was the crown princess of Belfast. No one else seemed to have met Yumina before, so there was no need to worry about her identity being exposed. Even the rest of the Belfast knights had never worked at the castle.

Lyon was also the only one aware of my tentative status as Yumina's fiance. I wasn't informed of anything of the sort, but I wouldn't be surprised if he was tasked with protecting her.

"Sir Lyon, I apologize for causing trouble." Olga came to him and expressed her gratitude with a bright smile on her face. The young knight entered a flustered state in response.

"Ah, n-no need for that. Th-This is merely part of my job! Don't mention it, really!" His cool attitude completely gone, the golden-haired youth's face turned red as he spoke to Olga. Looking at him, the foxy beauty giggled in a bemused manner.

Ohoho... So that's how it is. I slowly backed away, making sure they didn't notice me. Standing behind one of the carriages, I silently observed as the two made some gleeful small talk.

"Ah, young love."

"Yes, it is indeed beautiful…"

"Yep, sure is."

"Such a wonderful thing…"

When did you guys get here…? The twins, the samurai girl, and the princess, with Kohaku in her hands, were all right next to me, watching the two as I did.

"Does Olga-dono know how Lyon-dono feels about her, I wonder…?"

"I'm sure she does. Unlike a certain someone, she doesn't seem very dense," Yumina said. *Huh? What're you guys looking at me for?*

"…Density is one thing, but I also think that Touya is far too kind to everyone he meets," Linze muttered.

"Oh, I totally agree," Elze proclaimed as she nodded her head.

"I'm not sure what to make of that attitude of his, I am not." Yae chimed in, uncertain.

"Do you even know what we're talking about?! Sit down!" Elze suddenly yelled at me, clearly angry for some odd reason.

"Wh-What?!" *I don't understand. What's this all about?* Unable to resist them, I was forced to sit down and be exposed to a ridiculous amount of unreasonable scolding. Why, though? With most of their words just flying over my head, the strange event continued into the dead of night.

"You're kidding me, right? This isn't a river; it's a whole ocean..."
Water. Marine blue as far as the eye could see... Though, I *could*
make out the outline of the opposite shore if I squinted hard enough.
It reminded me of when I went to Aomori as a kid and could see
Hokkaido from Cape Omazaki. So, this river was about as wide as
the Tsugaru Strait...

After six days of journeying, we finally arrived at Canaan — the
southernmost town in the Kingdom of Belfast. The plan was to take
a ship and cross over to the Mismedian town of Langley.

Naturally, being a town that connected the two kingdoms,
Canaan had a significant number of demi-humans. With dog and
cat beastmen being a given, there were also some who had wings
sprouting from their backs or horns adorning their heads. Not to
mention the dragonfolk with scales covering certain parts of their
bodies and thick tails trailing behind them. From what I could tell,
the humans and demi-humans around those parts coexisted just
fine.

Once we reached the riverbank, which looked more like a
harbor, by the way, we saw a great number of boats. However, all of
them were quite small. I could see some medium-sized barges, but
none that really stood out in terms of size.

They were all sailing boats, but none had many sails on them,
making them all look extremely plain. I was told that the passengers
were always joined by users of wind magic who could get the boat
to the other side in about two hours, so such simple designs were
actually optimal. Considering how gentle the river's current was, I
could fully understand the reasoning.

*Okay, so we'll leave the carriages here and cross over to Mismede
by boat.* Apparently, there was another carriage waiting for us on the
other side.

We left the actual boat-hiring to Olga, Garm, and the other Mismedians. On the side of the road, not too far away from the boat, there was an open-air market.

"Oh, that's a handicraft stall."

"And this one here sells silks... Wow, you can find lots of things here." Arma and Yumina looked at the wares being sold. *Well, this is the last Belfastian town before Mismede, after all... Guess it makes sense that there's a bunch of merchants hawking souvenirs.*

"Oho? Touya, look at that..."

"Hm?" I followed Yumina's gaze and saw Lyon standing before a jewelry stall. It sold various accessories such as brooches, rings, and necklaces. He had a strained, pensive expression on his face as he stared at their wares. *Huh, I thought he was off sending a letter to the royal palace.*

Instead, he seemed to be seriously considering which accessory to purchase. *But those trinkets were meant for girls, so... Ohhh, I get it. So that's how it is...*

"Hey, Lyon. Getting something for your family?"

"Eh? S-Sir Touya?! W-Well, I was just, uh, m-my mother, she's... Yes! I was thinking of getting something for my mother..."

"Heh..." His oh-so-splendid complexion made it very clear that it wasn't for a member of his family. Also, there was something really off about buying souvenirs for a Belfastian in Belfast, rather than waiting until we got to Mismede. But, at least for the moment, I decided to spare him the embarrassment and keep any such comments to myself.

"Boy, sure is a good assortment here. Oh, actually... Arma, how about you pick something? I'll buy it for you. It'll be a little present to remind you of Belfast."

"Really?! Wow!" Arma quickly and joyfully chose one of the brooches. It had the shape of a bunch of grapes, but the "grapes" themselves were replaced by neatly-placed purple crystals. *The fox and the grapes… Man, this reminds me of that old fable.*

"It really suits you, Arma."

"Ehehe… thank you so much!" Arma smiled broadly as I paid for the item. *Alright, here's my chance to help Lyon out.*

"Does Olga like brooches like this, too?"

"Hmm… Sis prefers flowery designs. Like, uh, she really loves elius flowers. I've seen her buy a bunch of them." As she spoke, Arma pointed toward one of the accessories on display. It was decorated by cherry blossom-like flowers. A little plain, but still quite pretty.

Lyon, eavesdropping on us, smiled a little. *Bingo.*

"Right then, I'll be off. Don't take too long to get back to the boat, Lyon. We're setting off soon."

"Ah, of course. I'll be there in a moment." A few moments after we left the scene, we turned around to see Lyon buying the elius hair ornament and getting it gift-wrapped.

"Excellent work, Touya," Yumina praised me. *Guess she noticed my handiwork.* The sister of the young knight's beloved, however, seemed quite clueless.

"Although, I would have liked it if you also bought *me* a present, Touya."

"…Sorry."

"Well, I'll be satisfied so long as I get a ring on my left ring finger eventually." With a bright smile on her face, Yumina wrapped her hands around mine. *Darn it, Touya. You should've bought her something! That alternative's too scary…*

As such thoughts spun through my head, we returned to the boat.

"That was fast."

"It was only two hours, after all, it was." Elze and Yae left the boat while carrying the box containing the large mirror meant for the Kingdom of Mismede. They were followed by Arma and Yumina, who carried our baggage. Then came Kohaku and finally there was me, carrying Linze.

"…I'm so sorry, Touya."

"It's fine, no worries. I don't mind at all." She got seasick about an hour into the journey. It was clearly because she was reading. The boat itself was pretty steady, after all. I tried using **[Recovery]** on her, but it didn't seem to have much effect. Strange, since it was clearly a negative status ailment.

Wonder why it didn't work… That aside, how come she's fine with carriage shaking, but not boat swaying?! Then again, I knew people who could handle cars, but still got seasick, so this is probably similar.

Once off the boat, I took a good look around Langley. We were now in the country of demi-humans — the Kingdom of Mismede. Not like the mere two hour journey resulted in some massive change, but compared to Canaan, the town in Belfast, this one had significantly more demi-humans than humans.

There were stalls, just like on the other side, but just about every merchant was a demi-human. And they were so varied, too. It was quite a sight.

"The town's bigger than I expected."

"…That's probably because it's heavily influenced by Belfast." Still on my back, Linze replied to my mumbling. As we eyed the town, Olga led us to three carriages, which looked about the same as the ones we left in Canaan.

"What do we do now, Touya? If Linze isn't well, we can always stay here for the night and move out tomorrow." I could make out some concern in Olga's voice.

"Ah, I-I'm fine now. I got better once we left the ship." Linze slipped off my back. Suddenly, Elze came up to her and whispered into her ear.

"You could always ask him to carry you a little more, Linze."

"Wh-What are you s-saying, Sis?!" She suddenly grew flustered, yelling at a volume she likely didn't intend. She was looking away from me, so I couldn't see them so well, but I could tell her ears were red. *Getting carried must be embarrassing or something, I guess.*

"Then, let us leave in an hour. I'll send a letter to His Majesty the Beastking."

"Ah, th-then I shall accompany you. There's no telling what could happen, ma'am!"

"You are right indeed. Do join me, Sir Lyon." She smiled at him and the two walked away. *Well, that's enough to make anyone feel all warm and fuzzy.* It felt like I could finally understand those obliging people who found their vocation in arranging formal marriage interviews.

"Mister Touya, once we leave, we won't come across any large towns for a long while. You should buy everything you need here." Garm, the Mismedian captain, explained the situation to me. We decided to spend an hour stocking up for the trip.

Kohaku, Yumina, and I went to buy an assortment of things, such as emergency rations and tea leaves. *What was that...?* I looked around and sharpened my senses. *Did I just imagine that...?*

"What's wrong?" My strange behavior got Yumina's attention.

"Nothing... kinda. Felt like someone was watching us. Probably just imagined it, though."

"Sure it isn't just someone curious about Kohaku?" In Mismede, white tigers were considered sacred. Even capturing them was a serious offense, let alone hunting them. If I put a collar on Kohaku and dragged the little furball with a chain, I'd be sent to the gallows without a trial. We had to make it obvious that he was following us of his own free will. Though, that was a bit troublesome as well.

«No, my lord... You're right. There is someone observing us. Specifically, the two of you, not me. They've completely concealed their presence now, however.»

Kohaku's words made me look around again. *Who could it be, then...? I should be on my guard, just in case.*

We went on to buy ten or so fruits I had never seen before. They looked like pears, but were orange in color and had the smell of apples. After that, we returned to the group. Everyone else had already met up at the carriages, so we were the last to arrive.

"That's everyone, then. Let's head off." At Olga's words, the knights and soldiers entered the carriages at the front and back. The rest of us filed into the one in the middle. Elze and Yae sat up front, and when the rest of us were about to step into the carriage, I noticed the cherry blossom-like hair ornament glimmering in Olga's hair.

"Oh, that's a fine piece of jewelry. It really suits you, Olga."

"Eh? R-Really? Thank you very much." Yumina noticed it as well, and when she praised it, Olga gave a bashful smile. *I guess Lyon gave it to her when they went out together. Good for him.*

"I'd love to receive something like that from my beloved. I believe that expressing feelings through such trinkets is part of being a true gentleman. Of course, I have nothing against those who prefer to show it in their behavior, like through an embrace, or..."

"Well alright, let's get going!" The conversation was heading down a dangerous path, so I rushed into the carriage.

CHAPTER II: TO THE DEMI-HUMAN KINGDOM

Yumina might actually be the type to hold grudges, I didn't expect that... Damn, I really messed up by buying something for Arma, but not for her. Still, I can't bring myself to embrace her instead... I've gotta think of an alternative. Wait, no... if I get her something, then the other girls will notice too. Won't be good if they take it to be proof of my love or something. Maybe it'd work if I give them all gifts and present it as thanks for everything until now?

When I got inside the carriage, I took out my smartphone and began an image search for the latest accessories back home in my original world. Figured I'd get some inspiration for something to make with **[Modeling]**.

Once we left Langley, the surroundings grew shockingly different. Unlike Belfast, there were a lot of overgrown plants all over the place, and the road was rough. Our carriages were slowly making their way through a place that was less of a forest and more of a jungle.

I could totally see why people said that Mismede had far more monsters than Belfast. Woodlands like this were the perfect habitat for them. Every now and then, I could hear the howls of creatures I couldn't hope to identify, but it seemed like they were just part of everyday life in this country.

From what I'd heard, the high amount of monsters didn't really have much of an impact on life in the settlements, though. That was because the forests were already full of creatures fit to be prey for the bigger ones. The monsters didn't need to dig up people's fields to find something to eat.

However, every now and then, villagers who went out hunting ended up having an unfortunate encounter with a monster or two. In those cases, the people were the intruders, so they had to be prepared to be attacked. *Wonder if there's some bear-warding bell that could keep them away or something...*

"Doesn't seem like we'll make it to Eld village before dusk." I checked my map app and saw Eld on the road from Langley to the capital, right beyond this forest. Just as Olga said, at the speed we were traveling, it was too far away to reach before sunset. Plus, I didn't like the idea of heading there in the dead of night, either.

"Mismede is like a colony composed of several individual clans. Towns and villages here are still made by separate clans just doing what they do. And, just as there are clans that have friendly relations with each other, there are also those that can't stand one another. His Beastliness included, there are seven clan leaders responsible for gathering the distant races."

According to Olga, the seven Patriarchs each represented a type of demi-human: there were the beastmen, the winged races, the horned races, the dragonfolk, the dryadic people, the aquatic races, and the fairies, too. And, as things were, the Patriarch of the beastmen — the beastking — was the current ruler of this country. That might've been because beastmen were the majority race, so it was easier for the country to function.

Also, even though the king's seat was hereditary, the other patriarchs held a great amount of power. Guess they were comparable to influential nobles. In any case, Mismede, being an emerging nation, seemed like it had a number of problems going on.

The sun was slowly hiding behind the horizon. I realized it was a good idea to start making camp while it was still light out. We would not go any further without resting first.

We stopped our carriages at a wider part of the road and began setting up our camp. Once the firewood was gathered and a bunch of well-placed rocks turned our campfire into a little stove, we began making food. I contributed by cooking up a large pot of vegetable soup. Minestrone, to be precise.

When the sun completely set and night truly blanketed us, we could hear lots of noises from the forest. There were probably lots of nocturnal animals.

"I'm a bit scared..." Yumina inched herself closer to me as she nervously ate my soup.

"Basic beasts won't come close as long as Kohaku's around. Hell, even monsters should notice, so there's no need to worry. Giant insects and Slimes are another story, though." Kohaku transmitted those words into my head, so I was just quoting what was said to me. In response, Yumina pulled the little tiger into a tight embrace.

"Thank you, Kohaku."

"Worry not, Mistress. It will be fine as long as I'm here." Kohaku whispered in such a way that no one but Yumina could hear. In response, Yumina smiled widely and patted the tiger's head.

Some people were taking turns keeping watch while we ate, and due to how unfamiliar the lands were, the Belfastian knights seemed really tense.

"I'll go pick up Yae and Elze. Kohaku, look after Yumina and Linze."

«Understood.» I walked away from everyone near the campfire, entered the large carriage, and used a [Gate] to return to my home back in Alephis, the Royal Capital of Belfast.

I appeared in the living room to find Elze and Yae enjoying some chill-out time. Standing not too far from them was our super-butler, Laim.

"Oh, is it time already?"

"Why the rush, Touya-dono...? My hair still needs to dry, it does." Yep... They went home just to take a bath. We gave them thirty minutes, so that people wouldn't get suspicious and grow aware of the fact that I could teleport.

We were able to magically create water, so we just told the others that we'd fill a tub and heat it up with hot rocks, but in reality, they were taking a normal bath back at home. They decided to go together so that one could keep a lookout while the other bathed, or so the story went.

"Come on, let's head back before someone notices that something is off. Did anything happen today, Laim?"

"Nothing worth mentioning, sir. Ah, yes, I almost forgot. Julio was thinking of making a vegetable garden. What do you say about that?" *A vegetable garden, huh... Dedicating land to growing fresh veggies sounds good to me...*

"Gotcha. He has my permission. Let him do whatever he wants."

"As you wish, sir." With that settled, I soon realized that I couldn't see Lapis or Cecile anywhere. *What're they up to...?* I asked Laim, who said that Lapis already went to sleep due to business in the marketplace early in the morning, while Cecile went to see a friend who was visiting the capital.

"Is there anything you wish for me to tell them, sir?"

"Nope, I was just curious. Alright you two, let's go."

"Okay!"

"Indeed." I opened a [Gate] and traveled back to our carriage with the girls. It only took a moment for me to realize that something was off. The forest was overflowing with the cries of countless animals. It was completely different from when I left. The sounds were on another level entirely. I ran out of the carriage, quickly finding everyone else. The soldiers and knights were brandishing their blades and looking out for any hint of danger. *What the hell did I miss?!*

"Touya!"

"What's going on here?"

"We don't know. The animals in the forest suddenly started panicking." Yumina ran up to me, completely perplexed. Soon after, the rabbit beastman, Lain, looked upward.

"U-Up in the sky… S-Something huge is heading our way!" Everyone followed his gaze. As sudden gusts of wind rustled the treetops, I saw something large glide through the night sky. *What on not-Earth was that?* I could only make out a dark silhouette, but the beastmen, having eyes that could see in the dark, clearly saw what it was.

"A Dragon… Why is it here of all places?!" Garm spoke words that conveyed his evident confusion as he stared straight up into the sky. His eyes were open wide, clearly showing his lack of understanding.

A Dragon? A giant, winged… lizard? A Dragon flew over us just now?

"B-But why would there be a Dragon here?!" Olga rushed to her sister, speaking in a frantic voice as she cradled the little girl.

"Huh? Is it not normal to see Dragons in this area or something?" Arma looked scared beyond belief, but I had to get an answer from her sister.

"D-Dragons... They normally inhabit the Sanctuary Grounds in the middle of this country. That's their territory. No one's allowed to go there, and Dragons don't terrorize the people as long as no one intrudes on their land. That's how it's supposed to work, but..."

"Did someone enter the Sanctuary?!" Olga's words made Garm's voice turn rough. *So this might be the Dragons' reaction to trespassers in their home... This is bad. In their eyes, it's probably justified anger. If they believed their land was being invaded, they were only acting how you'd expect them to...*

However, Olga shook her head, clearly denying that idea.

"No, that's not the only explanation. Every few years, Young Dragons appear in our settlements and wreak havoc. Even if we cut down the adolescents that leave the Sanctuary, the others never come over to avenge them. That's because *they* are the intruders in that situation. That being said, though..."

"Can you beat a Dragon?" Garm turned to answer my question.

"If we had a hundred of our best, like the elite royal soldiers, it might be possible. But any attacks that don't critically injure them only make them even angrier."

What? A hundred of Mismede's best soldiers? And even then, it "might" be possible...? Are Dragons really that strong? That aside, if this Dragon really is just some teenager running wild, it means that even the proud flying lizards have unruly brats among them, huh? I can't think of anything more irritating. It's basically a living natural calamity, right next to tornadoes, tsunamis and volcanic eruptions in terms of disaster potential.

I took out my smartphone, started the map app, and ran a search for "Dragon."

A number of pins dropped down somewhere in the middle of Mismede on the map. *Guess that's the Sanctuary Grounds, then... So that means this lone pin over here is the Dragon that was just above us. Hm... it's gradually moving toward... Oh. Crap.*

"Hey! The Dragon's flying straight for Eld…!"

"What?!" Everyone was shocked at my words.

"Why's it heading to Eld of all places?!"

"There's a large pasture south of the village. Is it aiming for the cattle, maybe?" I had the thought that maybe if the Dragon ate some cows or sheep, it'd be satisfied enough to spare the village. Garm quickly dispelled that theory with a harsh truth, however…

"Once it gets itself a taste of meat, the Dragon will just strike again. And when it comes to Dragon food, we're as good as any cattle. Well, I'm sure some Dragons have individual preferences, but my point still stands."

At the rate things are going, the village is gonna be wiped off the map. Hmm, my Smartphone Strike has a limited range... With this much distance between us, nothing I try will work.

"What do we do? Our mission is to protect the ambassador. We cannot allow ourselves to let any harm come her way."

"Khh…" Lyon's words made Garm grit his teeth. To a man that serves his country, orders from higher-ups were absolute. If we were to go to the village and something happened to Olga, it would become an international incident. However, having half of our guards stay behind and making the others go save the villagers wasn't a great idea, either. And I'd never visited Eld, so I couldn't create a [Gate] to fast travel there. *What am I supposed to do?*

"Do you not have something you can do, Touya-dono…?"

"The problem is exactly that, Yae. I don't." I folded my arms and began thinking. *Unlike the soldiers here, we aren't obligated to do anything. We aren't under any orders; we simply took a quest from the guild. And protecting Olga wasn't a part of that arrangement at all. Our only role here is to deliver the fake teleport mirror to Mismede…*

"Wait…!" *Right, that's our task!* I took the mirror from the inner carriage and leaned it against the outside of the carriage. The mirror itself was as big as the door, so it was hard to pull out quickly.

"Touya, what's this?" Lyon looked at it with a puzzled expression on his face. In fact, just about everyone was tilting their heads in confusion.

"Err… right. This is my Teleport Mirror. It's one of two. The other is in the royal palace back in Belfast, and you can get there in an instant by using this one as a door. I was thinking of letting Olga and Arma take refuge in the palace while we deal with this situation. What do you think?"

"I had no idea you had something so powerful…" Olga muttered.

"Our job is to get it to the Kingdom of Mismede. King Belfast himself gave us permission to use it in emergencies." I spoke all the lies I could think of. I told them that it could only be used for one round trip per day and that it couldn't handle crowds of people. I spent most of my rant trying to talk about how safe an item it was. Most of my appeal was directed toward the Mismedian soldiers.

"Understood, then. We will use this to take refuge in the royal palace. While we're gone, please do your best to protect the villagers in Eld."

"Very well, ma'am. Touya, do what you have to." Garm gave a nod upon hearing Olga's decision.

"Got it. Now, Olga, Arma, Yumina, and… Garm, would you like to confirm what's on the other side with your own eyes?"

"M-Me? I don't know if I, uh…" Garm sounded a little concerned. I placed my hand on the mirror.

"[Gate]." Careful that they didn't hear me, I spoke my magic word. The portal of light appeared a few centimeters in front of the mirror. *This is actually a much better method than having to use* [Enchant] *on the thing so soon. We're not at the Mismede Palace yet, after all.*

The first to enter was Yumina. She was followed by Garm, Arma, Olga, and myself, after which the portal silently closed. Standing in Yumina's room in the palace, I turned around to see the connecting mirror. *Good thing we prepared this in advance.*

"So... th-this place is...?"

"Belfast's royal palace, yes. Alright, Yumina. Go and explain the situation to His Majesty."

"Very well. Be careful, Touya..." I briefly clarified where we were to Garm, who was so dumbfounded his mouth was hanging open, and told Yumina to handle the rest.

"Hey, Garm. Did that ease your mind a little? We've gotta hurry back now."

"Ah... y-yes. Time's wasting, you're right!" Just as I did the first time, I created a [Gate] a few centimeters in front of the castle's mirror and passed through it.

By the time we returned to the woodland, everyone was ready to move out.

"Alright, you lot! The ambassador is safe now! We will now move to protect the villagers of Eld from the Dragon!" Seeing that their captain had returned safe and sound, the beastmen let out an enthusiastic roar in response to his orders. I watched them as I walked over to Lyon.

"What about you and the knights, Lyon? There's no obligation for Belfastians to help out here..."

"If I were to claim that this was no concern of mine, my father would surely strike me with a fiery fist. We're helping too, naturally. I am certain His Majesty would will it as well." Lyon declared his resolution with not a hint of hesitation in his voice. Apparently, the soldiers had already discussed the matter at hand. *Works for me.*

My map showed that it would still take a while for the Dragon to reach the village. Nonetheless, we had to hurry. *Lucky for us, this beast seems to be a bit slow. If we go as fast as our carriages can manage, we'll get there about an hour after the Dragon makes contact.*

Desperately hoping that we'd be able to avoid any fatalities, we jumped into the carriages and rode off at full speed.

The village was a sea of flames. People were running, screaming, and stumbling in a panic. A Black Dragon was flying above the carnage, vomiting fireballs upon the settlement like the place was some kind of playground.

It had mighty, robust limbs, a long, scaled tail, and large, menacing wings that sprouted from its back. Its red eyes, shining in the darkness of night, made it seem as though the Dragon was deriving some kind of sadistic pleasure from the destruction below.

"Prioritize saving the civilians! Carry those who can't move to safety!" Garm barked orders to his men. The beastmen hastily began helping those who couldn't move due to injury and pulling out people buried under support beams, burning wreckage, and other such debris.

"You heard him, men! Let none be left behind!" By Lyon's command, the Belfastian knights joined the beastmen in helping the villagers.

"Alright, we have to lure that Dragon away from the village." *I'll get that scaleface's attention and have him glide away from here. With any luck, that'll give Garm, Lyon, and their men all the time they need to evacuate the villagers. It's a basic plan, but that's probably for the best right now...* The men's mission was to protect Olga. They couldn't afford to lose their lives to some random Dragon attack. Also, our target was high up in the sky. Standard weapon attacks wouldn't reach it. It was all up to magic users like me and Linze.

"Strike true, Light! Sparkling Holy Lance: [Shining Javelin]!" A single ray of light tore the veil of night asunder. However, the Black Dragon gracefully evaded it and puked out another fireball.

"Ghh! [**Boost**]!" I buffed my physical abilities and hastily switched positions. The fireball hit the ground and created an explosion that only served to spread more flames.

This is bad... If we keep fighting here, it's only going to result in more damage.

"Kohaku!"

"Very well!" In response to my call, Kohaku reverted to its true form.

"Linze, hop on!"

"O-Okay...!" I climbed on to Kohaku's back, pulled Linze up to me, and made her sit up front. With that, we sped off away from the village.

I turned around to see the Dragon spew a number of fireballs in our direction. We rode Kohaku through the grove as the tiger skillfully evaded the onslaught. *Good, we've got that brat's attention now.*

I brought Linze with me because she and I were the only ones capable of fighting the Dragon while it remained in the sky. *We just need to take out its wings... Once we manage that, the real battle will begin.*

We came out of the grove and entered a wide pasture. A good place to fight. There was nothing to block our sight or hinder our movements. The collateral damage would be much smaller here, too. It didn't have any good cover, but beggars couldn't be choosers...

"GRRrrRrraAaaAaAAGGGHhhH!!" The Dragon let out a deafening roar. In response, Kohaku suddenly began to snarl furiously.

"Impudent whelp! You dare insult my master?! You are naught but an airborne newt!"

"Huh? You can understand that noise?" Surprised, I dismounted Kohaku as the tiger began translating the Dragon's words.

"It said 'How dare you try and spoil my fun, you insolent worm. I'll rip you to shreds and eat the gristle off your charred bones.' What a disgraceful creature... You snot-nosed brat, you cannot even speak a civilized language! I swear, this is among the many reasons why I so despise the Azure Monarch's kin!" Expressing more fury through expression than I thought a tiger capable of, Kohaku glared up at the Black Dragon in the sky.

"...'Spoil my fun'? So you're telling me it attacked the village as some kind of prank? What a selfish little..." *I could totally understand if it was looking for something it needed to survive, or if it was exacting revenge for the defilement of the Sanctuary Grounds. If it was something like that, I had planned on chasing it off with a little pain. But now it turns out that this thing came and attacked the people for nothing but its own amusement?*

I refuse to hold back against something so sinister.

"Linze. I'll bring it to the ground. Get ready to slice off its wings."

"U-Understood, then..." Linze gave me a slight nod. I focused my magic and cast a Null spell.

"[Multiple]!" Several magic circles appeared around me, all aimed at the Dragon. One became two, two became four, four became eight... Once the number crossed the triple digits, I cast my next spell.

"Strike true, Light! Sparkling Holy Lance: [Shining Javelin]!" In a flash, the Black Dragon was assaulted by a barrage of one hundred and twenty-eight sparkling lances. I couldn't use high quality magic yet, but I was unmatched when it came to quantity. It was much like not being able to use bazookas, but being skilled with machine guns.

"GRrrYyYAaaAaAGGhH?!" The Black Dragon tried evading the shining onslaught, but dodging a hundred and twenty-eight of them seemed far too tall an order. Many of the projectiles dug into its body, drawing blood from its wounds and causing it to slump to the ground below.

Unfortunately, it quickly got up and spread its wings in an attempt to rise again, but Linze didn't allow that to go through.

"Come forth, Water! Feel My Blade, Both Cold and Clear: [Aqua Cutter]!" A sharp edge of compressed water went flying toward it. With a slicing sound, about half of one of the Dragon's dark wings was sheared off, and it fell to the ground with a crash.

"GHhhrRRraAaAHHhH!!!" The Dragon released a louder roar this time, one I assumed to be out of pain instead of an attempt to speak. It tried to get up and fly again. But alas, unable to balance itself, the Dragon fell to the ground moments after taking flight. We had taken its ability to fly away.

The Black Dragon suddenly glared at us with those intense red eyes. I could feel hatred swirling and brewing within them as it opened its maw. The motion was unlike the times it launched fireballs at us. I had no idea what it was trying, but I knew it was bad news. Taking Linze into my arms, I double-checked that [**Boost**] was still active before speeding across the ground on my enhanced legs.

Seconds later, the Black Dragon opened its mouth, unleashing a flow of burning crimson that quickly engulfed the area. It spread from its mouth like a flamethrower's nozzle.

Guess it has different types of flame breath. We were unable to get closer to the Dragon, and that new menacing blaze was doing a good job of keeping us at bay.

Linze tried launching another [**Aqua Cutter**], but the wall created by the beast's fiery breath reduced its power and dispersed any damage it could've done.

Suddenly, a silhouette dropped from above the Dragon.

"Hyah!" It was Yae. As she fell, she sliced into the Dragon's right eye.

"It's [**Boost**] time!" Following Yae's display, Elze jumped out of a grove, gathered all her might, and launched a fortified strike into the Black Dragon's side.

"GHhRRraAaAHhH?!"

"Ow… damn it! Its hide is way too tough!"

"At least this one does not regenerate as the crystal creature did, it does not!" Complaining here and there, Yae and Elze distanced themselves from the Dragon.

With its eye lost, the beast became enraged and released an onslaught of fireballs and blaze flows at the two.

"Whoa?!"

"We must get back, Elze-dono!" Yae and Elze hastily retreated. The fire that appeared behind them lit up the whole area.

With the Dragon's attention shifted to the girls, I looked for an opening, took out my katana, and closed in on it. With a quick jump, I landed a katana drop strike on the head of the repugnant reptile.

What followed was a snapping and clanging sound… Even with the effects of [**Boost**] amplifying my body, my attack did nothing but let out a metallic sound and break my katana in half.

"Gah…!" *This guy's tough as nails… I should've followed Yae's example and taken out its other eye.*

The Black Dragon bent its head in my direction, its sole eye fixing itself on me and narrowing. Moments later, the raging beast gaped its maw and readied itself for another blast of flaming breath.

Well… shit. Just as I thought my end was nigh, a knife flew in out of nowhere and dug deep into its left eye.

Screaming in pain after losing its second eye, the Dragon threw its head backward and released an unrestrained flow of flame.

"[**Slip**]!" Seeing an opening, I magically reduced the friction of the ground around the Dragon, making the senseless beast lose its balance entirely. Its gargantuan, heavy body suddenly came crashing to the ground.

Man, that was close… That [**Slip**] *spell of mine is super useful… Just a shame it's useless against enemies in the air. That knife was a real lifesaver, though. Yae must've thrown it. I'll have to thank her later. Actually, hold on… wasn't Yae on the opposite side of where the knife came from? Well, whatever. I'll worry about that later.*

The Dragon let out another furious roar. I had already lost my katana. Just as one would expect from a Dragon, it wasn't an easy foe to do battle with. I needed something with more penetrative power. *In that case…*

"Yae, Elze! Buy me some time! Linze, build a giant ice wall in front of me! Kohaku, you make sure that no harm comes to her!" Linze quickly began focusing her magic and speaking the incantation.

"**Come forth, Ice! Eternal Frozen Ridge: [Ice Wall]!**" A thick barrier of frost materialized before me. It was beautifully clear and without any visible faults. Perfect for what I was about to do.

"**[Modeling]!**" I placed my hand on the ice and began reshaping it. The object I was making wasn't complicated at all. Magic ice was harder to melt than normal ice, but I was changing its shape without heating it, so that was really an unrelated piece of trivia.

After a few seconds, I reformed it into the shape I needed — a large, icy magnifying lens. Complete with a stand that wouldn't let it fall.

"**[Multiple]!**" Small magic circles started appearing and expanding, all pointing toward the lens. *One... Two... Four... Eight... Sixteen... Thirty-two... Sixty-four... One hundred and twenty-eight... Two hundred and fifty-six... Five hundred and twelve!*

"**Strike true, Light! Sparkling Holy Lance: [Shining Javelin]!**" All five hundred and twelve spears of light were fired into the lens. They were absorbed and refracted, focusing into a single point. I quickly used **[Modeling]** on the lens to fine-tune its thickness and set the focal point onto the Black Dragon.

"Eat this!" In a flash, a strange sound pierced the air. When I looked at the Black Dragon, it had a gaping hole where its chest once was. Soon enough, the beast tumbled forward and fell to the ground, making the earth tremble something fierce. The fresh blood flowing from its chest painted the surrounding field a vivid red.

"We really beat that thing?!"

"We did it, Touya-dono! We did!" Elze and Yae cheerily ran up to me. And Linze, riding Kohaku, wasn't far behind them.

"Well done..."

"I'd expect nothing less from my master. Truly, I can rest at ease now." As I exhaled a sigh of relief at Kohaku's words, the lens I built suddenly shattered into countless pieces. *Whoa, that scared me!*

But, moments later, another fright came. A shadow cast itself upon the ground. I looked up to see yet another Dragon floating in the sky and blocking out the moon.

"What... another one?!" This one was considerably larger than the one we'd just killed. It had red scales and a white mane trailing from the back of its head to the tip of its tail. Its horns were thick and its tail long.

As we stood there in perfectly reasonable confusion, the Red Dragon, still floating in the air, began to talk.

"I have no intention of fighting you. This child of my people seems to have caused much trouble. For that, I sincerely apologize."

"Wait, you can talk?!"

"I am the Red Dragon, he who rules the Sanctuary Grounds. I came to bring back the unruly youth, but it seems I was too late." The Red Dragon surveyed the fresh corpse with a sad expression, then slowly closed its golden eyes.

So that was the reason it came here, huh? I'm sorry, if you were a bit faster it could've been different, but...

It was kind of hard for me to say anything at that point, so Kohaku took a step toward the Red Dragon.

"Red Dragon. If you ever meet with the Azure Monarch... tell it to properly discipline its kin."

"What? This presence... but that cannot be... The White Monarch?! Why are you in such a place?!" The Red Dragon was completely taken aback. I stared at Kohaku in utter blank, confused amazement. Was there even more to this tiger than I was unaware of?

"I see… So the Black Dragon was defeated by none other than the White Monarch. I can see why it stood no chance. What a foolish child it was…"

"Do not misunderstand. Your foolish ilk was exterminated by my master, Touya. The brat had the gall to insult this venerable young man. This end result is but a natural consequence of arrogance and idiocy."

"What?! A mere human is the master of the White Monarch?!" The Red Dragon directed its golden eyes toward me. It was clearly having trouble processing this information. Shortly after that, it gently landed on the ground, lowered its whole body, and bowed its head.

"I humbly request you pardon my insolent manner… I also hope you can find it within your heart to forgive us for this Black Dragon's actions. If possible, I would prefer the punishment—"

"Hey, enough of that. It's fine so long as you understand, but you're not getting a second chance, understand? Make sure it doesn't happen again by telling your kids to behave."

"Of course, sir. By all means. I will return immediately to the Sanctuary Grounds and voice what must be said. If that is all, I shall take my leave now. Thank you." The Red Dragon stood up, bowed once more, and spread its wings before taking flight. It made a circle above us and disappeared toward the south.

"Goodness gracious, how vexing… This is why I so detest that Azure Monarch." Mumbling some complaints, Kohaku popped back into tiger cub form.

The White Monarch and the Azure Monarch didn't seem to have a very good relationship. Wonder if it had something to do with one being a tiger and the other a Dragon. *Wait a sec…* I looked around to see that the three girls were on the ground.

"What's wrong with you all?"

"What's wrong is that... we couldn't move..." Elze spoke in a slightly hoarse voice. Ah, it was probably similar to Yumina's condition when I initially summoned Kohaku. That Red Dragon was probably among the more powerful ones. I wondered if he too was a bearer of the Mystic Eyes. They certainly were exotic and golden enough.

"Touya... were you really not scared at all through that?"

"Yep. I was just fine."

"That feels somewhat unfair, it does..." *Well, what am I supposed to do about that? Not like I can control whether or not I'm affected by stuff like that. It's probably just another of God's gifts.*

Now that I think about it, no matter how scared I've been, there's never been any time I was petrified with fear.

As those thoughts ran through my mind, I cast some Healing magic on the girls.

"Sheesh, I'm tired." I spread myself out on the grass and got comfy. The sun rose from the eastern sky, blinding my eyes with light. *It's dawn already...?*

After we beat the Black Bragon, we had to do a lot of running around the village. Linze used magic water to put out the fires, Elze searched around for the injured, and I restored them using Healing magic. Also, by the time I realized that I could've just run a map search for "injured person," we were already done. No one died in the event, but the village was basically reduced to rubble. The financial cost was great indeed.

"Ah, Sir Touya. So this is where you were."

"Ah, Lyon. Great work today." The good knight approached me. Apparently, the situation was cooling down. I could even smell some food being made for the victims.

"I must say, though, to defeat a Dragon with only four people... I am far past surprised. In fact, I'm simply deep into that feeling where you lose the ability to fully articulate a comment."

"Well, it was only a Young Dragon, so it wasn't super strong yet or anything. That's probably the only reason we won." I explained that part to him, but conveniently left out everything regarding the Red Dragon. Suddenly, the wolf captain, Garm, came over to us.

"Oh, Mister Touya. What do you intend to do with the Dragon?"

"What do you mean?"

"Well, just think of the ingredients. Selling it would net you a great amount of coin. Though, transporting it would be a problem..."

"You're telling me I can sell the Dragon's corpse?" Apparently, draconic scales, claws, horns, fangs, and bones were great weapon and armor crafting materials, while the meat was rather delicious. It seems dead Dragons were extremely expensive commodities. And since I was the one to defeat the Black Dragon, I had the right to decide what to use it for. *Hmm, in that case...*

"The villagers can have it. It should help them get back on their feet."

"All of it?! To them?!"

"Mister Touya, do you know what you're saying?! The price of a Dragon is staggering! That carcass alone would not go for anything less than ten royal coins!" *Ten royal coins? Seriously? It was worth more than a hundred million yen?! Awesome! I'll definitely keep it in tha— Oh. Damn.* Right as I was about to reconsider my decision, I saw the villagers huddled together in my peripheral vision. *Crap, they heard me.*

"...I-IT'S A SMALL PRICE TO PAY TO HELP THIS LOVELY VILLAGE. I TRULY HOPE THEY USE IT WELL." I couldn't retract my statement, so I forced out a sentence that made me seem far more benevolent than I actually was. I bet the truth of it showed on my face, though.

"I think I speak for all of Mismede when I say this. Thank you, Mister Touya."

"Hah... indeed. Just as father said, you are truly a man of fine standing. I cannot help but admire you, Sir Touya." Gazes of appreciation and respect converged upon me. *No. Stop. I was just keeping up appearances...* I could only hope that the girls would tolerate this mistake.

I used the fake teleportation mirror to bring Olga, Arma, and Yumina back to us, and Olga didn't hesitate before thanking me. Most of her gratitude was for defeating the Dragon and saving the village, but I had nearly nothing to do with there being no fatalities. That was likely due to our escorts doing a good job.

Speaking of those guys, they were completely exhausted and getting some well-deserved sleep next to the carriages. And honestly, I really wanted to join them. As if to deny me that luxury, however, an old beastman hobbled over to us, supporting himself with a stick.

"I am Solum, the village chief. I would like to give you my earnest thanks for defeating the Dragon that attacked our village, and giving such great support to our restorative endeavors." *By "support," you mean my generous donation, right? Man, did I screw up by just handing it over... But with the village in this sorry state, they'll need anything they can get. Ah whatever, no use crying over spilled milk.*

The chief called over some villagers who were carrying something. *What's that? Looks about one and a half meters long... A big, black curved cone? Oh, I've seen this thing before.*

"This is one of the Dragon's horns. Please take it for yourself."

"Huh? But I…"

"We hear you damaged your weapon. You can use this horn to craft a new one, or sell it and buy something already made." *Well, he's not wrong. Guess I should just take it, then.* Once the chief passed it over, I couldn't hide my surprise at how light it was. Despite that, I heard it was far harder than the finest steel. I began to understand why a creature as large as that could actually take off from the ground.

As far as I was aware, the only materials stronger than Dragon parts were hihi'irokane, mithril, and orichalcum.

Either way, I graciously accepted the horn and walked away from the village chief and the rest. To be honest, I was close to collapsing from exhaustion. But by some miracle, I was able to drag myself to the carriage. Looking inside, I saw Elze, Linze and Yae sleeping peacefully. I couldn't really join them, so I simply slumped down and spread myself out on the grass next to the carriage.

"Here, Touya. A blanket." A moment later, Yumina came over with something I really needed. *Perfect timing…* I gave her my thanks and covered myself, all while trying to prevent my eyelids from drooping there and then.

Ah, sweet warmth… I couldn't hold it back any longer. My eyes closed and drowsiness set in.

I woke up to see Yumina with the wide open sky behind her. Still not fully aware of my surroundings, I looked into her eyes as she stared at mine.

"Are you finally awake?" I could feel something soft under my head as I heard her say that... *Wait, is my head on her thighs or something?* I rolled off to the ground to escape the situation. *How long was I sleeping like that?!* I hastily got up and noticed the villagers and now-awake guards who were grinning and looking at me like I was something adorable. *Whoa, this embarrassment is next level. Resting on a girl's thighs in front of a group of people...?! I'd be lying if I said I didn't find it pleasant, but it's still way too embarrassing, man!*

"Oh. He's awake."

"...S-Seems like you slept well."

"Indeed. He looked quite satisfied, he did."

Chills ran down my spine. I fearfully turned around to see the reason for that. Three girls, silently standing there with full smiles on their faces. Their eyes, however, reflected no joy at all. *W-Wait a sec, are they mad at me?*

"Err... did I miss something?"

"Nope." "No..." "You did not." They were clearly lying. I could see it on their sulking faces.

"Now now, ladies. Let's leave it at that! The results of rock-paper-scissors are sacred. No grudges allowed, okay?"

"Geez, I know that much..."

"Mhm..."

"This is rather vexing, it is..." Yumina made a little clap and spoke words that made the three look away and calm down. *What was so important that they'd get mad at losing rock-paper-scissors over it?*

"Mister Touya, you should begin getting ready to depart. We have to report what happened here to the capital." Garm came over with Olga in tow, telling us to get prepared. It broke the uncomfortable air, so I used the opportunity to head to the carriage.

The stares boring into my back were distracting, but I pretended not to notice.

«Kohaku, what exactly happened while I was sleeping?» I telepathically spoke to Kohaku, who seemed to be inside the carriage. I figured the tiger might know something, after all.

«Well... How should I put this...? I suppose you could say that there was a catfight.»

«Huh?» I had no idea what that meant, but it was clear that no one other than Yumina was in the best of moods. I had to do something about that... *Aha!*

Struck with a sudden idea, I went to the chief's house and made a little trade to acquire a certain something.

As the carriage shook and rattled, I exhaled a sigh of relief while looking at the satisfied girls. There were silver bracelets shining on Elze, Linze, Yae, and Yumina's wrists.

They were made by me, of course. I bought some silver objects from the chief and used [**Modeling**] to reshape them into bracelets. The design was based on one of the more moderate ones I found on the internet. Once my work was done, I gave one to each of them, to express my thanks for everything up to that point.

They seemed pretty surprised at first, but none of the girls hesitated to take theirs. From the way they looked at the bracelets every once in a while, I could easily tell that they liked them. Though, the occasional grins were a tiny bit unsettling, honestly.

"Olga, how long will it take us to get to the capital?"

"We should reach Berge in just over two days. Touya, you should get a weapon in one of the towns along the way."

Good point. Garm told me the best place to get a weapon crafted from a Dragon's horn is the capital city. But being unarmed until then probably isn't smart. I mean, sure, I can fight just fine with magic alone, but being without a weapon at my side makes me feel a bit helpless. Hm? Wait. Can't I just use [**Modeling**] *to shape the horn myself? No, wait, I shouldn't risk screwing that up...*

"Well, it's only two days, so I'll just make do with magic." *No point in buying a weapon if I'm just gonna use it for two days. Berge is the capital city anyway, so it'll have way better goods.* Olga suddenly seemed to remember something and pulled a cloth-wrapped object out of her bag.

"I just remembered, the village chief gave this to me." Olga passed it over, and I instantly realized that it was a cloth-wrapped knife. It was black, single-edged, slightly curved, and had a length of about twenty centimeters.

"What's this...?"

"Hm? I heard it was found in the Dragon's eye... Isn't it yours?" *Oh, it's that weapon. So the chief retrieved it, huh?* I took the knife from Olga, wrapped it up again, and tried passing it to Yae.

"Here you go, Yae."

"Hm? But that is not mine, it is not." *Huh...? If it's not Yae's, then Elze, maybe?* It wasn't Elze's either. *Linze? No, she couldn't even hold something like this properly. Whose knife is this, then? Weren't we the only ones there? Did someone help us from the shadows? That means they weren't our enemy, but it's still super creepy...*

«Kohaku. Was someone other than us present during that fight?»

«There was someone there. I could sense a presence at the top of a tree in the grove. No, there were likely two, actually... I sensed no killing intent, so I had assumed them to be mere villagers.» I telepathically confirmed it with Kohaku. Apparently, it was certain that someone was observing our battle with the Dragon. Why, though? I suddenly recalled that someone was watching Yumina and me back in Langley. Could it have been the same people?

That wasn't something I could figure out just by thinking about it. I examined the knife, but it didn't seem like anything in particular stood out.

For the time being, I decided to keep the blade on my person. Not having its sheath was a real pain, though.

Seriously… who could it have been?

"Hah… so that's how it is…" That was all I could say upon catching sight of the pure white royal palace in the capital of Berge. To be blunt, it reminded me of the Taj Mahal. The all-marble tomb a certain emperor built for his beloved. That huge white building with a name meaning "Crown of the Palace."

Well, I said it reminded me of it, but there were a number of small differences too. When compared to the townscape, built primarily of sun-dried bricks, the palace really stood out. If I had to describe it, I'd have said that it felt as though an Indian palace got mixed into the world of the Arabian Nights folk tales.

As our carriage ran through the town, I couldn't help but notice just how undeveloped it was compared to Belfast. Even so, the inhabitants didn't disappoint when it came to liveliness. Many species walked the streets, creating a nice hustle and bustle. Various cultures mixed, merged, and developed in a single direction. I could only assume that it was the way the town was supposed to appear.

We left the streets, all lined with tall buildings, and crossed the long bridge toward the palace. Once we were over the town's waterway, we entered the palace grounds.

The five of us, along with Olga, left the carriage and met up with Garm, Lyon, and their eight soldiers before making our way through the garden. It was a beautiful sight. I could see birds frolicking around, and I even noticed some squirrels staring at us from up in their neatly arranged trees.

We went up a long staircase and entered the palace interior. Bright sunlight fell through the skylight windows, only to become even brighter upon hitting the white marble floor.

Surrounded by ornate pillars, we followed the corridor going through the middle of the courtyard until we reached a large, ornate door.

The soldiers posted next to the door opened it for us with a loud creak.

Sunlight shone through the windows and fell upon a large red carpet. Standing at either side of this carpet was a royal audience of various demi-humans. All of them were dressed in gaudy clothing, so I assumed them to be the ministers of the country or something along those lines. Some were horned, others were winged, so they were definitely a vivid group of people.

Beyond the audience, seated on his throne up high, I saw the ruler of the country.

Beastking Jamukha Blau Mismede. Apparently his beastman subspecies was Snow Leopard. At a glance, I thought he was in his early fifties or so. His face, surrounded by white hair and a beard, gave off a regal aura of power and awe. From his sharp, feline eyes, I could feel an indescribable force and even a little bit of mischief.

We gathered before the beastking, making sure to bend our knees and bow our heads.

"My liege... I, Olga Strand, have made my return from the Kingdom of Belfast."

"Hmph. Well done to you." The beastking gave her a light nod. Then, he spoke to Garm and Lyon, who were kneeling right behind Olga.

"Garm… and you, Belfastian knight. I am most pleased by your success in protecting Olga."

"Thank you, Your Beastliness!" "Thank you, Your Majesty!" Following those responses from the two, the beastking looked at me and the girls, squinted his eyes, and adopted a faint smile.

"So, you are the ones sent by Belfast's king, I presume? It has reached my ears that, despite being few, you were able to slay the Dragon wreaking havoc in Eld. Is this true?"

"Yes. You have heard correctly. I was unable to participate, but the other four besides me were indeed the ones who felled the black Dragon attacking Eld." Yumina stood up, confidently and resolutely answered the beastking's question.

"…And who might you be?" The girl showed no hint of apprehension at being in the presence of nobility. In addition, she looked at the ruler with unwavering eyes, so naturally it would make someone like him slightly suspicious.

"Pardon my late introduction. I am Yumina Urnea Belfast, daughter of Tristwyn Urnes Belfast, king of the Kingdom of Belfast." Her words caused a stir among just about everyone present. That was only natural. The crown princess just appeared, seemingly out of nowhere. Olga and Lyon were aware of the situation, but Garm couldn't help but widen his eyes in shock.

"My… what business brings the princess of Belfast into my domain?"

"This is to show just how important we consider this alliance with Mismede. Here is a message from my father. I humbly ask that you read what he has written." As she spoke, Yumina took out a letter and handed it over to him.

When did she get that…? Oh right… she probably got it when I had her return to the Belfast palace during the attack.

With a reverent dignity about him, one of the beastking's aides took the letter and brought it over to him. After removing the seal and running his eyes over the paper, the ruler of Mismede looked at Yumina and smiled.

"Interesting... I think I understand the situation. Give me time to consider what I've just read. Don't worry, I'll be sure to give you my response soon enough. Until then, feel free to make yourselves at home in my palace." The beastking passed the letter over to his aide.

"Right, now we've got the formalities outta the way... There's something I've been wanting to ask." The beastking's tone suddenly switched to a lighter one as he looked over at Kohaku. *Well, it makes sense he'd be interested in that...*

"Is that white tiger with ya?"

"That's correct. It is Touya's... servant, of sorts."

"Rawr." Kohaku gave a short response, as if to affirm what she said. In Mismede, white tigers were considered sacred. There was a thing or two to be said about calling Kohaku a "servant," but since I didn't use a collar or a leash or anything like that, no one seemed to mind too much.

The beastking spent a moment looking at Kohaku before slowly shifting his gaze to me.

"...How very interesting. So, a white tiger-taming hero downed a Dragon, eh? Geheheh, s'been a while since my blood's boiled this hard! So then, boyo! Wanna spar with me?"

"...Huh?" A small sound leaked from my mouth, signaling my confusion. The ministers surrounding us heaved a collective sigh of resignation as well. *Wait... what?!*

There was a gigantic arena behind the white palace. It reminded me a bit of the Roman Colosseum. *Man, this country is way too inconsistent.*

I'd been inexplicably brought there for a duel with the beastking. *Why is this even happening?*

"Do forgive us, good Touya. His Beastliness is the type who cannot resist fighting anyone he thinks is strong. In all honesty, we are quite troubled by it, too." Chancellor Glatz turned to apologize to me. He was an avian with gray wings. By his looks, I'd say that he was in his late forties. He was clad in a robe as dull as his wings. His mustache stuck out prominently too.

"I would be truly grateful if you gave him some serious pain! Fight with all your might, please."

"Wait, hold up! Isn't he your king? Are you sure you're okay telling me to do that?" I looked at Glatz with obvious confusion in my eyes. Soon enough, the people next to him began backing him up.

"We do not mind. Fight as you please. His Beastliness always looks down on the importance of state affairs! There are times when he just disappears and we find him training with the soldiers, overpowering every single one of them!"

"There was also that time when he got an idea for a new weapon and just walked out to the blacksmith's! It ruined our schedule and caused me so much trouble!"

"Don't forget when he said something about starting a grand tournament... Did he even consider the budget?!" *Damn... the ministers of Mismede really have it tough, huh? The king of this country is kind of a weirdo, I guess. Well, it's not like Belfast's king is much better in that regard, but still...*

Pushing those thoughts aside, I took a wooden sword and headed for the center of the arena. The audience was made up of my friends, the Mismedian ministers, and a number of Mismedian soldiers, all ranked captain and above.

The beastking was wielding a wooden sword and shield. I had the opportunity to take a shield, but I turned it down. I was no good at using them and preferred to be agile anyway, so it was fine.

"The fight will last until one side receives an injury that would be fatal with real swords or if one side admits defeat. The use of magic is also permitted. However, offensive magic aimed directly at your opponent is forbidden. Do both parties agree to these rules?" The referee, a horned fellow with dark skin, explained the rules to us.

No offensive magic on the opponent, huh? Hm... that narrows down my options a bit. Still, the state ministers told me to go all out, so I guess I shouldn't hold back.

"Hey uh... are you sure you want to fight me?"

"Heheheh. Of course, and don't you dare hold back! Consider this a real battle. Use all you have and try to win!" I asked him for confirmation, and His Beastliness replied with a full smile. *Man, is he really serious here? His body is really well built... Not the kind I'd expect for a man of his age, honestly. He's probably done some serious training.*

Guess I don't have any other option. If he's so serious about it, it'd be rude not to go all-out. I'll just take the liberty of treating this as a real battle.

The horned referee raised his arm high and took a look at both fighters before speedily casting his arm down.

"Round one. Begin!"

"[Slip]."

"Wha-?!" The beastking fell over in a way that was almost magnificent. I quickly closed the distance between us and placed my wooden sword against his neck.

"Alright. That's a wrap."

"W-W-Wait a sec! This ain't fair! What was that all about?!"

"It was my Null spell, **[Slip].** Non-offensive magic isn't against the rules, right?"

"No no no! That's cheating! That's not allowed! It wasn't even a proper duel!" His Beastliness childishly protested. Seems he was unable to accept the outcome.

Well, he does have a point... But all things considered, that's the most efficient way of taking down an enemy, isn't it? Well, so long as I'm up against an enemy that can't fly.

"I want a rematch! No magic this time!"

"Hmm, well... what do you think, Chancellor?" I looked at Glatz and the ministers surrounding him. They seemed pretty confused at first, but once they realized why I brought them into the conversation, a few of them developed sly grins.

"Well... We would prefer it if you refrained from delaying our governmental affairs any further."

"G-Glatz! Don't say that! This won't take long! I promise! Just give me a moment, okay?!"

"Hmm... I'm not sure if I should..." His Beastliness ran over to the Chancellor and they began to talk about a few things. I could hear the beastking say things along the lines of "I'll be more serious, I swear!" and "I'll be where I have to, promise!" over and over.

In response, the ministers gave him several conditions, which made him drop his shoulders in resignation. Still, he ended up agreeing to whatever terms they had given. *Did I just do something bad...?*

"Sir Touya. If you do not mind, we would like you to have another battle with His Beastliness!" The beastking took up a position opposite me as Glatz asked for another round. He sounded a lot happier this time... *Is it just me or does the king look a little annoyed?*

"That spell is forbidden this time. Got it?"

"Got it." We readied ourselves once more. And again, the referee raised his right arm before swinging it down.

"Round two. Begin!" The beastking attacked me the very moment the duel began. I faced him head-on and twisted my body to gracefully evade the blow. Then, after backing down a bit, I charged toward him.

"Come forth, Sand! Obstructing Dust Storm: [Blind Sa—]."

"You're slow." The beastking leaped to me with the speed of a bullet and bashed me with his shield, forcing me to reposition myself. *Crap, he interrupted the spell!* I parried his wooden sword, launched a feint attack, and backed away again.

But it was no use. He predicted my movements and lunged right where I retreated. He went for my chest. I somehow evaded his attack, but he followed it up with an attack against my throat.

The second thrust surprised me, but I was able to bend my head in a way that caused him to merely scrape my ear. *Whoa, that was close! Backing away was a bad idea... I've gotta go on the offensive!*

"[Multiple]!" Small magic circles began to form on the ground around my legs.

"Hm?!" The beastking halted his charge when he saw them. Though just about anyone would do that, honestly. *Hook, line and sinker! You fell for my bluff!*

"[Boost]!" I used magic to buff my physical abilities and quickly utilized my explosive speed to close in on the beastking. *Victory is mine!*

"[Accel]." The beastking suddenly whispered something. The moment the words escaped his lips, his large body disappeared. My blade came down on nothing but thin air.

"Wha—?!" Dumbfounded, I suddenly felt someone behind me. I ducked down by reflex alone and saw the beastking's wooden sword fly above my head horizontally. I rolled away from him and adjusted my stance. *What the heck was that?!*

"You were able to dodge that, huh? Not bad at all, boyo."

"Was... Was that a Null spell?"

"You're right. It was my own Null spell. I call it [**Accel**]."

I knew it. So it's a spell that accelerates your movement... No wonder I completely lost sight of him! What's more annoying is that I don't know anything about it. Does it have a time limit? Does it boost his muscles?

"How does it work?"

"It simply makes the body a bit faster. That's all there is to it. Though, when used, it creates this magic barrier around the body that eats magical energy like crazy, so you can't really keep it up for long. Normal humans can't even see the speed I move with when it's up, so I've gotta hand it to ya for being able to dodge that." *Ah, so it's just a simple acceleration spell, then. The magic barrier was probably there to protect the body from the high speeds.*

"I see. I get how it works now. That's a good spell you have there."

"It is, isn't it? I'm pretty prou—"

"In fact, I like it so much that I'm gonna use it too! [**Accel**]!" And, just like that, I used the beastking's signature move against him. In but a moment, I dashed past the beastking and my wooden sword cleaved through thin air.

Huh? Aww shit, I messed up the timing. Could've sworn I aimed at his torso, but I was way off. This spell's gonna take some getting used to... I tried to move a bit, but my own perception of speed couldn't keep up with my body.

"Wha—?! You just… But… that's my—!"

"Wow… it's harder to control than it looks! I won't miss again, though." I kicked into hyperspeed and closed in on the beastking once more. He cast [Accel] too, and we began an extremely fast exchange of attacks, dodges, backsteps, and parries. The barrage of his attacks was as fast as lightning, but my defense wasn't far behind. I was quickly getting used to the speed. I could only assume that the spell accelerated my brain power and reflexes, as well.

Our battle in this supersonic world felt just about normal for the both of us, but it was probably extremely hard for normal humans to see.

However, I had a trump card. *I'll just combine this* [Accel] *spell with…*

"[Boost]!" With a flash, I gained even more speed! Magical acceleration stacked on top of my enhanced leg muscles. I reached a speed bordering on divine. No naked eye could follow my movements. Though it lasted only for a moment, I had completely exceeded the limits of [Accel] alone.

"How?!" In less than a heartbeat, I was behind the beastking, pushing the wooden sword against his neck.

"Checkmate."

"…I'm not sure what that word means, but it seems I've lost." His Beastliness raised his hands and accepted defeat. Accepting his admission of defeat, the referee raised his right arm.

"The winner is Sir Mochizuki Touya!" Following that declaration, everyone in the arena's audience began applauding. In truth, I had expected a barrage of booing and jeering, mostly because I had just defeated the country's king, but apparently my worries were unfounded.

"I didn't expect you to know how to use [**Accel**] as well... I had extreme confidence in that spell, so I became a tad conceited. I guess I should rethink my strategies!"

"Well... maybe? Hahaha..." I laughed it off. Null magic was personal magic. People who could use the same Null spell were few and far between. Though, I heard that those from the same lineage might've had similar spells. Regardless, it was only natural for the beastking to be unprepared for my display. It was basically foul play.

Shame I didn't get to use any elemental magic. I can't cast spells properly if the incantation is interrupted... Though that was rarely a concern for mages. They were nearly always backline fighters anyway. *Still, it'd be really convenient if there was a way to use elemental magic without having that pesky incantation in the way...*

Come evening, there was a minor party in the palace. The guests were mostly Mismede's ministers, the elite nobles, and important merchants. From what I could tell, it was meant to celebrate Olga's return and to welcome Yumina, since she was the princess of Belfast and all.

It wasn't a proper feast, so attire didn't matter all that much, but it just so happened that I ended up in formal wear.

Both my upper and lower body were covered in white, but the vest coat they gave me was black. Then there was a broad, navy blue sash. All I needed was a turban and I'd look like some kind of Sinbad or Aladdin cosplayer.

The party had a buffet, so most of the attendees were taking bites from the selection and enjoying some small talk.

The guest of honor, Yumina, still wasn't there. Neither were Elze, Linze, or Yae. *They're probably getting changed into their formal clothes. They won't be in any trouble, Kohaku's looking after them anyway.*

"Hey there, Sir Touya. That looks really good on you." Champagne in hand and clad in a snazzy tailcoat rather than the usual armor, Lyon came up to me with a greeting. Being the son of the baronial Blitz family, he was probably used to fancy events already.

"Wait a sec, Lyon, why wasn't I given clothes similar to yours…?" Regardless of whether or not my outfit looked good, I had to ask. Though, I guess it was for the best. I'd feel pretty low if I had to stand next to him while wearing the same suit. My fragile heart would receive a crack each time someone compared me to this handsome devil.

"Er… Sir Touya… you haven't seen Olga around, have you?"

"Can't say I have." Lyon tried to casually ask me about Olga, trying to put on airs and hide the fact that he was anxious to see her. *He has a point, though… It's kind of weird that I haven't seen the other guest of honor anywhere. Well, she's probably just not here yet. Hope she gets here soon though, there's only so much grinning I can do at fidgety Lyon over here.*

"Touya!" The moment those words reached my ears, I felt someone hug me from behind. I turned around and looked down to see a twitching pair of small, fox-like ears.

"Well, if it isn't Arma." I patted the head of the small foxgirl. She was wearing an adorable dress. When I looked behind her, I saw a well-built gentleman with white facial hair. There was a pair of ears poking out of his hair and a long, thick tail trailing behind him. *Could this guy be…*

"A pleasure to meet you. I am Olba, Arma's father." *Called it.* I shook the hand he extended, then took a moment to look at both the man and his daughter. Apparently, the hair on their ears and tails also turned white with age…

"Nice to meet you too. I'm Mochizuki Touya. Ah, Touya is my given name."

"Hoho, so you're from Eashen, then?" *It's been a while since I've heard that one.*

"I-I am Lyon Blitz, a-a knight from the first order of B-Belfastian knights!" *Get it together, Lyon...* Lyon shakily shook Olba's hand right after I did. Guess he couldn't help it. Arma's father was also Olga's father, after all.

"You have my heartfelt thanks for protecting my daughters."

"N-No need for that, sir! I-I was merely following orders!" *Lyon, please. There's no need to freak out that much, man...* With no intention of helping Lyon out of his sticky situation, I decided to begin some small talk with the old fox.

"What do you do for a living, Olba?"

"I'm a merchant. I deal in various high quality goods, some of which come from Belfast." *A merchant, eh? Various goods...*

"Recently, I've been trying to get my hands on this new game called 'shogi.' I'd quite like to sell it here. I hear the king of Belfast himself enjoys it quite a bit."

"Hmm? Shogi?" *How did news of the game spread out this far?* As it turned out, Olga wrote about it in one of the letters she sent him, and it wound up catching his interest.

"I just so happen to have a shogi set with me. Would you like it?"

"Oh, could I really take it? I'd be most grateful. I've wanted to see it with my own eyes for a while." Luckily for him, I still had the shogi set I made during the trip.

"No problem. I'll make sure you have it by tomorrow. Though, I have some business to take care of, so... Lyon, could you bring it to Olba? Olga already knows the rules, so I'm sure she'll teach you both."

"H-Hm?! Me?!" Once I brought him into the conversation, Lyon began to panic once again.

"Lyon's father is General Leon, one of the king's most trusted aides. I hear he's one of the king's top picks for shogi opponents, as well."

"Hoh? A son of *the* General Leon?! Oh my, I would be really glad if you visited our home. There's so much I want to ask you." Olba spoke gleefully to Lyon, a full smile across his face. When it came to personal background, the young knight was a fine match for his daughter. I quietly hoped he'd make a good impression on the old fox. Well, whether they'd get married or not depended entirely on how the lovebirds felt, so I might've been doing something unnecessary in the end.

"Yes! I'll be sure to come and visit you tomorrow, then!" Lyon positioned himself like a proper soldier. The guy was as needlessly serious as ever.

As I worried about the extremely diligent knight, the people gathered in the palace grew a bit noisier.

What's all the fuss about? I looked over to the entrance of the hall, where I saw His Beastliness, Olga, Yumina, and the rest of the girls.

Olga was clad in a gaudy Belfastian party dress, while Yumina and the rest were wearing costumes that reminded me of Indian saris. Elze's was red, Linze's was blue, Yae's was purple, and Yumina's was white. Though different in color, they all looked really good. Kohaku was walking alongside them.

"Oh, hey again, boyo. You're looking pretty good. I almost mistook you for a Mismedian noble."

"Er, thanks... I guess." The beastking stared at me with a grin on his face. *This feels kinda awkward... I don't really know how to deal with situations like this at all.*

I looked to my side to see Lyon intently looking at Olga in her fancy dress. *Oh my... I could see a familiar hair ornament shining in her hair. I think it's safe to say he has a shot with her at the very least.*

"I love your outfit, Touya. You look wonderful," Yumina said, lavishing me with praise.

"Yup. It just works."

"...I-It shows a different kind of charm..." Linze muttered.

"Amazing, Touya-dono! It's very flattering on you."

Everyone seems to think I look pretty nice... You guys better stop it or I'll blush!

"You all look really good, too. Oh hey, can I take a photo?" I took out my smartphone and brought up the camera. Once I got them all in frame, I took the picture, making my phone emit a flash.

Surprised by the burst of light, the Mismedian soldiers posted next to the palace walls placed their hands on their swords. *Uh-oh, guess the flash is a no-no.*

"What was that?" His Beastliness looked at the smartphone in my hand. *Well, guess I'd have to explain it sooner or later...*

"Sorry, this is one of my Null spells. I can use it to record what I see and look back on it later."

"Hoh? Sorry, I don't really understand." I showed him the photo I just took. The four girls were on it, lined up and smiling.

"Oho! A spell that lets you draw pictures right away, eh? I've heard of someone with a similar spell over in the Refreese Imperium! Is it possible to take this picture out, though?"

Hmm... so the Imperium has someone who can do something similar to me? Now I'm a little curious about what kind of person that could be... Putting those thoughts aside, I decided there was no need to give a full explanation of how photos worked.

"I can actually take it out, yeah! I just need a piece of paper and something to write with." The beastking had someone bring me what I requested. I looked at the photo I took and cast [**Drawing**] to transfer it to the paper. Soon enough, the blank paper displayed a discolored, sepia-like version of the photo showing the four girls. It was like one of those old, monochrome photos. I could have colored it, but this much was enough to get the point across.

"Incredible! That's amazing, kid— er, Sir Touya! Could you draw a picture of me as well?"

"Sure, no problem." Since he was right there, I didn't have to use the camera. I simply cast [**Drawing**] while using him as reference.

When I gave him a photo… well, sort of a photo, of him doing a cool pose, he was completely overjoyed. But it very quickly got out of hand. Caught in the flow of the situation, I drew out Olba's family, after which countless random party guests asked me to draw them, too.

A single drawing took less than ten seconds, so I had no qualms about doing it over and over, but there were a number of people who weren't satisfied with their poses or something and took multiple tries to satisfy. *What am I, a Polaroid camera?! I'm getting tired… C'mon already.*

Lyon took advantage of the chaos and had me draw him next to Olga. I had no reason to refuse, of course. But still, when I did that one I felt less like a Polaroid camera and more like a photo booth.

After I finished up with the requests of the more important guests, I ran out of the party hall to take a rest. I noticed a couch in the corner of the corridor, so I plopped down onto it and tried to relax. That was pretty easy, considering how silent the place was compared to the party.

As I blankly stared at the corridor up ahead, something strange walked through the place where the corridors intersected.

CHAPTER II: TO THE DEMI-HUMAN KINGDOM

"What the—" An expression of disbelief passed my lips.

There was one thing I noticed about the... *thing* walking down the corridor in the distance. To be blunt, it was a bear. Well, sure, the country of demi-humans was bound to have some bear beastmen. I'd actually seen quite a few of them at the party. The issue wasn't that, but the fact that the thing I saw was not a beastman. It was a stuffed bear toy.

I couldn't say for sure, but it seemed about fifty centimeters tall, and no matter how many times I re-evaluated what I was looking at, it was clearly a plush toy bear... *Why is there a toy bear walking around... Am I more tired than I thought I was?*

Suddenly, it stopped and looked in my general direction. *Oh cripes, it's looking me dead in the eye!*

Staaare...

Staaaare...

Staaaaare...

Staaaaaare...

Hasn't this happened before...? What? The bear was moving its arm, clearly beckoning me over.

Is it trying to ask me to come with it? Should I actually follow it? I pondered for a moment and decided to oblige. I reasoned that if things started to look bad, I could use [**Accel**] and get out of there.

The waddling bear led me to a room not so far from the party hall. It was short and stubby, so it couldn't reach the doorknob. Undeterred, it skillfully jumped up and spun the knob to open the door. It headed inside, but not before beckoning to me again.

Guess it wants me to keep following... I entered the dimly-lit room and saw moonlight beaming in through the window. The room was spacious and properly furnished.

"Oh? You brought over quite a strange guest this time, Paula." Perplexed by the sudden voice, I started looking around. Moments later, I noticed a girl sitting on a red chair in front of the window.

Age-wise, she seemed close to Yumina and Arma. She had white hair tied in twin-tails and eyes of gold. Wearing a frilly black dress, black boots, and black headdress, she looked like a proper gothic lolita. Normally, my eyes would be fixed on her clothing, but I couldn't keep them from shifting to the things behind her.

A set of thin, semi-clear wings, shimmering in the moonlight. They weren't like those you'd see on birds, more like those of an insects. It was safe to assume that she was a fairy.

"So? Who might you be?"

"Ah, I'm Touya. Mochizuki Touya. Touya's my given name."

"Born in Eashen, I take it?" *Oh, how I'd love for that to stop. Well, it's similar enough, so I can't really say much else...*

"I see. So you're a guest of this party. The famed Dragon Slayer, yes?"

"Dragon Slayer? Well, I mean... I guess that's not wrong. And you are?"

"Oh, do forgive me. I've forgotten to introduce myself. I am Leen, the clan matriarch of all fairies. And this little darling here is Paula." Clan matriarch?! This girl?! The surprise made my words catch in my throat, to which Leen giggled, clearly amused.

"Despite appearances, I am far older than you. Longevity is but one of the main characteristics of the fairy race, after all."

"You're older than me?! By how man—?" *Wait, I better stop right there. It's definitely not appropriate to ask a woman her age.* Leen, however, didn't seem to mind my train of thought.

"Well, I'm not too sure... I'm at least six centuries older, that much is certain."

"Six centuries?!"

"Thinking about this is a bother, so just assume that I'm six-hundred and twelve years old." *W-Wait, that's a pretty major assumption... I can't believe this petite-looking girl is over six centuries old... No holds barred in this world, I guess. That said, now that I know her age it's easier to accept she's the clan matriarch.*

"Do fairies age slowly?"

"...That isn't the case, no. We merely stop aging when we reach a certain age. Normally, it happens when we reach the appearance of a human in their late teens or early twenties, but it came earlier for me. That's all there is to it." I could see her pouting as she muttered those words. I figured she wasn't too happy with the body she was stuck with for eternity. *Man, no matter how I look at her, I can't see her as anything other than a person Yumina's age.*

As if to comfort Leen, Paula clambered behind her and patted her on the head.

"So, about Paula... is she some kind of contracted familiar?"

"She isn't, actually. She's a genuine stuffed bear. She can only move thanks to my Null spell, [**Program**]."

"[**Program**]?"

You mean like a computer program or something? Is this bear a robot?! "The Null spell, [**Program**], allows the user to give certain orders to inorganic objects and make them act accordingly. For example..." She took a chair from the side of the room and brought it over to me. Leen held her hand before the chair and focused her power, making a magic circle form under it.

"**Begin [Program]/Motion: Two meters forward/Starting Condition: Someone sitting/End [Program].**" The magic circle on the floor quickly faded away. Once Leen sat down on the chair, it slowly moved about two meters forward before stopping.

"Oh, I forgot to set the speed. But you get the general idea. It allows me to give magical orders to objects."

Yeah, I think I get it now. A name like **[Program]** *is more than appropriate for this one. Even if it's limited by the programming, the ability to make objects move on their own is super useful.*

"So, can you make Paula fly by adding an order that forces her to?"

"Something like that is impossible, I'm afraid. It isn't that great of a power. **[Program]** only allows for simple movements. Though flight would likely work fine for small model birds."

Alright, I think I understand better now. Seems like the spell has some reasonable limits. Doesn't make it any less useful, though.

"I'll have a go at it."

"Sorry...?" I focused my magic on the chair. A magic circle formed on the floor, and I began to prepare my own **[Program]**.

"Begin [Program]/Motion: Five meters backward at standard human walking speed/Starting Condition: Someone sitting/End [Program]." Once the magic circle disappeared, I quickly tested the program by sitting on the chair. It began moving backward at a slightly higher speed than before and stopped after five meters. *Yup, this is useful.*

"What... What did you do just now?" Leen was staring at me, blinking hard and slow.

"Well... I used **[Program],** didn't I?"

"Why are you phrasing it like a question...? No, forget that for now. You were able to use **[Program]** just like that?"

"Erm... ahaha, I guess so..." She looked at me with great suspicion in her eyes.

Staaaare...

Staaaare...

Staaaaare…

This happened with Paula already! They say pets resemble their owners, but I don't know if that's quite right here… Soon enough, she heaved a sigh and folded her arms.

"There's a lot I'd like to ask you, but I'll leave it for another time… I told Paula to bring any interesting humans to me, and she didn't fail me in that regard. You might even be a better find than Charlotte was."

"Charlotte?" I couldn't help but react to the familiar name.

It can't be the same Charlotte, can it? "Yes, one of my disciples. I hear she's Court Magician in Belfast now." *Oh. I guess it could. Wait, then, hold on… That means…!*

"Ah! So you're the demonic teacher that made her cast spells until she collapsed, then forcibly restored her magic and made her cast more spells until she collapsed again, right?!"

"What?!"

Oh man, she's scaring me. Please don't glare at me like that, I'm fragile. I'm not the one who said it to begin with! S-Sorry? Should I say sorry?! I should say sorry!

"Well, never mind that… Charlotte will be getting a slap next time I see her, though. That aside, Touya, your magical talents are really quite remarkable. Besides Null, what other elements do you have the aptitude for?"

"All of them."

"…Well, at least nothing will surprise me anymore." After another long sigh, Leen pondered something before slowly opening her golden eyes. She looked over at me and clasped her hands together.

"Very well, then. You shall be my new disciple."

"Come again?" The twin-tailed gothic lolita made her wings quiver as she smiled in my direction.

Yesterday, the matriarch of the fairies, Leen, told me to become her disciple, but I politely refused. Seriously, who would willingly work under someone so relentless? I'm not a masochist or anything, you know? Still, she seemed pretty annoyed by my rejection.

Later on, the party reached a calm end. We returned to the rooms we were given and went to sleep on our soft beds. It'd been a while since I slept on something nice, so it took some time for me to fall asleep. Before I realized it, however, it was already morning and I was well rested.

Alright, there's something I wanna try out today! I browsed several sites on my phone and used [**Drawing**] to get transcripts and pictures of just about everything that looked useful. *Think that should be just about everything...*

Once I was done with the light breakfast they brought me, I gathered the bundle of papers I prepared and got Kohaku to join me in going to see Chancellor Glatz.

I told him that I wanted to leave for a bit, so he gave me a medal that doubled as a permit for crossing the castle gates. He also asked me if I could use [**Drawing**] to make a portrait of him. In all honesty, he was the one person I hadn't expected to request one.

After that, I met up with Lyon and gave him the shogi set. Sensing a small opportunity, I also told him that Reflet was planning on becoming the official town for shogi.

"Oh? Are you going out?" Once Kohaku and I were done with our business in the palace, we set off for the main town. But not before we ran into Yumina and Linze. It seemed they had just eaten breakfast and were about to go out for a walk in the courtyard.

"Yeah, Kohaku and I were gonna go shopping. You two wanna tag along?"

"Of course," Yumina responded immediately.

"I-I'll come too," Linze replied hesitantly. I was thinking of inviting Elze and Yae as well, but Linze said they were training alongside the Mismedian soldiers in the arena... I could only hope that His Beastliness wasn't there, too.

The four of us crossed the palace gate and went out to town. *Alright, now... wait.*

"Where can I buy metal?"

"M-Metal?"

"Yeah. Iron, copper, brass. Things like that. Ideally they'd be pressed into ingots."

"I'm not exactly sure what 'ingot' means, but I think you might find what you want at a blacksmith's," Yumina replied.

Well, that makes sense. I took out my phone and ran a search for smithies. There were some points here and there. I figured I couldn't go wrong by choosing the closest one.

We took the street heading eastward and found the place on the corner near an intersection. I could hear the hammering before we even got there.

"Morning. Welcome all. You here for a repair job? Or maybe your blade needs sharpening?" A horned employee greeted us with a smile. They were more than happy to sell pressed metals to me, so I bought some iron, brass, and lead. Several ingots about as thick as two small paperback books, to be exact. There was a tool shop right in front of the smithy, so I took the opportunity to buy some wood and rubber. The kind used on shoe soles.

"And now for the gunpowder..." I ran a search for it and easily got a hit. *Seems like it's at a magical goods shop... Well, I guess gunpowder is kind of magical.*

I went there and bought three medium-sized bottles of the powdery stuff. *I think that's everything I need, then!*

"...What are you planning to make?" Linze looked at all the goods I bought and couldn't help but ask.

"Gonna forge myself a weapon."

"A weapon...?" After they tilted their heads in confusion, I took them to a nearby back alley and used a **[Gate]** to return to my room in the palace. I grabbed the meter-long Dragon horn I had left there earlier, and used another **[Gate]** to go to the forest we crossed before getting to the Mismedian capital.

Good, nobody'll see us out here.

I placed my papers on a nearby stump and put an ingot on top to stop the wind from blowing them away.

"Now I just need to take this Dragon horn, and..." *Crap. I can't actually make use of the horn right now, can I? It's a little bit too long. Ah well, I'll just trim it a bit first... Wait, it was too tough to cut with any of my gear, wasn't it?*

"Linze, can you use magic to cut it? Somewhere around here, please."

"N-No problem!" I showed her where to cut and she got to it pretty quick.

"Come forth, Water! Feel My Blade, Both Cold and Clear: [Aqua Cutter]!" With a watery sound, the Dragon horn was cut down to a more proper size. *Whew, good thing I brought Linze along.* I took the result into my hand, and it was far lighter than it looked. I felt as though I was holding plastic. The lightness made me doubt its strength, but it was a cold hard fact that it was far tougher than iron. I was pretty amazed by it all.

Wait, I didn't come here just to admire this thing. I've got a job to do!

I glared at the papers I brought and memorized all the relevant parts. Well, even if they came out wrong, I could just use some fine-tuning to fix it up. *Alright. It's time.*

"[**Modeling**]." The horn began to slowly change shape. Barrel, cylinder, hammer, trigger... I made the parts, one after another. After that, I used the wood I bought to create a grip and put them all together.

Ten minutes later, I held a slick black revolver in my hand.

I based it on a gun known as the Remington New Model Army, but it turned out a bit short. Well, it wasn't *too* different, so I didn't really care.

Since I wanted something that could rapidly fire, I turned a single-action gun into a double-action one and messed around with the cylinder, so the insides of this gun ended up completely unlike the original. I only used it as basis because I thought the design looked cool. Taking it in hand, I examined how it felt.

Not too shabby, to be honest. Maybe it's a little light? Actually, that's probably not a negative.

"Now, for the bullets." Using the ingots and gunpowder, I made the bullet heads, cases, powders, rims, and primers, just as they looked on the internet.

By the time I was done, I had fifty bullets of several varieties. *That's enough for now,* I thought.

Alright, time to load up all six revolver chambers... Oh wait, before that...

"[**Enchant**]: [**Apport**]." I enchanted the gun with my item teleporting spell. *And now...*

"**Begin [Program]/Starting Condition: Wielder says 'reload'/Action Upon Start: Hastily eject empty cartridges, use [Apport] to refill any empty chambers using bullets located**

within a range of one meter/End [Program]." And with that, I was done. Manually reloading was a pain, after all. I could've just made an automatic weapon instead, but my taste was more important than that. I considered revolvers to be the coolest gun, that's all there was to it.

I filled the chambers, aimed at a nearby tree, and pulled the trigger. The bullet went flying with an explosive sound. *Whoa! The recoil's way stronger than I thought it'd be.* Linze and Yumina put their hands over their ears. Despite the grand presentation, it seemed that I actually missed my shot.

I followed it up with two more bullets and noticed that my accuracy was pretty low. *Am I just a bad shot? The bullets aren't firing straight at a— Oh...*

Right, I forgot to make the rifling. Rifling refers to the helical grooves in the inside of a gun's barrel. I read that it gyroscopically stabilized the bullet by forcing it to spin, which made it travel straight.

And so, with another [**Modeling**] spell, I crafted the rifling for my gun. I shot some more bullets, and the difference in accuracy was clear as day.

Once I emptied the whole cylinder, I decided to test the reloading mechanism that I'd programmed earlier.

"Reload!" The moment I said that, the empty cartridges were instantly ejected and fell to the ground. Then, six of the bullets I had placed on the stump disappeared and reappeared inside the gun. I pulled the trigger again. Another bullet fired out. *Yup, it works like a charm.*

"Are you finished?"

"Yep, I'd say so. This is something called a 'gun.' It's a weapon made to attack at long distances. You can use it with one hand and it's stronger than bows and arrows."

"...Amazing. It's like a small cannon." Linze quietly spoke, gazing at my creation. It was true that not-so-sleek cannons also existed in this world, but since any single wizard who knew the [Explosion] spell was far more effective, they didn't see much use.

"I finished making the gun, but there's still one more thing I wanna try." After removing all the bullets from the cylinder, I took one into my hand.

"[Enchant]: [Explosion]." I imbued it with explosive magic. *Let's see here...*

"Begin [Program]/Starting Condition: The bullet head escapes the gun's muzzle and impacts something/Action Upon Start: Activate [Explosion] around the bullet/End [Program]." I placed the enchanted bullet into the cylinder and shot the same hole-riddled tree.

With a fierce roar, the tree I shot and the ones unfortunate enough to be near it shattered into thousands of splintery pieces. The [Explosion] test worked.

"Wha...?!"

"W-Whoa!" Linze and Yumina fell to the ground, seemingly too shocked to stay upright. *Good. That solves my issue of using offensive magic without an incantation. Then again, having to [Enchant] and [Program] everything is a bit of a pain, too... Wait, I could just do it with multiple bullets at once, so it's not so bad.*

I could probably enchant some rubber rounds with [Paralyze] for non-lethal takedowns. Weapons this handy are few and far between indeed! Oh wait, [Paralyze] wouldn't work if they had any magic-warding amulets on them.

"Touya, may I also have one of these... guns, was it?"

"I-I'd like one, as well..."

"Huh?" Yumina and Linze's sudden request made me ponder for a bit. I could understand why they, being rearguard fighters, would want such a weapon, but I couldn't help but worry. *Am I just being too overprotective?*

Yumina has a bow, a pretty dangerous thing in its own right, and Linze has the ability to clip a Dragon's wings, so worrying about them handling a gun safely is kinda stupid.

Also, being able to use magic without any care for affinity would be pretty advantageous. With a gun, even Yumina, someone without any aptitude for fire, could use [**Explosion**].

"Sure, why not? Pick a design you like." I ran an image search for various guns and put them to paper using [**Drawing**]. After a long moment of staring at the options, Yumina finally chose a Colt Army Model 1860, while Linze went for a snub-nosed revolver known as the Smith & Wesson Model 36.

Linze's was fine, but I was a bit worried about how Yumina's choice would fit in her hand. Then I remembered that it was just a design and I could handle the size myself. My gun was also made to suit me, after all. Right down to the specs and caliber.

Honestly, my gun-crafting was rough. I was sure any gun nuts out there would give me a real earful. If I needed it to just shoot something out, a BB gun would've worked just fine. Even so, there were things you just couldn't help but get picky about. Basically, I always wanted to fire a real gun.

I had Linze cut the Dragon's horn again and used it to make their guns for them. Just to be on the safe side, I programmed their weapons in a way that prevented anyone else but them from pulling the trigger.

I created about a hundred rubber bullets, divided them between the girls, and let them get the hang of wielding and firing their guns.

Being made from a Dragon's horn, they were lighter than standard firearms and weren't too hard for girls to use.

Alright, now it's time for the main event. The gun was actually nothing but a base for the creation of my *real* weapon.

"[**Modeling**]." I took more of the Dragon's horn and once again began giving it the form of a gun. However, unlike the other ones, this one was building up to be a bit strange.

Extending from the trigger guard and tracing the lower part of the barrel, there was a blade. The grip made a bit of a curve and gave the whole object a somewhat straight shape. Overall, it was less of a gun and more of a shortsword.

An unholy fusion of gun and knife! Though, "knife" wasn't too apt either, considering the blade was thirty centimeters long and pretty broad. However, there was a reason for that broadness.

"**Begin [Program]/Starting Condition: The wielder says 'Gun Mode' or 'Blade Mode'/Action Upon Start: Use [Modeling] to quickly transform the blade piece from shortsword to longsword in the case of 'Blade Mode,' or from longsword to shortsword in the case of 'Gun Mode'/End [Program].**" I also programmed it with the same reloading mechanism I'd tried earlier. I reloaded quickly, readied my weapon, and pulled the trigger. A gunshot rang out, and the bullet easily destroyed a branch. *Great, the gun works just fine!*

"Blade Mode." In response to my words, the thirty centimeter knife instantly became an eighty centimeter sword. The broad blade lost about two-thirds of its thickness and gained some length instead.

I swung the elongated blade around. It didn't feel the least bit heavy.

"Gun Mode." The blade became short and broad again. *Alright, the transformation function works just fine.*

"Amazing. So it can be both a gun and a blade?"

"Elze and Yae are purely vanguard fighters, while you two are purely backliners, so I decided to be a little more flexible in my approach." *To be honest, I've been wanting to do this for a while. The duel with the beastking made me consider that there'll be situations where I can't effectively use magic. The answer to that problem? A gun.*

"...So, what are you going to name your weapon?"

"Well... 'Brunhild' works fine, I guess." I answered Linze with a grin on my face. Instead of using the name of some legendary weapon like "Excalibur" or "Balmung," I went for the name of the strongest weapon in one of my favorite retro games. Man, did I have fun playing that one... It was really old, though. In fact, it was a part of my grandfather's collection.

As I looked at my new weapon, Brunhild, I realized that I was actually part of those fantasy worlds I yearned for in my younger years, which made me aware of just how much my life had changed.

After a few test shots and debugging of my program, I tested the durability of Brunhild's blade mode.

Though it was made of many parts, the whole section that was unaffected by the transformation was almost perfectly merged with the blade and the entire object had the toughness of a Dragon horn. I could easily cut down a rather thick tree. The sharpness was incomparable to my previous sword.

Soon after that, we returned to the town around the palace and bought three leather sheaths for daggers and one for something a bit larger. I turned them all into holsters for our guns with my [**Modeling**] spell. They really stood out, after all.

While I was at it, I also took the opportunity to buy three waist pouches for bullets. Since we were in town, we didn't have to worry about being attacked by monsters, so I only gave the girls rubber bullets imbued with [**Paralyze**]. I still had a bunch of real bullets with me, though. It suddenly dawned on me that there was the possibility of them standing next to me while reloading and accidentally getting my real bullets into their guns...

To prevent such a disaster, I reprogrammed their weapons. Now, the guns would only load the bullets that the wielder wanted. That was perfectly doable thanks to [**Apport**].

That meant we only had to consider the enchantments to put on the bullets. Since Linze used [**Explosion**] back in the ruins of the old capital, I was fully aware that it had the firepower to blast away a whole load of ruins, and it was lacking in utility. *Maybe* [**Ignis Fire**], *then? One shot and they'd be engulfed in flames... No, that's totally overdoing it as well.*

Well, as long as the opponent is human, [**Paralyze**] *should work just fine. Even if they have amulets protecting them, the rubber bullets'll still hurt a lot. Hm… guess I'll need to think about it more later.*

"Wanna grab some food while we're in town?"

"Great idea. I'd love to try the local cuisine."

"Y-Yes, me too. I've heard a lot about this local dish called 'Cully.'"

Cully…? Hmm… that's piqued my interest. Guess I'll try it too. It was sold at a nearby food stall, so we went right for it. There was a menu with "pork cully," among other variants. *That smell's pretty familiar…*

Yumina ordered a beef cully, Linze got a chicken cully, and I got a pork cully. Kohaku didn't want any, for some reason. We sat at the nearby table and waited for only a few minutes before it was ready.

This color, and this smell… I knew it! It's curry. Not rice curry, though, since there was no rice.

"Uh, guys? Just so you know…" I was about to warn them about the potential spiciness, but they had already brought some of it to their mouths.

"Ack!" "Gah?!" They covered their mouths as tears formed in their eyes.

Ah. I guess it is spicy, then. Shame it isn't the sweet kind. Judging from how those two are acting, it must be super hot…

They reached for the water jug on the table, almost fighting one another over it, as they poured some water into their cups and quickly gulped it down. As I watched them, I tried the curry myself, and wow, was it hot. That evaluation was coming from yours truly, who'd tasted quite a number of spicy curries, so I could only imagine how hard it hit the girls.

"Whath a shtrong tashte…" "Ow, it'sh like my tongue ish on fire…" So hot they couldn't even speak properly… Once we left the cully wagon, we went to get some fruit juice from another vendor. A few quick sips of that neutralized the deadly spice.

"It's not that bad once you get used to it."

"You hadh a chance to eat khullay before, Touyah?"

"Well, something similar to it, at least." I gave Yumina, who was still having trouble speaking, an ambiguous answer. Linze took the ice that came with the juice and moved it around in her mouth. *Come to think of it, I haven't had much of anything spicy since I came to this world.* In my mind, Belfast was almost solidified as a kingdom of sweet foods.

…*Huh?* As thoughts of dinner circled my head, I felt someone looking at me. *This sensation's a familiar one…*

«Master. Someone is observing us. I believe it's the same people as before.» Kohaku spoke to me telepathically. *I knew it.*

«The ones who were watching us back in Langley? Alright. Let's say hello to them. Where are they located?»

«Atop the tallest building to your right.» Pretending that I wasn't aware of their presence, I looked up to where Kohaku had pointed out. I could see them on the roof of a three-story building. They were pretty far off.

"Guess I should get ready… Reload." I filled my holstered gunblade, Brunhild, with rubber bullets imbued with **[Paralyze]**.

"Touya." My sudden reloading made the girls look at me with apparent confusion, but there was no time to explain.

«Keep an eye on the girls, Kohaku.»

«Be careful.» *It's go-time.*

"**[Boost]**." I buffed my physical abilities and jumped upward. After landing on one of the buildings to my side, I made another leap toward the roof ahead of me. Roof after roof, I went straight for the building upon which I saw the mysterious observers.

"Yo."

"Gh?!" "Hm?!" My sudden arrival and nonchalant greeting left them stunned.

At least, I thought it did. I couldn't see their faces. They wore similar-looking black robes, and from the little I saw, the clothes under the robes were black, as well. The faces under their hooded heads were hidden by white masks. Not completely white, though, since there were strange symbols on the foreheads. For a moment, I thought they were the same on both, but then I noticed that one had a hexagon, while the other had a vertically stretched oval.

"Er, hey… can you talk? I'd like to know who you are and wh—" Suddenly, the one with the hexagon took out a test tube-like object and threw it on the ground. In a flash, the surroundings were bathed in an intense light.

"Khh…!" The flash momentarily blinded me, and once I regained my sight, the observers had vanished. *They escaped? Ha, not likely!* I took out my smartphone and ran a search for 'masked weirdo.' And there they were. The two were running through a back alley to the north. *There's still time to catch up, good.*

"[Accel Boost]!" Speeding myself up with magic, I ran across the roofs again. The view went by me with insane speed, and moments later, I could see the two running through the back alley.

I went ahead of them and stopped them in their tracks.

"Mmph?!" "Gh!" I still couldn't see their faces through the masks, but I was almost certain they were surprised. However, Hexagon Mask quickly reached for another one of those test tubes. *Not this time!*

Without hesitation, I took out Brunhild and fired at the one trying to blind me.

The sound of a gunshot rang out as hexagon mask fell to the ground. *No protective amulets, huh? Too bad.* Having lost an ally, oval mask looked at me, then back at the one on the ground, seemingly not knowing what to do next. *That's my opening.* Another gunshot rang out through the back alley.

"Alrighty! What now?" While they were still paralyzed, I tied them up with coils I made using [**Modeling**] and placed them against the wall of the alley. I could take their masks off and look at their faces, but with [**Paralyze**] active, they were still conscious. It would be pretty bad if they had some weird, cult-like laws that'd force them to commit suicide or kill me if I were to see their faces.

"I'll take away the paralysis, so don't struggle, okay?" I gazed into their eyes and focused my magic.

"[**Recovery**]." A gentle light embraced them both. That should've taken care of the paralysis. Now, if only we could have a proper exchange.

"So, who are you two? Why were you observing me?"

"……" *Hmm… using their right to remain silent, huh?*

A moment later, I noticed that Hexagon Mask was making slight movements. *Did I tie the wire too tight? No, probably trying to escape…* It'd be quite a pain if they used some weird tool, similar to the flash bomb, to melt away the wire or something. To be on the safe side, I decided to remove their gadgets and whatnot.

I placed my hand against Hexagon Mask's chest.

"Hyah?!" Hexagon Mask released a cutesy voice and I began to feel something soft in my hand. Once I realized what it was, I began to sweat all over.

"Y-Y-You're a girl?!" Hexagon Mask nodded slightly. I quickly withdrew my hand, but I could still feel the softness I'd held mere moments ago. *Oh geez.* My face was probably as red as a tomato. *Wait... wasn't that voice familiar?*

As I backed my hand away, I accidentally hit her and made the white mask with the hexagon fall to the ground with a clatter. The face under it was that of a woman I knew.

"What the—?! Lapis...?" With a blushing face, my maid, who should've been at my home back in the capital of Belfast, gave me another nod.

"We are 'Espion.' Intelligence operatives acting directly under the command of His Majesty, the king of Belfast."

"The king?"

"Yes. Our current mission is to protect the princess." Lapis' explanation was easy to process. With how he just handed her over to me, I always thought that the king's attitude with regard to Yumina was a bit too relaxed, and this explained it all. He was looking after her from the shadows.

Wait, I remember that time I heard something through the ceiling of the Silver Moon Inn... I thought it was a rodent or something at the time, but it could've been these guys. This "Espion" group sounds like a mix of traditional ninjas and modern spies.

"Are you the only ones protecting Yumina?"

"Nooo, there's several mooore. All of them are girls, toooo." My other maid replied with her usual needlessly stretched pronunciation. Cecile, who voluntarily removed her mask, was giving me a smile completely devoid of any fear.

They're all girls, huh? Well, since their protective detail required hiding up in the ceiling and similar places, girls were probably the better option as far as Yumina's privacy was considered.

"Wait, how long have you been following us? Since we were still in Belfast?"

"That's what our mission was, yes," Lapis responded.

"Now that I think about it, neither of you were home when I used a [Gate] to return there. I assume Laim is in on it, too, then?"

"Yes, hee is." Well, they sure had me fooled. I asked them some more questions, and apparently, they weren't lying about being part of the Maid's Guild. Maid skills were necessary for infiltration missions, so just about every female operative of Espion was also a guild member.

"Ah, wait. So, the one who threw the knife at the Black Dragon was…"

"That was Cecile, yes. She's a knife-throwing expert."

"Eheheheeh. Oh, I'm not *thaat* good." Cecile's cheeks turned slightly rosy as she blushed. *So, that knife was thrown by this… puffy girl? Never judge a book by its cover, I guess.*

Suddenly, Cecile grew a bit despondent and fearfully looked up at me.

"Sooo, uhmm… are we getting fiiired?"

"Hm? Why would you be fired?"

"Well, sir, we're your maids, and instead of fulfilling our duties, we're here on another job entirely…" *Oh, that.* So she felt bad about working for the king while being hired by me, then.

"No, I don't plan on firing either of you. The king only gave the order because he was worried about his daughter, after all. Also, if I fired you, I'd also have to get rid of Laim." *Do you girls think I'm that petty...?* I was pretty confident I had the emotional depth to sympathize with a father worrying over his little girl.

The two heaved a sigh of relief.

"So, what are you going to do now?"

"We will keep on secretly protecting Princess Yumina... but before that, we have something to ask of you, sir." This time, Lapis was the one to look up at me, readying herself to say something difficult. *Man, I just can't get used to being called sir...*

"Would you be kind enough to keep us a secret from the princess...?" *Ah, since it's a secret mission, being found out is obviously a huge problem.*

"If she were to find out about our protection, the princess would get reeeally mad at his Majesty." *Oh, never mind. The real reason is a lot simpler. Well, he acted as though he sent her off by herself because he believed in her, so the truth would make it seem like he didn't believe in her at all. Gotta be tough to be a dad, huh...? I don't mind keeping a secret, so it's fine by me.* I let them keep following their orders, walked away from them, and returned to Yumina.

I told Kohaku all about it through our telepathic link. To Yumina and Linze, however, I just lied by saying that they ran away. Well, it wasn't a *complete* lie, since they actually did run away once after blinding me. They gave me some strange looks, but I was able to fool them and we all returned to the palace.

The following day, the kings of Belfast and Mismede were to have a discussion regarding the details of the alliance between the kingdoms.

It was a proper summit meeting, but there was a minor bit of arguing over which side would come over to the other. In the end, it was decided that Belfast would come to Mismede, so I placed the mirror meant for teleportation (officially, anyway) in the conference room.

Besides me, the other people present were Lyon, the other Belfastian knights, His Beastliness, Chancellor Glatz, and a bunch of Mismedian soldiers led by the familiar wolf beastman, Captain Garm.

I opened a [Gate] just in front of the mirror, allowing His Majesty and his younger brother, Duke Ortlinde, to pass through.

The fact that a person actually walked out of the mirror surprised many of those present, but that didn't last long, for it was time to give the king a proper welcome.

"Welcome to Mismede, King of Belfast."

"Thank you for the invitation, Beastking of Mismede." They exchanged a handshake. It was time for matters of state. Being an outsider, I decided to take my leave.

I headed out of the conference room and into the corridor. All I could do was hope that the two kings would get along.

Suddenly, from one end of the corridor, I saw the stuffed bear, Paula, toddle along with her master, Leen. She was still clad in the same gothic lolita outfit as the last time we met.

"Seems like the Belfastian king came over to say hi."

"Yeah, just now. They're having a conference in there." I answered her while pointing at a nearby door, the only door with two guards standing by it.

"Well, do you feel like becoming my disciple yet?"

"How many times do I have to say no before you get it?" Refusing to give up after my first rejection, Leen had been asking me to be her disciple just about every time we met since then.

Last time she said I could be a "provisional disciple." Sounds too much like "provisional club enrollment" to me. Wait, isn't that a lower position than regular old disciple?! Paula stood by her side, beckoning me forward with a small gesture.

"Man, for a stuffed toy, Paula sure is lively… It's almost like she's alive."

"That just shows how many times I've used [**Program**] on her, doesn't it? I've been setting her with actions and reactions to various situations for almost two hundred years now. She might as well be autonomous at this point. You humans cry when in pain and get mad when made fun of, right? Same principle." *Two hundred years…? So Paula's behavior feels natural due to countless uses of* [**Program**] *over a long period, huh?*

Suddenly, I considered the possibility of creating a human-like doll via [**Modeling**] and then using [**Program**] to make a pseudo-android, but then I remembered that it took Leen two hundred years just for Paula. *I wonder if we could copy and paste her programming…*

In response to my intense stare, Paula seemed to get a little uncomfortable. She backed off slightly. *Oho, so even that kind of response is programmed too?*

"You said she's over two hundred, but Paula sure doesn't look it. Do you rebuild her regularly or something?"

"That's not the case, no. She's under the effects of my Null spell, [**Protection**]. As the name goes, it's a spell that, well, protects from certain things. Paula is protected against getting dirty, deteriorating, and getting gnawed on by bugs, among other things."

Protection magic, huh? I won't lie, it's pretty impressive that Paula still looks so good. Using it on clothing would remove the need for laundry, right? Hell, casting it on the body could remove the need to take baths… Though, that doesn't seem quite right. Even if it protects from outside filth, it probably can't do anything to the buildup of grime due to metabolic processes.

"Wait, how many Null spells can you use, Leen? There's [Protection], [Program], and the [Transfer] one that Charlotte told me about."

"Fairies have a high aptitude for Null magic. In fact, fairies that don't have a single Null spell to their name are few and far between. I only happen to have four at present, however."

Four of the elusive Null spells, huh? That's pretty amazing. But I guess I'm not really in a position to say that, given my own affinities. I can see why fairies are considered a species built for magic, though. Now I'm curious about what Leen's fourth Null spell is.

"Sir Touya? His Majesty, the king of Belfast wishes to see you. Please come inside."

Chancellor Glatz opened the door to the conference room and peeked out. Having no reason to refuse, I went in, which made both kings turn to stare at me.

"Hey, Touya my boy. The talks went very smoothly. Thank you for all your help."

"Well, that's good to hear." The Belfastian king's words made me heave a sigh of relief. My job was as good as done.

"Very well. We shall now return to Belfast. We leave the rest to you. Thank you for your time, Your Majesty."

Once they were done with their goodbyes, I secretly opened a [Gate] in front of the mirror and let the king and his brother leave. When they were gone, I began acting out our plan. With everyone watching, I took out a hammer and shattered the mirror into little pieces.

"S-Sir Touya?! What are you...?!"

"Ah, there's no need to be upset. Just give me a moment." Ignoring the flustered Glatz for a moment, I looked away from him and focused my magic on the fragments of the mirror.

"**[Modeling]**" The broken mirror and wooden frame lost their original shape and turned into a number of small, oblong mirrors. Basically, I created some small framed mirrors approximately two centimeters high and fifteen centimeters wide. I picked one up and quietly enchanted it with **[Gate]**.

"These mirrors are connected to Belfast. Now, when you have something important to tell someone there, you need only put a letter into the mirror. Though both sides will still have to use official documents to confirm their authenticity."

"I-I see… So messages that normally take a twenty day round trip will now reach them in an instant? That is most convenient! I will make sure to use it to further our friendly relations." I handed the little mirror over to the beastking, and he gave a small smile. With that, my job was done.

Finally, time to head home… Even though I have such a nice place, I haven't had a chance to live there properly yet. I feel about ready to take a long rest.

For the time being, Lyon and his knights decided they'd remain in Mismede. From what I heard, not having any Belfastians there could cause any post-meeting formalities to stagnate.

There were those who insisted on protecting Princess Yumina on her way back to Belfast, but she did a good job refusing. Basically, she just told them to do their jobs.

In all truth, however, them coming along would've been a problem. We were planning on getting home instantly using a **[Gate]** after all.

Before we left, I gave Lyon a set of "Gate Mirrors" for sending letters. I thought the name I gave them was cool. They allowed people to keep in touch despite all the distance. If he gave one to Olga, he could talk to her even after returning to Belfast. Man, did he get fired up when I handed them over. To be honest, it was a little unsettling.

I said my goodbyes to His Beastliness, Chancellor Glatz, Olga, and Captain Garm. Leen and Paula were nowhere to be seen, though, so I left without telling them anything. A shame, really, but there was nothing to be done about it.

We left the palace and decided to go around town to pick up some souvenirs for Sue and the servants. While we did that, we also ran a final check of our things. All that was left was to open a **[Gate]** and return to Belfast, but...

"Sorry, I forgot a souvenir I wanted to get." I slipped a white lie to the girls, blended into the crowd, fired up my map app, and searched for the people I needed. *Okay, up on this roof then?* I activated **[Boost],** jumped up, and got myself right to where they were.

"Eek?!"

"Uwahh?! Ohhh, it's just you, sir. Don't surprise us like thaaat."

It was Lapis and Cecile, still wearing the masks from the other day. They were my maids, but their primary employer was still Yumina's father — His Majesty, the king of Belfast.

Apparently, His Majesty made Laim hire them, so I entertained the thought of docking or outright canceling their pay, but since they seemed to be skilled maids, I decided to let it slide.

You're definitely not getting paid for the next ten days, though! If you've got a problem with that, bill the king!

"We're about to use a **[Gate]** to return to Belfast. I figured I should send you two first." With all the spying they'd been doing, they surely knew about my [Gate] spell already, so I figured I'd make the offer.

"Whaaat? To Belfaaaast?"

"Well, if we take the normal route home, we'll get back ten days after everyone else… The princess would likely grow suspicious."

"That's exactly why I'm here." Smiling wryly, I opened up a small [Gate] for them. I walked through, they followed suit, and we all ended up back in our mansion. The living room, to be precise.

"Welcome back."

My butler, Laim, was a bit surprised by our sudden appearance, but he quickly regained his composure and welcomed us home.

"We're back, Laim."

"We're baaack!"

"Please forgive us, the master of the house found out our true mission."

"So I see." Lapis began to explain what could be easily deduced from this situation. In response, Laim could only offer a resigned smile.

I had the two girls change into their maid uniforms and act as though they'd been here the entire time. Once they left to their rooms, Laim bowed his head to me.

"Sir, please forgive me. His Royal Majesty himself made me give the order to them…"

"Well, I can understand a father worrying for his daughter, and it's not like anything bad happened because of this, so I don't mind it too much. Not to mention that it was probably really hard for you to refuse." I had no intention of punishing him for such a minor slight. I wasn't *that* strict.

Sure, if this had connected to a life and death situation or made me lose something big, I would've reacted differently, but there was nothing for me to care too deeply about in this instance. Hell, if you looked at it from one angle, you could even say I had a new pair of guards watching my back... That might be a little bit of a stretch, though.

"Don't worry, I'll keep it a secret from Yumina and the others." Since I was about to leave and return with the girls, I asked him to be sure he'd welcome me as though I was just returning from my journey.

"You took ages! What were you doing?" Using another [Gate], I walked out to the same rooftop I left from, then headed straight for the others. Elze immediately voiced her displeasure. I gave them some half-hearted lies before we went to an empty alley, where I opened yet another [Gate].

Once we entered the living room, Laim welcomed us with a bow.

"Welcome back." After I accepted his greeting for a second time, the door to the living room opened. Lapis and Cecile walked through, looking like the proper maids they should've been all along.

"Welcome back, everyone."

"Welcome baack!"

"Lapis, Cecile. Nice to see you both again." We exchanged a natural enough greeting. Everyone walked back to their rooms and then went to take a bath. We were all pretty tired after the trip. I decided to go in after they were done.

It was a good chance to give everyone their souvenirs.

To Laim, I gave a necktie pin and cufflinks, while Lapis and Cecile received different-colored tea cups. They said they couldn't accept them, but it would've been weird if they were the only ones who didn't get anything from me, so I practically forced them to take the gifts.

Julio and his wife, Crea, got a straw hat and a Mismedian cookbook. I also gave the happy couple two matching bowls. The guards, Tom and Huck, each got a decorated ceremonial knife. Sue would be getting her gift the next day.

I dropped on my bed and stretched myself out. *Man, that was exhausting. Not just physically, either. I didn't expect so much mental strain from traveling into a new country, but it was actually a lot of stress. Then again, I guess this whole world is new to me though, isn't it...?*

All in all, I'm glad I made the trip, though. I came up with a ton of new ideas. I mean, hypothetically, I can send a mirror enchanted with [Gate] to Eashen and go there the moment it arrives. Plus, that new spell opens up a whole new world of things to do. I can [Program] a self-moving carriage or even create an automatic vehicle. The car idea is probably the best one... Wait, no, it'd probably stand out too much. Oh... I can use [Program] to give the map app an auto-targeting function! There's so much more I can do now... Man, this is all so great!

I thought about the autonomous doll, Paula. *I should make something similar, yeah... I'll use a cat or a penguin plush toy and... uhh... Getting kinda... sleepy.*

Huh? Oh, damn. Think I dozed off a bit there. Guess I was more tired than I thought. I didn't change into my pajamas, so my body felt heavy. I decided to head for the bath, thinking hot water would reinvigorate my spirit.

I took out a fresh pair of underwear and a bath towel from my dresser, then made my way to the bathroom on the first floor.

The bath in the room was large enough to fit five to six adults. It was like a modest public bathhouse. The girls often took baths together, but I always went in alone. The butler and I were the only males who used it, so it always just ended up that way. I had no intention of going in with Laim, after all.

"Well, it's one of the luxuries in my current life." My spirits raised, I placed my hand on the doorknob and entered the dressing room.

"...Hm?" All four of them looked up as I entered.

".........Whoops?" *Err... what are Elze, Linze, Yae, and Yumina doing here?* All of the girls were in their underwear.

Elze and Linze's were matching, having the same small ribbons, though they were different colors. Elze's was pink, Linze's was blue. Both pastel. The lower garments were tie-side panties. Yae, standing next to them, was wearing a sarashi breast wrap and a fundoshi. That wasn't too surprising. Guess that was the standard in Eashen. *Ah, the whiteness of it's just blinding. Also, the sarashi's a bit loose, so it's clear that she actually has the biggest pair out of all of the girls.* Last, but not least, Yumina. She was wearing expensive-looking, but not overly wild, white underwear with frills and laces. Just like the twins', the lower part was tie-side. I could only assume that it was the panty standard of this world.

Weird, I don't remember casting [Accel] *at all... It's impressive how much I can process in so little time.*

"KYAAHH!" All the girls screamed in unison.

"Gyaaah!!!" I screamed in abject terror. Their sudden screams returned me to my senses, but all I managed to do was respond in kind. Was I actually staring at them more than I should've been?! A teary-eyed Elze launched her fist at me. Judging from the vigor of the attack, I could only assume that she had cast [Boost] to amplify it. And with that, my temporal lobe was violently rocked. I lost all consciousness.

"Well, you're right that we were at fault for not locking the door, but…!" Linze muttered lowly.

"I would like you to be more aware of your surroundings," Yumina said. *I'm on the ground. The girls are surrounding me. How long has it been since they started scolding me? Eons, perhaps?*

"I thought you all were already done and out…" From what they told me, I wasn't the only one who took a short nap after returning to my room. I walked in just after they woke up, headed for the dressing room, and began to undress. *Talk about bad timing… Or, well, actually… maybe it was good timing?*

"…You *do* feel guilty, don't you?"

"Huh? Ah, of course!" Linze glared at me with scornful eyes as I responded to her question. Since she was usually docile, it was a strangely powerful expression.

"I would prefer such events to come after the proper steps have been taken…" *Wait, what steps are you talking about, Yumina?! Don't say weird stuff like that with your cheeks flushed red. You're really freaking me out here!* Well, it was a fact that I could've avoided the situation if I was more perceptive. On top of that, I couldn't deny that I'd spent a long moment staring at them. Honestly, I wasn't in a situation to talk back…

The scolding continued for a while after that, and when it finally ended, it was already the dead of night. In case it wasn't obvious, I didn't get any sleep. After all, that marvelous sight came back to me whenever I closed my eyes… Putting the painful punch aside, it was actually a really great day!

The day after we returned from Mismede, we made our way to the guild in the capital to receive our rewards.

As I looked at the quest board, which was just as surrounded as the one in Reflet, I gave my card to the receptionist. Since it was a direct request, the royal palace should have already informed the guild that it was completed. The lady at the desk looked over our cards and request papers before pushing that familiar seal against them.

"You've all done a great job. Your completion of this quest has increased your Guild Rank. Congratulations!"

I looked over the cards she gave us, and, sure enough, mine, Elze's, Linze's, and Yae's were Blue, while Yumina's was Green. Since the order was Black, Purple, Green, Blue, Red, Silver, and Gold, we were now in the perfect middle of the chain. Once we got to red, we'd be able to call ourselves proper adventurers.

"And here is your reward. It comes out to ten platinum coins." The receptionist placed ten white coins on the table.

Still can't believe just one of these is worth one million yen. I mean, that's ten million yen in total... Isn't that a bit much? Then again, it's a reward for a mission that'll help decide the fates of two countries, so maybe I shouldn't feel so bad about it. Plus, the whole plan depended on my rare ability to use [Gate]. If you take that into account, maybe the reward was just inflated because of the special conditions.

Each of us took two coins and turned to leave the guild. But before we had a chance to leave, the receptionist stopped us.

"Ah, could you wait just a minute? We were told by people from the royal palace that a party led by one Mochizuki Touya has killed a Black Dragon. Would that be you?"

"Well, yeah. We *did* defeat one… Can't help you if you're asking for proof, though." I didn't feel like showing off the guns I made from the Dragon's horn, and the pieces I hadn't used yet were all back at home. Plus, that stuff no longer resembled a horn, so I doubted they'd have believed me even if they saw it.

"Oh no, it's enough to just confirm your identity. The validity of your kill was assured by the royal palace, so there is no problem in that regard. With that in mind, the guild would like you to accept the symbol of your deed — the title of **'Dragon Slayer.'**" As she spoke, she took the cards of everyone who participated in the battle and pushed a different seal against them. She handed them back, and I quickly noticed a round symbol in the right corner of my card. It portrayed a sword piercing through a grounded Dragon. *The proof of a Dragon Slayer, huh?*

"If you present this card to weaponsmiths, armorers, tool shops, or inns that are partnered with our guild, you'll receive a 30% discount on all your transactions. I hope you enjoy the benefits."

Huh? There are bonuses to this? Well, no way I'm refusing something so nice. According to the receptionist, the Dragon Slayer title only went to those who had slayed a Dragon in a party of five or less. That seemed reasonable enough to me. After all, if a thousand people went and swarmed a Dragon to death, it wouldn't be fair to call those people Dragon Slayers.

The receptionist also said that a Blue member killing a Dragon was a very rare occurrence. Interestingly enough, the only Gold adventurer in the world was also still Blue when he killed his first Dragon. Putting small talk aside, I happily accepted my new title.

We left the guild, and as the girls began talking about buying clothes and other knick-knacks, I decided to head back home. But before I could leave, I remembered there was something I had to take care of. *Alright, now, to find a blacksmith...*

My shopping left me a tad overburdened, so I used [Gate] to return to my lawn, where I accidentally surprised my gardener, Julio. *Whoops, my bad...*

"Sir, what might that be?" Curious about what I had with me, Julio stopped his work on the flower bed.

"Steel, rubber, and a bit of leather. I'm about to try making a bicycle."

"Buy-sickle?"

"A simple vehicle. One that allows you to go really fast."

"I... see..." He replied, but was clearly oblivious to the idea. Couldn't exactly blame him for that, though.

As I was getting started on the tires, it hit me that I probably needed an air pump first. Then I remembered that the roads in this world would make them go flat very quickly, so I decided to make them full rubber. Riding on a bike with full rubber tires would probably be a lot less pleasant, though.

While I was using [Modeling] to give the rubber the shape of a bike tire, Laim came to the garden, accompanied by none other than Duke Ortlinde.

"Sir, His Highness Duke Ortlinde has come to visit and... If I may ask, what are you doing?"

"Hey there. What is that thing?"

Their reactions were the same as Julio's. My reply was exactly the same as well, and, as one would expect, they didn't understand at all.

"So, what brought you here, Duke?"

"I merely came to thank you for what you did. Oh, also... about those mirrors meant for sending letters... I was wondering if you could give me another one."

"You want another Gate Mirror? What for?"

"Well actually, this would be for my wife! I was thinking that she'd have such a smile on her face if I gave her the means to frequently talk with her mother. Her mother lives quite far away, you see."

You're looking pretty bashful there, Mr. Duke. Heh, how cute. I had Laim go to my room and fetch me a set of mirrors from the drawers in my desk. Then, I used [Enchant] to imbue them with [Gate]. Just to make sure, I put a piece of paper into one of them, and it came out the other just fine.

"I'd be thankful if you kept these a secret. I don't like the idea of someone shady going after me." Even if it might've been a bit late to stop the gossip, I tried my best to hammer that point home.

"Of course, no need to worry there. Both my wife and her mother always keep such promises." Since he happened to be there, I decided to also give him the souvenir that I'd bought in Mismede for Sue. It was just a silver hair clip, but I hoped she'd like it.

"By the way, how long will it take you to finish this... bicycle, was it?"

"Hmm, it's my first time making one, but I guess it'll be done in about thirty minutes. Though the fine-tuning might add a bit to that."

"I see… Then I shall take the liberty of observing you until completion, if you don't mind."

Duke, you have too much free time. Well, whatever. I have a tire to finish. I took a steel ingot and used [**Modeling**] to create a bike wheel frame.

"Okay, looks to be about done."

"Hoh. So this is a bicycle…" Laim, Julio, and the duke looked at the completed bike with great curiosity.

In the end, I opted for a standard city-bike design. Though simple, it was complete with a basket at the front and even had a rear carrier. However, bike locks and lights for night rides seemed like a pain to make, so it didn't have any of those.

Not wanting to waste any time, I sat down on the leather seat and began pedaling forward. Laim, Julio, and the duke looked on in amazement.

Alright, all good. Well, maybe it's vibrating a bit too much. I rode a lap around the garden, came back around, then hit the brakes. *Good, no problems there either.*

"Touya! Can I ride that too?!"

"Anyone can. Where I come from, even children ride these. Though, first-timers usually end up falling over a lot while they practice… Are you willing to go through that?"

"Of course!" *Seriously, man? You've got more curiosity than you ought to, Duke!*

Duke Ortlinde excitedly took the bike from me and imitated what I did by sitting on it and pedaling… only to fall over almost immediately. *Well, who didn't see that one coming?* Laim hastily helped him up, but the duke was undeterred. He hopped back up on his bike and… fell over again.

It made me remember back when I went through the same rite of passage. I thoroughly believed that repeated failures were what made the first success so satisfying. Shame I couldn't remember how long it took me until I could ride properly.

I ran an internet search, found a site on "How to learn to ride a bike in a day" and used it to give him some advice. I could only hope it would help him.

The duke was occupied with falling off the bike, Laim was occupied with helping him up after he fell, and Julio was occupied with watching the whole spectacle unfold. I decided that it was the best opportunity I'd get to make a second bike. After all, it was far too obvious that he'd want one of his own when he learned to ride it.

Once the second bike was done, I figured Sue would want one, too, so I began making a child's bike with training wheels. I also added a tool to remove the training wheels, just in case.

When I was done with the smaller bike and left with nothing to do, I decided I'd help the duke with his training. But it seems that wasn't necessary judging from the fact that he whooshed right past me as I turned around. *Well I'll be… he's actually riding it pretty well!*

"I did it! I finally did it! Hahahahahah!!!" The duke laughed uncontrollably as he rode his bike around with ease. His expensive clothing and regal face were covered in mud, but he seemed to be having the time of his life as he did several laps around the garden. *It's weird how people are able to control bikes so easily as soon as they manage to ride them.*

"What the heck is that thing?!" Elze exclaimed.

"It has wheels of some sort, it does!"

"Some kind of vehicle…?" Linze muttered, questioningly.

"U-Uncle, what are you doing?!" The four girls returned from their shopping spree, noticed the duke laughing as he made laps on the bicycle, and looked at him with confused and disturbed expressions on their faces.

Well, it certainly *was* a disquieting sight.

Soon enough, the duke stopped by me and said exactly what I was expecting him to.

"Touya! Please let me have this bicycle!"

"I knew you'd say that, so I made one for you already. I made one for Sue, too. But you'll have to pay me for the materials." I pointed at the two bicycles behind me.

The duke gallantly sat down on his very own bike, singing my praises all the while. I used a [Gate] to get Sue's bike to the duke's garden, but the man insisted that he'd ride his own bike home.

Just to be safe, I told him not to ride out into intersections before confirming that it was safe, to watch out for carriages and pedestrians, and to watch where he was going. Honestly, I felt like an elementary school teacher.

With an elated and soothed expression on his face, the duke returned home alongside the carriage he arrived in.

Man, that was tiring... I already know what's gonna happen now. He'll show it off to the king the first chance he gets. And then the king's gonna ask for one too. I should probably just make another one already.

After seeing off the duke and returning to the garden, I saw Elze gracefully falling off the bicycle.

"Owowow... This is harder than it looks." Elze said as she scratched at her bruises.

"I wish to be next to try it, I do!"

"I-I'd like to try it after Yae."

"Touya, could you make another one?" Yumina asked. *Linze, Yumina... I get that you wanna try the bike, but could you change into something other than a skirt first?*

After being finally freed from saving the duke from bicycle failure, Laim and Julio now found themselves having to save Elze and the others from the same fate. While they were at it, I went and made bikes for each of the girls and one for the servants to share as well. As expected, I ran out of materials and had to restock at the shop. As animated as I might've seemed about it all, I had absolutely no intention of becoming a bike salesman.

I was just being considerate of my servants. After all, a bike would be a great help when shopping or running errands. Besides, they were in for a world of pain until they learned to ride it properly.

Come evening — bath time, to be precise — I could hear some whining about the hot water stinging their wounds. I suddenly realized that I could've used Healing magic to get rid of their injuries, but in the end, I figured that the small grazes would serve as symbols of hard work and decided to leave them alone.

Alright, let's see what this new Null spell can do...

"**[Storage]: [In].**" A magic circle appeared on the floor, and the chair I had placed above it quickly sank into it. *Right, the storing part seems to work just fine.*

"**[Storage]: [Out].**" I cast the reverse of the spell while thinking about the chair. A magic circle appeared once more, but this time it forcefully fired a chair out from the middle.

"Whoa!" I caught the chair before it could drop to the ground. *Fine-tuning this thing's power isn't gonna be easy...*

The Null spell [**Storage**] did exactly what it said on the tin — it stored objects. It didn't work on living, animated creatures or anything, but it seemed to work well on plants. Apparently, the amount one could store depended on the user's magic power. So if I had to guess, I'd say my limit was probably an entire house and then some.

The stored objects allegedly ignored the flow of time, too. Soups and similar things would come out as warm as they were when they were taken in, even after a whole day of storage. It felt like a very useful spell to me.

After all, the most annoying thing about travel was the management of our luggage. The mirror we took to Mismede, the Dragon's horn we got... things like that were an absolute pain to carry around.

Even during the recent bicycle event, I couldn't help but be frustrated with the fact that I had to haul materials back and forth.

So that was where this spell came in. It was so I could finally say goodbye to the troubles of luggage management.

Now the girls can ask me to carry all their stuff and it won't even be a problem! If I use this alongside [**Gate**], *I can lead a comfortable life as a one-man home delivery service or something. And on that note, it's time for shopping! No matter how much I buy, nothing'll drag me down anymore! Ahaha!*

I took my wallet, left my room, and walked down the stairs to the first floor, my chipper mood shining all the while. I saw Kohaku in the living room, stretched out on the sofa and sleeping without a care in the world. *You're becoming more like a house cat, my fluffy widdle tiger...*

I crossed the terrace and walked out into the garden. Soon enough, I saw Julio and his wife, Crea, looking over our vegetable garden.

"Hey there, are the crops doing well?"

"Ah, good to see you, sir!" Crea replied.

"Why yes sir, they're growing beautifully. For now, I only planted some cumbers and tomatoes, and it looks like it won't be too long until we can harvest them." Julio seemed quite happy with his work. He was right to be proud, of course, considering he was going to be responsible for our freshly-grown produce.

Just in case it wasn't obvious, "cumbers" were cucumbers. This world had some vegetables with the same names as the ones in my previous world, but there were also those with completely different ones. Well, tomatoes were still tomatoes, at least. Still, I wasn't sure if they'd wind up different to the ones I was familiar with.

Man, if we're able to harvest fresh veggies, we should get some fruits too... Maybe I should plant some chestnut or persimmon trees... Wait, is a chestnut a fruit?

"Sir, do you have any requests for lunch?" Crea asked me about today's menu. I mostly let her make whatever she felt like making. Her food was *always* good.

"Well, it's kinda hot today, so I'd like something refreshing... like chilled Chinese noodles."

"Chilled Chyne-ease noodle? I've never heard of that. Is that another dish from your homeland?!" Her eyes began to gleam with joy. Crea didn't seem to know a single one of the meals I wanted to eat, so I always had to give her a recipe. The exotic cuisine I presented her with never failed to spark her curiosity.

"Well, it's obviously a noodle-based dish. It uses a cold, sour soup, vegetables, meat, and sometimes an egg. I'll give you a detailed recipe, so try your hand at making it."

"Yes sir! I'm looking forward to it!" Excitement was good and all, but we happened to be in a different world. She probably wouldn't be able to get all the necessary ingredients. Regardless, Crea was just so good that I had no doubt she would whip up something delicious. It wasn't the first time I had her make some noodles, so it was safe to expect something just as good.

I ran a search for chilled Chinese noodles and used [**Drawing**] to get Crea the recipe. *Heh, I'm looking forward to lunch now.*

Okay, time to head out! I opened a [**Gate**] and went to the outskirts of the capital. The southern district, to be precise. It was focused on commerce, so there were lots of shops and services lined up next to one another. To the west, you could find elite stores like Berkut, while the east had an entertainment sector full of taverns, theaters, and other facilities.

The western district, where we lived, was the residential area of the wealthy, while the commoners inhabited the opposite district to the east.

Compared to the western district, the east was quite dangerous. I had heard it even had slum-like areas. Among all the rumors, I heard that people who lost their jobs and orphaned children formed criminal gangs there. I'd even heard rumors of roving pickpockets. Guess it was only natural for a great city to have a big shadow.

After stepping through my [**Gate**] to the back alley in the southern district, I made my way to the bustling main road. I decided my first order of business was to make my way to the guild to take out some money. On the way, I saw a number of street peddlers and performers.

Whoa, that guy's juggling knives! Reminds me of the time my grandma tried to teach me how to do it with beanbags, but I just couldn't get the hang of it... As such thoughts ran through my mind, I forgot to watch where I was going and accidentally walked into someone. It was a young boy. He was wearing a worn-out jacket, ragged trousers, and a large, but grimy cap, which he put on in a way that covered his eyes.

"Oh, sorry about that! I wasn't looking..."

"Oi bruv, watch yer step. Make sure that doesn't happen again, aye?" After saying that, he ran off and disappeared into the crowd. *What a brat! He looked even younger than Sue. His parents are probably good-for-nothings...*

I entered the guild, which was as bustling as ever. Various adventurers stood before the quest board and glared at the many missions posted there. Ignoring them, I walked up to the receptionist and asked if I could withdraw some of my money.

"Certainly. May I have your guild card, please?"

Alrighty, lemme just... Oh? Front pockets, chest pockets, side pockets, back pockets... Wait... wh-what? Where's my wallet? Did I leave it back in my room? No way. Did I drop it? No, I... Oh. Shit. It was probably the kid. That brat stole my wallet! Goddammit! I didn't have much money in there, sure... but he made off with my guild card!

I hastily left the guild, took out my smartphone, sighed the greatest sigh of relief I could at the fact that he didn't steal my smartphone, and then ran a search for "my wallet." Sure enough, I got a hit. *Great, he's still in this district.*

Hmm... judging from the speed this pin's moving, I guess he's running. Oh, he stopped in a back alley... Probably planning on looting the contents and tossing the actual wallet there. Well, if that

happens, I'll just run a search for "my guild card." Don't really care if
he takes the money. For now, I've just gotta make my way to that alley.

Once I got there, I saw two boorish-looking men kicking the little boy, who was huddled down on the ground in the fetal position.

"Doin' business in our area again, ya little shit?! It's yer fault the patrols've stepped up, innit?!"

"Oi, you fookin' listening to us?! Ya blew our whole operation! Get ready fer yer jus' desserts, gobshite!" One of them took out a knife and pushed one of the boy's arms against the ground. The blood drained from the boy's face, and his expression became one of sheer terror.

"I-I'm sorry! I'm really sorry, please lemme go!" The boy cried and pleaded with them, but the two men only laughed at him, clearly having no plans to release him.

"Bit late for sorries, y'little runt! As friends of the trade, we'll let ya off with jus' one finger. Don'tcha dare let us catch ya in our area again, aye? Cause next time we'll just snuff ya out. Bwahaha."

"N-No…! Please! No! Somebody help!!!"

"How about you just stop right there." The two hoodlums shot a collective glare in my direction. The boy, who had closed his teary eyes in fear, opened them up and looked my way as well.

"Th'fook're ya after? This ain't none of yer business. Piss off or we'll kill ya!"

"Where I come from, it's normal to get in the way of people who get their kicks hurting kids. Judging from what you said, I think it's safe to assume that you're thieves, too, right?"

"Aye? So what?"

"Well, nothing really… Just means I don't have to hesitate." I pulled out the Remington New Model Army and fired at them both as if it was nothing.

"Whuh?!"

"Argh!" The rubber bullets imbued with [**Paralyze**] hit their mark. The men crumpled to the ground like wet paper bags. I holstered my gun and ran over to the boy.

"You okay?" His face wet with tears, the boy nodded. I could see a number of bruises and injuries on him.

"**Come forth, Light! Soothing Comfort: [Cure Heal]!**" The Healing spell quickly made the wounds fade away. The boy observed the changes in his body with surprise in his eyes.

Once done with the spell, I took out a small cube of steel, used [**Modeling**] to turn it into wire, and tied up the two hoodlums so they couldn't move. Sure, [**Paralyze**] was supposed to stay active for a few hours, but you couldn't be too careful. I figured I'd call some guards over to apprehend them anyway.

"Can I have my wallet back now?"

"Ah..." He quickly searched his sides, took out what was mine, and returned it to me with quivering hands. I looked inside to confirm the contents. *Alrighty, there's my guild card.*

"Well, I got my wallet, so I won't report you to the guards this time. Later!"

"H-Hey!" As I turned to leave, the boy called out to me. *Hm? What does he want?*

"Th-Thanks fer savin' me just there..."

"If you're actually grateful, just stop stealing. You might get caught next ti—" Suddenly, I heard a strange, low growl.

It was his stomach. It actually made a sound loud enough to cut me off. Silence reigned for a few moments.

"...You hungry?"

"Haven't eaten in three days..." The boy let his head hang forward. He looked kinda pitiful.

Well... crap. Guess I lack the mental capacity to understand that his hunger has nothing to do with me. I'm a total sucker, huh? Fine then, if it's gotta be this way...

"Come on then, kid. If you come with me, I'll give you some food."

"For reals?!" *Wait, I totally just sounded like a kidnapper right there.* But it seemed that if I was actually a stereotypical kidnapper, it would've worked out just fine. The kid was clearly an idiot and eagerly ran toward me. Suddenly, the spring in his step made his cap lose its balance. It shifted slightly on his head, revealing a long head of hair beneath.

Once the boy realized that, he took off the cap, which was coincidentally the moment my perception of him switched from "that's totally a boy" to "that is definitely a girl."

What. She had light beige hair that flowed down past her shoulders. The entire image that I'd had of the kid was shattered in an instant.

"Wait... you're a girl?!"

"...Aye." Her green eyes looked up at me as if I was a weirdo for ever assuming otherwise. And that was how I met the thief girl, Renne.

Now that she's scrubbed some of that grime off herself, Renne's actually a pretty sweet-faced kid…

"Oi, bruv. What're ya gonna feed me, then?" *The way she talks is a lot less sweet, though…*

I figured that hard food would be too much for a stomach as empty as hers, so I bought some fish soup from a food stall next to the guild. Then I put it in a cup and gave it to her.

Renne fearfully took it into her hands and slowly began drinking it. Looked like she couldn't handle hot stuff. But that was fine by me. If she took it slowly, she wouldn't overwhelm her stomach.

"Wait here for a moment." I left her there and went into the guild. I gave them my guild card and withdrew some of my money. Not a lot in total, though. Once I left the guild, I took Renne with me. I considered entering a proper restaurant, but with her appearance, she was bound to get kicked out.

So, I settled on going to another stall, getting some roasted meats, and eating them on a bench in the plaza.

"There's no need to rush, just take it slow."

"Nngh." Renne, seemingly out of her mind due to her hunger, greedily gnawed at the meat. She didn't pay me much heed. *She's almost a match for Yae…*

"So, uh, where do you live?"

"Lotsa places. Sometimes the park. Sometimes the alleys. Lived at an inn with my dad before that."

"Where's your dad now?"

"He was an adventurer. Went off ta kill a beast 'bout a year back. Never came home."

Oh... Oh no. Her dad totally got killed by a monster. It wasn't rare for adventurers to get killed while on hunting quests. If it happened while they went solo, they were usually treated as missing persons.

"What about your mom? You have any other relatives?"

"Dead. Right after I was born, said old dad. Dunno any other family. Never got told much at all."

Finished with her meat, Renne wiped her dirty hands on her pants as she told me her story.

So her father vanished and she was left as an orphan? I'm just amazed she survived a full year all alone...

"After me dad up and vanished, a kind old lady rolled through town and taught me how to nick things off people. Knew it wasn't right, but a girl's gotta eat..."

Well, that old lady sure did something she shouldn't have... Still, it was the stealing that allowed Renne to survive so long. Man, this girl's a complicated case. I don't know what I should do here. She doesn't have any parents, and no other family either... I could try taking her to an orphanage, but she's already a criminal, so... She says she only steals when she needs to, but I don't know if they'll let it slide since she's a poor kid. Kids like her aren't unusual here, I get that. If they stop stealing, they'll just drop dead. They're just doing their best to survive with the hand they were dealt. They lead unfair lives, sure. But that doesn't mean stealing is the right thing to do... Maybe I could get her a job? Nah, that's not gonna happen. But if I leave her here, then she'll just go back to stealing again. And that might lead to her getting caught...

People probably would've called me a huge softie for my actions. But I really couldn't have cared any less at the time. After all, I really wanted to help her.

"Renne… would you like to come work at my home?"

"You wot mate?"

"You'll have a place to sleep and food wouldn't be an issue either. You will have to work properly, though. You'll be paid for the work you do, don't worry about that part. How about it?"

"Wait, wait… You're gonna hire me?! You havin' a laugh or what?!" Renne looked at me with obvious surprise and suspicion on her face. Though she was clearly perplexed by my sudden offer, her eyes were gleaming with hope.

"But I'm offering you this job on the condition that you never put your thieving skills to work again. If you do, I won't be able to let you keep working for me. Think you can handle that?"

"Y-Yessir! I'll never use 'em again long as I live! Cross me heart!" As Renne excitedly nodded, I gave her head a light pat.

I should've probably waited and had Yumina look at the kid with her Mystic Eyes, but I don't think Renne's a bad person. Well, now that's settled… let's go home.

I could've used a **[Gate]** to get us there immediately, but I decided to lead her on foot just so she'd know the way.

"Hang on a tick. It's not over here?"

"Nope, my home's over there. I live in the west district."

"The west?!" Renne, who was facing the east, suddenly turned around. She looked even *more* surprised for some reason.

Is it really that big of a deal…? We left the southern district and entered through the western gate. We headed through the gradually widening residential area, and eventually came across the gentle hill on which our home stood. *I kinda hate this hill… It'd be way easier if we didn't have one.*

"Hold up, bruv… Uh, Touya… you some kinda noble?"

"Well, can't really say I am. Very nearly became one, though." She was probably feeling extremely insecure and out of place. Most nobles chose to live in the inner district rather than the outskirts. But nobles with lesser influence or disgraces would often move out into this area. This district had a number of affluent merchants, too.

Once we hiked the hill, we could see the red roof of my very own home. Renne stood still, dumbfounded, before slowly turning to me.

"This the place? You're not havin' a laugh?"

"Yep, this is it. Oh, hey there, Tom."

"Oh? Good day, sir! It's rare for you to come home through the front entrance." The guardsman spoke with a broad smile on his face. Well, I always used a [**Gate**] to go to and from the mansion, so it was only natural for him to make that comment.

We entered my territory through the pedestrian entrance next to the main gate. We walked through the garden and made it to the front door, which I opened to find Lapis and Cecile cleaning the entrance hall.

"Oh, what a welcome surprise, sir! It's rare for you to use the front door."

"Ohhh? Who is this?" Cecile looked at Renne, her stare almost boring holes into the little girl. Renne hid herself behind me, likely out of embarrassment.

"Her name is Renne. She's gonna work here from now on, so try to get along with her. Go on, Renne. Introduce yourself to them, they don't bite."

"Errm... I-I'm Renne. It's a great p-pleasure to meet you!"

Wow, she turned so meek and formal. Guess she's nervous. Not unreasonable, given the gaudy place I brought her to.

"Where's Laim?"

"He went to the living room to give Miss Yumina her tea." Lapis pointed the way, so I took Renne along with me. I let the little girl sit on a comfy chair while I explained the situation to Laim.

Yumina silently listened to what I was saying, staring at Renne all the while. It didn't take a genius to tell that she was using her Mystic Eyes. Soon enough, Yumina adopted a light smile. *There, I knew it! Renne isn't a bad girl!*

With a sidelong glance, Laim confirmed it himself.

"Very well, sir. I understand the circumstances. However, I need to be certain she is serious about working here. I cannot have our efficiency as a team hampered by anyone. You there, your name is Renne?"

"Y-Yup…"

"Do you truly intend to work here? We won't mind if you fail or cause a bit of trouble for us servants at first. However, you must promise to learn from your mistakes and not to flee from your responsibilities." Laim glared at Renne with the sternest expression I'd ever seen him adopt. I thought it was a slightly harsh thing to do to a child no older than ten, but it didn't seem like I had any business intruding, so I held my tongue.

"…Yeah. I wanna work here. I wanna be where Touya is." Renne stared right back into Laim's stern eyes. After staring at her for a good moment, the butler softened his expression and stood up with a smile.

"Cecile. Take young Renne to the bath. I want her scrubbed down until she's spotless."

"Okaaay. Come with meee, little Renne. It's bath tiiime, eeheheh."

"Uh?! What?!" And so, Renne was taken to the bathroom. Though it might have been more apt to say that Renne was dragged into the bathroom.

"Lapis, go buy her some fitting clothes. Oh, and order a custom-made uniform for her."

"Understood, sir. If you don't mind, I will use the bicycle." Lapis hurriedly went outside. She and Cecile learned to ride the bike in just a few hours. I wasn't too surprised, given that they were this world's equivalent of the ninjas.

Yumina suddenly spoke up after hearing us speak.

"When she's done bathing, she can wear my clothes, for the time being at least. They'll probably be too big for her, but it'll only be until Lapis returns." Yumina got up off her seat. She was probably headed to get some clothes to the dressing room. Once she left, I spread myself out on my chair and drowned myself in thoughts for a while. Soon enough, Laim came over and placed some tea on the table in front of me.

"...Should I have just handed her over to an orphanage? Did I do something uncalled for?"

"That is for Renne to decide, sir. For now, if you'll permit me to say... you should only accept the truth. The truth is that you have saved a young girl from poverty."

Guess you're right about that, Laim... I shouldn't overthink it. I did exactly what I wanted to do, anyway. That's all there is to it. Man, I can see why Laim used to work directly under the king. He's got a way with words. Putting all that aside, though, Renne is still a criminal. I'll have to make her atone for whatever it is she's done. Maybe I should consult someone about that? Well, whatever. I'll just talk to the king or something.

...Hm? I could hear someone running through the corridor. Suddenly, the living room door flung open, and Renne ran in, wearing nothing but a bath towel. In her arms, she held my dear little white tiger.

"T-Touya! Bruv! There's a little tiger over 'ere!" Kohaku looked at me with an annoyed expression on his face. I could totally understand why.

"Master... who is this child?"

"You wot?! It can bleedin' well talk!"

...She's noisy, and that way of talking came back pretty quick, too. She should really put on some clothes, honestly. Doesn't look very proper at all. As I started to think about just how lively my home would become with her, I noticed something strange. There was something hanging on her neck. It looked like some kind of pendant.

"Renne, what's with that thing around your neck?"

"This? Dad gave it to me. Said it was to remember my mum by. It's the only thing I ever had for myself."

"Can I take a look at it?" Renne took it off and gave it to me. Moments later, Cecile, with her sleeves rolled up, came and dragged her back to the bathroom. *Things got way too chaotic, way too fast...*

I shifted my gaze to the pendant in my hand. From what I could tell, the thing was gold... It would clearly fetch a considerable price on the market. Since Renne kept it around despite the fact that she could feed herself by selling it, the pendant must've been very dear to her.

The design was a pair of spread wings, in the middle of which was a gem in the shape of a downward triangle. *Is this... an emerald? No, it's a wind spellstone.*

There was a crest on the back.

"Laim, do you recognize this crest?"

"A Griffin, a shield, two swords, and laurels... I cannot say I do."

"If this is really a memento, could it mean that Renne has some blue blood in her?"

"I would not be so sure. It might be something her parents or grandparents merely happened upon."

And it went from generation to generation until it ended up in Renne's hands, huh? That's definitely a possibility. But usually something so gaudy would've been returned or sold, right? Well, with Renne's dad gone, there's no way to know for sure...

"As far as I am aware, there is no such crest among the ones used by Belfastian nobles. Though, I do know that Griffin crests are quite popular in the Empire..." *The Empire... which is that again...? Oh, the Regulus Empire? I think that was to the east? The one that isn't on the best of terms with Belfast. Was Renne's father a fallen noble who escaped from that place? Whatever the case, this doesn't seem like something I should talk about more than necessary.*

I made a mental note to ask about the crest if I ever met someone from the Regulus Empire.

"Yep, it looks good on you."

"R-Really?" Renne slightly raised the skirt of her new maid uniform and did a little spin. The pendant hanging around her neck swayed along with her.

"That thing might get in the way of your work, so you should put it under your clothes."

"Ah, gotcha. No prob, Touya!" While I wasn't lying about it obstructing her work, it was better for it to be hidden away from those who'd like to steal it.

Laim, who was standing at my side, looked straight at Renne.

"Renne, from now on, you are one of us. You are among the servants. When referring to the one you serve, you must use 'sir.' None of this 'Touya' or… 'bruv,' as you put it."

"Ah, erm… Got it! I'll do my best, Mister Laim!"

"Excellent, young lady. Your job right now is to help the servants working here. Go to Crea to learn about how we prepare our meals. The rest you can learn from Lapis and Cecile."

"Gotc— 1 understand." Renne's answer was proper and straightforward. Even so… I couldn't help but worry a bit.

"Okaaay, Renne, let's gooo!"

"Alright. I'll be off, bru— sir."

"Do your best out there." Renne left the dining hall, led off by Cecile. *All she needs to do is get used to it.*

"Don't think you have to worry about her, Touya," Elze said.

"Y-Yes, I feel the same way…" Linze muttered. As they drank their post-breakfast tea, the twins expressed their approval of my decision. I had told them everything that led up to me employing Renne the day before.

"Yes. She has a very strong heart, and I am certain she properly considers everything, I am." Yae was still eating breakfast. Her hunger was as great as ever. I couldn't even imagine how many croissants she had consigned to the void within her this morning.

I heard the door to the dining hall open and turned around to see Yumina walking in. She was holding a piece of paper in one of her hands.

"It's from my father. He requests that you pay him a visit today, if you have the time." The Gate Mirror through which we kept in contact with the royal palace was in Yumina's room. The letter probably came through there. The royal palace was only a thirty minute walk away, but the Gate Mirror was useful nonetheless.

"The king? What does he want from me?"

"He said something about uncle boasting to him about his bicycle, so I think it has something to do with that." Yumina smiled wryly. I had predicted this a few days ago, and now it had come true.

Well, guess I better make another one. At least this'll be a good excuse to talk about Renne.

I walked out to the garden and used [Storage] to take out the bike materials. Since I had made so many of them already, I had the king's order done in a mere ten minutes. Using [Storage] again, I took the bicycle with me. *Man do I love this spell.*

"Alright, I'm off."

"I'll come with you." Yumina walked out into the garden. *Well, I can't freely walk around the castle without her, so her presence will be a big help anyway.*

"Hold up there! I'm coming too. I wanna fight the general again." Elze ran out, her asymmetrical gauntlets dangling on her side. General Leon, the supreme commander of the royal army, had fought her countless times by this point, making their relationship sort of like that of a master and apprentice.

It just hit me that this country has both an "order of knights" and an "army." What's the difference? If I remember right, Reflet was being protected by the knight order.

So, are they responsible for policing duties, while the army are the ones handling monsters and outside threats? With those thoughts in my head, I opened up a [Gate].

"Well, you know, Al... No, ah... Duke Ortlinde showed me a most peculiar vehicle. He also said that you were the one who provided him with it. So, er... I was wondering if you would be able to give one to me, as well." The king told me why he called me over, acting strange all the while. It was just as I had thought.

He and I were having a little talk in one of the smaller palace rooms. Since Elze went to see the general, and Yumina went to meet the queen, the king and I were alone together. Well, alone if you ignored the guards.

"I thought that was why you called me over, so I prepared one before coming here."

"Oho! How considerate of you, my boy! So, where is it?!" I cast [Storage] and created a magic circle on the floor. From it, I summoned the bicycle I had prepared earlier.

"As always, you do the most unexpected of things, Touya my boy... Is this different from those [Gate] things of yours?"

"This one's a storage spell. It allows me to keep many things on demand, so I use it a lot." The king simply sighed before shifting all of his attention toward his new bike. I figured he was out of things to say about my spells at that point. He stared at it from every direction and touched it all over to see how it felt.

"Did Duke Ortlinde let you ride his bike?"

"He did, but I was unable to grasp the proper technique... Al told me that it requires practice. How much, exactly?"

"It took the duke about a day, but my maids got the hang of it in just three hours. I'd say three days should be enough for anyone." The king was a busy guy. He probably didn't have any days he could dedicate entirely to bike practice. But it was still a fact that he'd be able to ride it sooner or later.

As the king joyfully hopped up on the saddle, I began talking about my own business.

"Now that we've settled this, there's something I'd like to ask... or maybe just discuss with you."

"Hoh? It's rare for you to ask for my help, Touya." As the king raised his brow slightly, I told him about Renne. He was intently listening to me, and when I finished, he began speaking in a highly serious tone.

"Crime is crime. She must pay for what she has done. However, we must take her circumstances into account as well. If you, Touya, are able to properly look after her and turn her into a proper member of society, we will let her off with only a hefty fine and a warning. However, she will not receive a second chance. Be sure to inform her of that fact." His words made me feel relieved. I was definitely serious about protecting Renne. I couldn't be more thankful for the king's rationality.

Moments later, the king turned ominously silent. *D-Did I do something wrong?*

"Hmm… I just cannot understand it."

"What do you mean?"

"Why are there so many vagrant children? The funding I direct to the capital's orphanages should be more than enough. Could it be that…" The king clapped, and a masked figure clad in black silently fell down from the ceiling. *Whoa, that caught me off guard!* For a moment, I thought it was one of my maids — Lapis or Cecile — but then I noticed that the symbol on the forehead of the mask was different. Lapis' was a hexagon; Cecile's was an oval. This one was a pentagon. Whatever the case, it was clearly another member of Espion — the intelligence officers who answered directly to the king.

"Who is responsible for the funding of orphanages?"

"Baron Sebek… There are rumors that his influence has been growing unusually strong over the last few years."

"Thoroughly examine the flow of money and have anyone clearly guilty of embezzlement dealt with accordingly."

"Yes, my liege." He disappeared through the ceiling just as swiftly as he appeared. A ninja if I ever saw one.

"My apologies, Touya. The circumstances of the child you took in might be the result of my own carelessness. Forgive me for my negligence." He bowed his head.

So the money meant for the orphanages was probably embezzled by someone who managed the flow. Which means the orphanages couldn't operate at full capacity and weren't able to take in all the kids. So people like that exist in this world too, huh...? Scumbags who get fat and fill their own pockets by exploiting positions of power...

Still, the king sure was a person of good moral character. Not everyone would bow to another over something like that. The public might disagree, but I couldn't help but think that this country was blessed to have such a ruler.

"You sure have it hard, Your Majesty."

"Indeed. If only there was someone who could take my position and allow me to retire." The king grinned broadly.

...Are you referring to me and Yumina, old man?! Even if I do marry her, I have absolutely no intention of being king! I had a great amount of respect for King Belfast, that much was true, but it was completely unrelated to me succeeding him.

I should meet up with the head chef of the castle and give him a recipe for a dish that gives a hearty boost to stamina. Maybe then the king can just make another baby. Garlic, yam, turtle... do those things even exist here? That doesn't matter, I need to get them, and fast!

"We're back." Yumina and I walked out of the [Gate]. We arrived just outside our front door. Elze said she'd come back on foot as soon as the training was over.

We walked through the door and into the main hall, where we were welcomed by Laim.

"Welcome back, sir."

"Good to see you too, Laim! It all worked out with Renne."

"Most excellent. Oh, and you have a visitor."

"A visitor…?" I nonchalantly looked down the corridor beyond Laim, where I saw something strange bobbing over to us.

Fifty centimeters tall. A red ribbon around its neck. It was a stuffed bear with round, cutesy eyes.

"Paula?!" The bear heard her name and greeted me by raising her right hand. She came up to me, so I picked her up.

"Did you come all the way from Mismede? By yourself?"

"Of course not, you silly little man. She came with me." The door to the parlor opened, and out came a girl in gothic lolita clothing. Her long white hair was in twintails.

"Leen?! What're you doing here?" Well, I guess I shouldn't have been too surprised. Paula wouldn't have just been here without her creator.

"I'm just here for research. Oh, and I had to punish Charlotte, too. I slapped her already, so that's done and dusted."

Man, she sure is one to hold grudges… Kinda immature. Aren't you over six hundred?

As I stared at her with slight disappointment, Yumina pulled on my sleeve.

"Touya? Who might this be?"

"This is Leen, the clan matriarch of Mismede's fairies. She doesn't look it, but she's way, way older than us."

"Fairies? But…" Yumina looked at Leen with a puzzled expression.

Wait, where'd her wings go? Sh-She didn't cut them off, did she?!

"Oh, I concealed my wings with Light magic. They attract far too much attention in this country." She removed the spell, causing a set of see-through wings to gradually appear behind her. The sunlight coming through the windows made them gleam and shimmer. I couldn't help but wonder whether fairies and avians had trouble sleeping because of their wings.

"Why are you in my house, though? How'd you even find out where we live?"

"Charlotte told me. I had something I wanted to ask you. Specifically, I wanted to ask you about that 'crystal creature' you defeated some months ago."

"...What?"

The crystal creature. I know exactly what you mean, Leen. That mysterious beast from the ruins underneath the old capital. The one that regenerated, absorbed magic, and couldn't be hurt by blades.

"For you see, that crystal creature... One has appeared in Mismede, as well." Leen's words not only surprised me, but made a strange chill go down my spine.

"It was a day before you returned home. The palace received an urgent message from Lairesse, a town in western Mismede. It warned of a strange phenomenon that had been happening there over a period of a few days."

"What was that?" Leen took a sip of the black tea that had been prepared for her, then leaned forward in her seat slightly. On the other side of the table, there was Yumina, Linze, Yae, and myself. Paula was seated right next to Leen.

"The ones who discovered it were a group of children from Lairesse. What they found was... a crack, of sorts. A crack, suspended in thin air in the middle of the forest. No one could touch the strange crack, but everyone knew it was very real."

A crack in empty space...? What the hell? Was it a spell or something?

"Soon enough, the children noticed that the crack was growing bigger each day. One of them decided they should tell the adults about it. After that, the village chief sent a message to the capital." Leen placed the teacup back on the plate. *So, the messenger reached capital the day before we returned to Belfast, did he?*

"What we found was carnage. Utter carnage. What was once a home was now a warzone, teetering on the edge of annihilation. A crystal creature was killing them… No, it was slaughtering them. It had no remorse. The soldiers and I tried to fight, but we stood no chance. Swords could not harm it, spells were absorbed by it. It regenerated when shattered… It was like battling a nightmare. Half of the soldiers were maimed beyond recovery. The village could not be saved."

"Sounds just like the one we fought… Did you manage to defeat it?"

"Somehow, yes. Just barely. When I found out it was vulnerable to magic that dealt physical damage, I used Earth spells to hit its head with a boulder that weighed several tons. Once I shattered the core in its body, it stopped regenerating."

The red core again… So it ceased all activity when it was destroyed. That meant it was definitely the same type of creature that we fought.

"I wanted to do more research on that monster, so I went to Charlotte to get her to help me. It was then that she informed me of a similar event in Belfast. I was quite surprised when she told me that you were the ones who defeated it." Leen looked straight at me with quite a wicked-looking grin. I felt like a frog being eyed by a snake. It was actually making me sweat, so I would've preferred her to stop sooner rather than later.

"There was another thing she told me. You can cast any Null magic, right? That explains why you could use [**Program**]."

"Well… what can I say here? I'd be thankful if you didn't talk about it too much." *Dang it, Charlotte, don't spill all the beans! Come to think of it, the poor girl was probably forced to talk under duress… Guess she couldn't keep anything in when this demonic teacher got in her ear.*

"The few surviving villagers told us that the crack in space was destroyed, and the crystal creature came out of it." *From the crack…? So it wasn't like with us, where it just awakened in the ancient ruins.* Leen took out a piece of paper from her pocket and spread it out on the table. The creature displayed on the paper was unlike the crystal creature that we had defeated. This one had a different shape.

The one we encountered in the ruins had an almond-like body and six thin, long legs. Overall, it was like a cricket. But the one Leen presented us with had an almond-shaped head — rather than body — and instead of having legs, it was just very long.

If the one we fought was a cricket, then this one was a snake. A crystal snake with a winding body. Kind of shaped like a katana that had been bent one too many times.

"This one's shaped differently to the one we fought. The one here in Belfast was more like a cricket. It attacked us by extending its legs."

"Ah. The one we faced in Mismede used its tail to impale people and shred groups apart. It was like a sharp, precise blade."

The shapes of the two creatures were different. Still, it was clear that they were the same type of creature. If I had to compare, I'd say it was similar to grouping butterflies and praying mantises into the same group. That group being "insects," of course. It seemed pretty reasonable to deal with it like that.

"…A long time ago, when I was still a young girl, an elder of my kind told me a story. She spoke of a race of monstrous beasts that emerged as if from nowhere. They brought the world to the brink of ruin, and were known as the 'Phrase'... Their bodies were pure crystal, said to be completely invincible. But in the end, they disappeared as spontaneously as they had appeared. The world simply returned to normal..."

"So, you think the Phrase and the crystal creatures could be one and the same?"

"I'm afraid I do not know. The elder is no longer with us, and she told us that it was merely a tale she heard when she was a child. Also, we fairies only began to have contact with outside species a mere hundred or so years ago."

If those beasts were really the same as the stuff in the story, where did they come from? Is someone controlling them like summoned creatures? But then why would they attack people? No amount of thinking could answer those questions of mine.

They're strong, but they aren't invincible. If one appears again, we just have to kill it. And if there's a mastermind behind it all, we'll just drag him out and beat the crap out of him, too.

"Well, nothing will come from us just thinking about it. They aren't creatures I'd be pleased to meet again, but if they do appear, we'll simply defeat them like the first one."

"Reasonable indeed. Oh, by the way, while Olga is away, I will be staying in this country as the Mismedian ambassador." *Is this fairy serious? Oh Charlotte, you poor girl...*

"I'll be visiting here every once in a while, so let's get along. Also, Touya, you can use **[Gate]**, right?" *Ah, dang it... She's sharp.* I went out of my way to resort to trickery to keep it a secret, but since it came out, Mismede would likely turn wary and begin doubting the alliance.

As if reading my thoughts, Leen adopted a faint smirk.

"No need to make that face. I won't tell anything to the beastking or the other clan leaders. I'm gentle to my own, you know?"

"Your own?"

"Oh yes. You will be my disciple, won't you?" Leen's grin had turned sadistic. *Good lord. This is the textbook definition of blackmail.* As I wracked my mind trying to figure out how to respond, Leen started laughing.

"Eheh… it was a joke, silly. I don't like forcing people to do what they don't want to do."

That's a total lie. You were at least half-serious there! As I glared at Leen, the door to the living room opened up. Through it came Cecile and Renne, carrying trays with a teapot and sweets.

"I-I've gone and b-brought more tea for you's— you!" Renne's way of speaking made it clear that she was extremely nervous. Fidgeting something fierce, she placed the plate with the sweets on the table and refilled our empty teacups. Cecile was watching over her with a smile on her face.

"E-Excuse me." *Ah, she stuttered.* The two left the room after that. *That wasn't too bad at all. In fact, it was pretty good, considering it was her first time. Go Renne!*

"I see that you employ someone exceptionally young. It didn't seem like she was used to dealing with guests. A newcomer, I assume?"

"She just started, yes. I'd be grateful if you tolerated any clumsiness from her." I took a sip of the tea Renne just gave me. *It's a bit too hot, and it's brewed way too strongly. Well, it's only natural that she wouldn't be as good as Lapis or Cecile yet. Not a huge deal in the grand scheme of things.*

"Back to what we were discussing, though. You can use [Gate], right?"

"I can, yeah. Though, it has the negative of only letting me go to places I've visited."

"Ever heard of the Null spell, [Recall] at all? It allows you to read people's minds and gather their memories. By using it, you should be able to open a [Gate] leading to places known to the person whose mind you read."

Really? I'd never heard of that. Wonder where she learned about it… Oh, right, most fairies are born with Null spells, so maybe it's only natural for her to know.

"I want you to use this spell in conjunction with [Gate] to get me to a certain place. There's a ruin I want to examine in that country."

"I'm not fully getting it, but… what place are we talking about?"

"The far east — the easternmost part of the world, even. The Divine Nation, Eashen."

"Eashen…?" I instinctively looked at Yae. She looked pretty perplexed, too.

Eashen was the country which had lots of similarities to Japan from my original world. I had always been quite curious about it. And now I had a chance to go there.

"This girl was born in Eashen, right? If you read her mind, you should be able to make a [Gate] that leads to Eashen."

"W-Wait! T-Touya-dono is going to read *my* mind, is he?!"

"Don't worry. As long as you're properly conscious, [Recall] only lets the caster take the memories you allow them to have. You don't have to worry about him seeing memories you don't want to be seen." Unable to properly fight back, Yae turned pensive. Well, it was natural for people to have sides to them they wouldn't want anyone else to see. Even if there was no risk of that, she couldn't help but worry. I was confident I'd be just like her if our roles were reversed.

After a long moment of hesitation, Yae nodded.

"The Null spell, **[Recall]**, works by harvesting memories from the person's mind through touch. The most efficient way of touching in this case is a kiss."

"What?!" All of the girls screamed in unison.

"It was a joke." Leen's words seemed to drain everyone of their strength. *I'd really like it if she wiped that grin off her face. Curse this sadistic gothic lolita! She played us like a fiddle!*

"Alright, now calm down, stand here, and face each other. Hold each other's hands, too." Leen dragged both myself and Yae, and made me stand before her. There were other methods, apparently, but until I got used to the spell, we had to do this to have the greatest chance of success.

Leen grabbed my hands and connected them with Yae's. *They're soft... Way softer than I'd expected... I didn't think anyone could use swords as much as Yae and still have such lovely hands... Crap, now I'm getting all nervous!*

"Ahh…"

"E-Eek…" When I raised my head, my eyes met with hers. She was staring at me, face red as a beet. *That expression is just unfair! It's making me even more embarrassed.*

"Alright, close your eyes. Now Yae, try to picture the landscapes of Eashen. Make sure the image is as clear as possible. If you picture something vague, the **[Gate]** will have a small chance of transporting us to a place that's only similar in aesthetic. When the image is clear, Touya, place your forehead against hers and cast **[Recall]**."

Doing as I was told, I began focusing my magic and placed my forehead against Yae's. The pleasant smell that assaulted my nostrils almost made me lose my focus, but I was able to keep myself together and cast the spell.

"**[Recall]**." Something began to flow into my head. *A large tree… Is it a camphor, maybe? There's something near its base… It looks like a torii arch, one of those traditional gate arches you'd find at a shinto shrine… Oh, I can actually see the little hokora shrine as well… Two lion-dog statues on either side of it…* What I saw was clearly a hokora shrine inside a forested area. I could only assume I was observing Yae's memories of Eashen.

"I see it." I opened my eyes and met Yae's gaze. Sharing memories with someone was quite a strange experience. I felt as though I had been there countless times.

"Ahem!"

"Whoa!" Yumina's forced cough made me come back to my senses and let go of Yae. The fact that we were just holding hands and looking into each other's eyes made us both turn bashful and look away from one another.

"If you actually saw Eashen, I would like you to open a **[Gate]** now. Are you able to?" *Oh, how I'd like to wipe that grin off your face…* I pictured the place in Eashen I just saw and opened a **[Gate]**.

Once I walked through the portal of light, I stepped out into a forest with a large camphor tree, under which there was a torii arch with a hokora shrine, protected by the two lion-dog statues. Everything was exactly as I saw in Yae's memories.

"There is no mistaking it. This is indeed my homeland, Eashen, it is. We are at the grove of the village shrine near my hometown of Hashiba."

Yae walked through the **[Gate]**, looked around, and confirmed my success.

There I was, at the easternmost country in the world. I'd finally taken my first steps in Eashen, the Divine Nation.

"So this is Mismede. What a bustling place!" A few days after I made the bicycles, I fulfilled my promise of using a [Gate] to take Sue to Berge, Capital of Beasts.

We weren't alone, of course. Yumina, Kohaku, Leim — Ortlinde family's butler and Laim's younger brother — and a number of escort knights of both genders accompanied us.

That was only natural, given Yumina and Sue's royal status. Well, I didn't think the guards were really necessary, considering that this stealthy little adventure of ours wouldn't last more than two or three hours, but it never hurt to be careful.

The knights and Leim were wearing clothes that allowed them to blend in, but they were still armed.

"They are selling so many strange things! I must buy something for mother and father! Touya, let us go over there!"

"Yep, yep. As you wish." Sue innocently pulled on my hand, leading me through Berge's streets.

Compared to Belfast, Mismede isn't exactly a safe place to be. Well, both are kind of on the same level when compared to the safety of the world I used to live in. I don't mean the crime rates or anything. More the general roughness of the population. It was especially common to find brutish people among the beastmen, even compared to other demi-human species.

Many might assume that the king's nature has something to do with it, but I disagree. It's more likely that beastmen — especially those with predator qualities — are predisposed to aggression from birth.

Oh, look. There's a street brawl starting right now, even. Doesn't look like a fight to the death or anything, just fisticuffs. The people passing by didn't intervene, treating it like a daily occurrence not worthy of a second glance.

Not only that, the fighters themselves didn't look like strangers to each other. It felt like a fight between two great friends.

I'd began to realize that what looked like "fights" to outsiders was merely "messing around" to the beastmen. But again, that was probably their nature.

It was nothing I wanted to get involved with, at any rate. As Sue and I walked through Berge's streets, I put more force into the hand that held hers.

She led me straight into a fancy-looking accessory shop. The nonchalant manner in which she chose such a luxurious place made me aware of just how blue blooded she was.

"Father should like this pipe. The tiger carving makes it look very cool! What should I get for mother, though…?" Sue took a pipe with a silver tiger decoration embedded in it, and handed it over to Leim. Then, she stood before a case full of other accessories and began thinking. While she did that, Leim paid for the pipe and had it wrapped.

As I was looking around the shop, trying to find anything the girls would like, Yumina tugged at my sleeve.

"Touya, isn't that Arma?"

"Hm?" I followed her gaze and looked through the window to see a girl walking through the streets all by her lonesome. A pair of twitching fox ears and a fluffy tail… There was no mistaking it. It was Arma, the younger sister of Olga, former Ambassador to Belfast.

I lightly knocked on the window. Arma heard it, stopped walking, noticed us and ran over while wagging her tail. She made her way to the entrance and ran into the shop.

"Heya Arma. Didn't expect to see you here."

"Me too! I didn't even know you were in Mismede!" I gave Arma a casual greeting, and she responded in kind with a cheery smile on her face. Yumina and Arma held hands, seemingly overjoyed. The fox girl didn't seem to care that Yumina was a princess.

"Are you shopping, too, Arma?"

"I am! What're you buying, Yumina?" Yumina introduced Sue, and the three began a peaceful little exchange.

Hesitant to take part in their girly chat, I went back to searching for accessories. Getting something for the girls seemed like a good idea.

«Master, is that not Olga and Lyon?»

"Huh?" Kohaku suddenly beamed a telepathic message into my head.

I took a look through the window and, sure enough, I could see a man and a woman walking through the streets with wide smiles on their faces.

Indeed, the fox was definitely Olga, and she was accompanied by Lyon, the steadfast Belfastian knight.

Lyon's still in Mismede? He's dressed pretty casually and has a dumb look on his face, so I guess he's off duty.

"What's wrong, Touya?"

"Look at that." I pointed outside, causing both Yumina and Arma to close in on the window and take a look at the two.

"Think they're on a date?"

"Most probably."

"Wait, big sis is on a date?!" Arma's eyes opened wide, as if she didn't expect it at all. *Why are you that surprised, kid? Olga seems like the kind of beauty who'd be super popular with boys.*

Then again, you can't deny the fact that her serious vibe wards people off. Combined with her beauty, it sort of creates an air of coldness and unapproachability. That image melts away as soon as you meet her, though. The girl's sweet as candy.

"We have to go after them!" Arma hastily left the shop. *What?! We're following them now?*

"This sounds interesting. I shall also make haste!"

"Hey, Sue! No, c'mon now!" Sue and Yumina chased after Arma. And, like clockwork, Leim and the knights responsible for their safety also charged behind them.

Staying there by myself didn't seem like a good way to spend my time, so I took Kohaku with me and went after them. *Good grief...*

We followed the duo through the streets, keeping just the right amount of distance behind them. I didn't worry about Lyon too much, but Olga — being a beastgirl — could have easily noticed us. Arma did a good job at keeping us out of the reach of her sister's perception.

"They seem so innocent." We were spying on the two from behind the corner of a building, Yumina felt the need to comment.

As he walked by her side, Lyon repeatedly reached for Olga's hand. Though he clearly wanted to go for it, he repeatedly failed to reach his goal. *Well, I guess "innocent" is one word to describe it.*

"Man, that is *so* irritating!"

"Get a grip, Sir Lyon! You're being pathetic!"

"This is too good..." Out of all of us, the ones who seemed to care about this the most were the group of knights escorting us. Guess seeing a co-worker on a date upped their curiosity to the max.

"What is he doing?"

"He wants to hold her hand, Sue. But he can't figure out if he should."

"It is naught but a hand. He should just hold it if he wants!" She was completely right, but love was an emotion that needlessly complicated such things... Not that I had any right to say that.

Nonetheless, the two — despite being quite mature — seemed to be really awkward about stuff like this. To my knowledge, Lyon was twenty-one, while Olga was nineteen. In this world, marrying young was the normal thing to do. About half of the normal citizenry had husbands and wives before their twenties. There were no such things as coming-of-age ceremonies (though, some tribes had coming-of-age rituals), and if both sides were independent and stable, they didn't even need their parents' permission.

Though, that completely changed with nobles. Lyon had baronial blood, while Olga was from a powerful Mismedian merchant family. They couldn't marry just because they felt like it.

There were even families that gave fiances to their newborn children. Luckily that didn't apply to either of those two.

Either way, they'll need to hold hands before anything else.

"Ah, they're going into a shop!" The two entered a nearby cafe. They'd easily notice us if we went after them. None of us were strangers to them, so we would need disguises.

"Touya, can you do anything about this?"

"Well, I can't say that I can't, but..." I disapproved of what Sue wanted from me. I had to consider their privacy, after all.

"This event might change big sis' life! As her sister, I have to know about it!" Even Olga's family was insisting that I do it...

Everyone besides Leim was pushing me to hurry up and get on with it, so I caved in, took out my smartphone and ran the camera app imbued with [**Long Sense**].

The screen began to display the inside of the shop. It presented exactly what it could perceive through [**Long Sense**]. Even sound came through just fine.

"I've never been here before, so I don't know if you'll like the food here..."

"No no no! Don't worry about me! This is a great place, really!" I could hear the knights behind me try to hold back their laughter. Lyon was tense out of his mind, but that was only natural, really.

"You're heading back to Belfast soon, aren't you?"

"Ah, yes... B-But with the alliance between our two countries, I'm sure I'll have many more chances to come here! I-I'm thinking of doing so the next time I get a long enough holiday!"

"Heheh, be sure to tell me when you visit... I'll take you to a better restaurant."

Heh, they're not doing too badly at all. Olga seems pretty happy with the situation.

"Ah, r-right! I-I have these things with me."

"Is that a... mirror? It looks somewhat strange..." Lyon put his hand in his pocket and took out two mirrors held by strangely long frames. *Oh, it's the Gate Mirrors I gave him. He still hasn't given her one?*

"These are a set of magical items. S-Sir Touya gave them to me... please have a look. When you put something in one..."

"Ah, it came out the other one...!"

"They allow the instant exchange of letters over long distances. I-I was thinking of giving this one to you today…"

"…Thank you so much. I'll treasure it." Olga held her Gate Mirror against her chest and smiled widely.

Hohoh, so she accepted it. Yep, she definitely likes the guy. Look at how happily her tail's wagging, it's way too obvious.

"Sis looks so happy…"

"Seems like he really has a chance with her."

Arma and Yumina made their comments, their eyes not straying from the screen for a moment.

I'd say they just need one more big push to close that distance between them.

After a light meal in the cafe, the two left the building. I asked Arma, who was obviously the most knowledgeable about Berge, for directions.

"The central plaza is off in this direction. There are many stalls selling rare imported goods or bargain accessories. That's probably where they went to." *First a meal, now shopping? Pretty basic progression for a date.*

"He should just buy a ring for her."

"No, this is definitely *not* the time for rings. Wayyy too heavy."

"If she likes him, wouldn't it just make her happy?"

"Thing is, we still don't know if she really likes him. Messing up the timing of such things can lead to tragic results, y'know…" The knights behind us nonchalantly spoke their opinions. I couldn't help but feel that they were amused by the situation. Then again, I would be lying if I said I wasn't curious myself.

Once they reached the central plaza, the two began looking at the stalls. Just as Arma said, I could see some strange things being sold there.

Honestly, I wanted to take a good look around myself, but I couldn't leave Arma's side as long as we were following the happy couple.

"Leim! Let us buy these masks! Souvenirs for father and mother!"

"Very well." Sue went off to buy some fox and cat masks, right next to the dating duo. The level of freedom she displayed made me jealous.

At the front, I could see Lyon buying souvenirs for his family while Olga was helping him pick them out.

With all the people crowding around these stalls, we almost lost sight of them.

Well, even if did lose them, I could use my smartphone's search function to find them again, so there was no need to worry.

However, Arma was unaware of this, so she rushed a bit and ran into the person in front of her.

"Owie…" Arma fell on to her backside, having ran smack-bang into a large, hooded figure.

"Oh, my bad. You okay, kid?"

"Ah, y-yes. Sorry. I forgot to look where I was going…" The hooded person took Arma's hand and helped her up.

"Arma, are you alright?"

"Ah, yes. I'm fine…"

"Sorry about that, we're in a rush, so…" As I began to apologize for Arma, I looked straight at the face under the hood, but what I saw made my eyes open with surprise. I turned numb. The other party reacted in the exact same way.

"HUH?!" "WHUH?!" We simultaneously screamed, pointed at each other, and closed our mouths. *Ack, too loud! Lyon and Olga could've heard that…*

"What the heck are you doing out here?!"

"That's my line! Didn't ya return to Belfast?" *No, no, no! Me being here is way less unusual than a king walking around without anyone accompanying him!* His Beastliness, King of Mismede, lowered his voice and spoke to me.

"Well, ya know… I like leaving the castle and taking a walk now and then. Also, I recently heard about a buncha thugs who think they're hot stuff, so I came to beat them up." *You came out to beat thugs? Seriously? What kind of king does that…? I'm sorry, Chancellor Glatz… This man clearly just does whatever he wants.*

"Wh-Wha—?!" *Oh, guess Arma finally realized who it is she bumped into. That's right, they did both attend that party a while back… Guess they know each other.*

His Beastliness put his finger against his mouth to tell her to be quiet, which made Arma put both of her hands over her mouth.

Yumina, who came a moment later, also recognized the beastking. However, Sue, Leim and the escort knights weren't familiar with him, so they assumed he was simply an acquaintance.

"So what're you guys doing out here anyways?"

"Well, if we have to answer that question… we're tailing someone." I tried to be as honest as I could get. His Beastliness tilted his head slightly while I took out my smartphone and pinpointed where the two had gone off to. They were in a park a short distance ahead. Looked like they were sitting on a bench.

Once again, we hid behind the corner of a building as we kept an eye on them. We could easily see them from where we were.

"That's… Olga and the young Belfastian knight. Bwahah, I see… So that's what it's all about, eh?"

"Nothing more, nothing less." His Beastliness joined us for some reason, so I told him to be quiet.

Probably wasn't the best way to deal with a king, but we've been pretty friendly ever since our battle. Though, it might've had something to do with me being engaged to Yumina.

The presence of a king usually forced people of lesser standings to abase themselves. However, with him being such a candid guy and a bit of a meathead — or, er, a man ruled by instinct — he probably didn't care about me being so buddy-buddy with him.

As I shifted my attention back to Lyon — still sitting on the bench — I saw him try to casually yawn and put his arm around her shoulder, only to end up failing and looking really awkward. Clearly, that was too high of a hurdle for him. Then again, he couldn't even hold her hand.

"Oh dear."

"This hurts to watch…"

"Get a grip, damn it!"

"Well, you can't really say it's not like him…" The whispering of the knights behind me made me grin.

"Bwaha… this is pretty sad. When I was young, men were more straightforward. I'll have you know that I—" Right as His Beastliness began talking about himself, things suddenly got rowdy a short distance ahead of the bench Lyon and Olga sat on.

I looked over to see a few men destroying one of the nearby stalls. The man who looked like the owner was being beaten up by a number of rough-looking hoodlums.

It clearly wasn't a simple squabble. The owner was the victim of a one-sided attack.

"Enough of that!" Lyon ran over to them. As befitted a Belfastian knight, he couldn't stomach the vile assault happening right before his eyes.

He sure has a strong sense of justice... Well, when you consider who his father is, it makes sense. Leon probably punched him every time he did something wrong.

"How about you back off and mind your own business, shithead."

"You will let that man go. I don't know what's going on here, but you will leave him alone. Who are you to gang up on and attack a man like this? Cowards. Have you no shame?!" *Whoa, he's so cool! What happened to that sad loser who couldn't even hold hands just before?!*

Since it was a day off, Lyon wasn't in his knightly outfit. The thugs probably thought that he was just a random guy with a sense of justice.

On top of that, they clearly had the advantage of higher numbers. There was no reason for them to back down.

"...What're the odds that those are the thugs you were looking for?"

"Pretty high. Pretty high indeed." There were more than twenty of them. All of them were beastmen, too. Lyon was weaponless, so it was clearly too much for him to handle by himself. Some of them were even wielding blades.

"Mind your damned business, human scum. I don't poke my nose into your shit, do I?!"

"Whether you're a human or a beastman is completely irrelevant here, cur. What you're doing is lowly and despicable, regardless of race!"

"Grr... what'd you just say?!" One of the beastmen ran to Lyon with a closed fist ready for a punch. The knight evaded the blow with a smooth movement of his upper body and hastily retaliated with a punch into his foe's stomach.

As the man fell to the ground, the hoodlums readied their weapons.

"Bastard! Get him, boys!" With that, they began to swarm Lyon.

This doesn't look good… They've got him totally outnumbered.

"Sue! Throw me a mask! One of the ones you bought earlier!" I took the fox mask from Leim and put it on. *Alright, this should do as a disguise.*

I looked to my side and realized that the beastking was nowhere to be found. *Where'd he go…?*

"Guah?!"

"Wh-Who the hell are you?! Where did you come from?!"

"Geheheh, I'm just a helping hand for this here lad. Prepare yourself, vermin!"

"I don't know who you are, masked stranger, but I'm thankful for your aid!" The beastking had already entered the fray. Donning the cat mask, he jumped in and blasted one of the ruffians away. *He's using* [**Accel**]! I quickly put on the fox mask, jumped out from behind the building and kicked one of the thugs in the back.

"Th-There are even more of these weirdos?!" *I'm not a "weirdo," thank you very much…* I could totally see why he said it, though.

One of the beastmen tried to punch me, so I grabbed his arm and used his momentum to throw him into the ground. As I threw a punch into his solar plexus, I evaded a knife thrown by another criminal.

In the midst of such a melee, one had to be careful not to let anyone come from behind. Focus was key, always try to keep as many enemies in sight as possible.

I hadn't expected Yae's teachings to come in handy so soon. That being said, the mask I was wearing definitely didn't help me with the "sight" part.

I looked to the side and saw His Beastliness, still masked, smash into a couple of beastmen with apparent glee. It didn't seem like the restricted sight even got in his way. He just looked like he was relieving stress. *Better just to leave him to it.*

Lyon, too, was fighting with great ferocity. As expected of a Belfastian knight, he was strong even without a weapon.

*This would be much easier if I could use [***Paralyze***] or something. But I don't want to run the risk of Lyon or Olga getting suspicious. I can't even use [***Slip***], this sucks...*

Well, it's not like small fry like these guys can't be beaten without spells.

As one of the hoodlums slashed at me with a knife, I knocked it out of his grip with a right hook and used a left swipe to smack him in the face. They really were pathetic. Standard thugs had no chance against seasoned knights and adventurers, after all. In the end, they were nothing more than scumbags who were only good at bullying weaker people.

It only took a few moments for us to defeat the whole lot. The last one was downed by Lyon.

"Did we go overboard?"

"Bwahaha... probably! Does it matter? Even if it does, these guys totally have a criminal record. We did nothing wrong." *Hrm... we were the ones that started it, though. Then again, if the most powerful man in the country says it's fine, who am I to disagree?*

I glanced at Lyon to see him staring at me. *Huh? What is it?*

"...You're Sir Touya, aren't you?"

"Whuh?! How did you—?!" I slammed my hand over my mouth, but it was too late. *How did he figure it out?!*

"Well, you are the only person I've ever seen who wears a coat like that. And I'm familiar with your voice." *Crap. Why did I even think this would work?!* That coat of mine was a one-of-a-kind I bought from Berkut. There was no other coat like it. *I should've taken it off before the battle began.*

"Lyon! Are you okay?!" Olga ran over to Lyon. She took his hand, making him turn red and flustered. He began to repeatedly assure her that he was quite fine.

She must've been in a panic too, given that she'd disposed of formalities and taken to just calling him "Lyon."

"Gahaha… it's high time to call the guards and hand these losers over to them! Actually, someone mighta called some already…" Olga slightly tilted her head and looked in my direction. Though, not directly at me, but at the one who just spoke.

"Your… Beastliness?" The old man in the cat mask suddenly went stiff. *Oh, I totally forgot. The mask is enough to fool Lyon, but Olga, being a Beastgirl, can recognize us by smell. Whoa, whoa. I can see an unnatural amount of sweat beading out from underneath that cat mask, old man! You're probably panicking hard because the chancellor's gonna find out about this, aren't you?*

"…[Accel]." His Beastliness activated the acceleration spell and swooshed away from us in a blink of an eye. *H-Hey! Don't just leave me here!* Right as I was about to use [Accel] and follow after him, Lyon grabbed me by the shoulder.

"Ah, ah, ah, Sir Touya. Where do you think you're going? We have something to talk about."

"Well, this is kind of accidental and also not. We saw you two, decided to help you out with kindling your passion for Olga and we got a bit carried away, so— **OWOWOW!** You're hurting my shoulder! Olga, help me out here!" I somehow escaped from Lyon's death grip and hid behind Olga. Standing between us, she looked straight at Lyon.

I piped up again, this time more forcefully.

"Lyon, it's your own darned fault for not making it clear, you know?! You have to say it loud and clear to make her understand! Do you like her?!"

"Wha—?! Of course I do! I couldn't like her more if I tried! I honestly believe women as great as her just don't exist! Cross my heart and hope to die!"

"So you're saying you want to have a serious relationship with her, right?!"

"Of course I am!" Leaving himself to the flow, Lyon finally made it clear.

Good man. That's what I wanted to hear!

"...Well, you heard him."

"A-Ah..." Lyon shifted his gaze away from me and toward Olga, who was right by my side. Her face was beet red. Lyon had professed his feelings. Now it was Olga's turn...

As she carefully chose her words, Lyon became stiff with fear. I moved closer to Olga and whispered into her ear.

"Don't make it vague. Say either 'I feel the same' or 'I'm sorry, but I don't feel that way.' Okay?" Her fox ears twitched a bit as she turned even redder. However, she was still able to word a proper answer.

"I-I feel the same..."

"Huh...? U-Uhm... S-So, you want to... go out with me...?!"

"Yes." Olga smiled a bashful smile.

Lyon's expression quickly went from worried to overjoyed, and a moment later, he let his emotions explode.

"H-HOORAY!!!" Overwhelmed by glee, he threw his fist into the air.

Seeing that, Olga smiled yet again.

Heheheh… just as I had planned… Well, no. I hadn't actually planned any of that at all. But it all worked out in the end. Whatever the case, it's pretty clear that the two needed something to happen or they'd have been stuck in limbo forever.

The knights all came forward and erupted into thunderous applause.

"You did it, Lyon!"

"Thanks!"

"Lad, you're getting better at this! Nice work!"

"Well, what can I say, hahahah!"

"You're making me jealous, damn it!"

"Haha, don't worr— Wait, when did you guys get here?" Lyon looked at his fellow knights, who were now patting him on the back.

From the expression they made when Lyon asked them that, it was safe to assume they ran out of hiding without thinking things through.

"Good job, sis!"

"A-Arma?! Why are you here?!" Apparently, the innocent little sister was so happy for her sibling that she couldn't help but come out and express it as well. Taken in by the flow of the situation, Yumina, Sue, Kohaku and Leim also came out and showed themselves.

The two — finally realizing that their date was observed — suddenly glared at me. Absolute terror engulfed the core of my being.

"Sir Touya! Explain yourself at once!" They yelled at me in unison, both red as beets. *Wait, why are you acting like I was the mastermind behind this?!* Though they were probably just hiding their embarrassment, Olga and Lyon began scolding me. *This isn't fair! This isn't fair at all!*

Seriously, I'm your cupid, you stupid lovebirds! If anything, I should be thanked!

Anyway, that was how the two began a serious relationship. They had regular letter exchanges over their gate mirrors, and on Lyon's days off, he occasionally asked me to open a [Gate] to Mismede.

Of course, he made a point out of telling me not to follow them again.

The day after, His Beastliness, King of Mismede got a heavy scolding from Chancellor Glatz. Or so I heard from Lyon, who was told by Olga.

If only that was enough to make the beastking stop leaving the castle unauthorized. But I knew in my heart it wouldn't be nearly enough.

I could only send positive vibrations out into the universe, and hope they'd give strength to poor old Chancellor Glatz.

"Slime castle?" With a stern expression on his face, the old man — the mayor of a small village named Zeryll — told us about the place.

After moving to the capital, we had taken on a lot of quests. Even though I had quite a lot of money, a life without work wasn't the kind of life I wanted, so we decided to take a quest or two every few days or so.

That's how we found ourselves at the village. There was a monster situation that needed investigation, so Elze, Linze, Yae, Yumina, Kohaku, and I all made our way to this little place north of the capital. We got there in only two days and asked the mayor for further details.

It wasn't hard to sum up what he told us.

There was an old fortress not so far from the village. Even though it was run-down and ancient, it recently received a new owner — a wizard, to be precise.

He had a strange obsession with monster research, with his focus being Slimes.

Most of the villagers were freaked out by the weirdo in the castle and never made any effort to get close to him, but the wizard himself started visiting the village and buying food or things necessary for research.

However, ten or so years ago, the wizard stopped making his trips entirely. The villagers began gossiping. Some said he succumbed to an illness, others spoke that he got eaten by a Slime that left no bones behind, while some even claimed that he cursed himself and transformed into a Slime.

Uneasy about the presence of such a castle near their village, the people hired adventurers to investigate it.

But the adventurers that went to the castle would always return ragged, say that they failed, refused to give any details, and leave quickly as if running away from something…

"Did they ever say anything notable, though?"

"Mostly things like 'The wizard in that castle is rotten to the core.' They'd often say something like that with a disgusted tone and just take their leave after that…" Such messages would leave the villagers even more worried. It got so bad that some would panic just by seeing the smallest Slime in the forest.

I distinctly recalled the guild's field guide saying that Slimes almost never attacked humans. Though, there were some dangerous ones, like the carnivorous Slimes that could melt flesh, Venom Slimes, or Lava Slimes.

All-in-all, there were many kinds of Slimes, and keeping track of them all was difficult. Many said that the dangerous ones had strong coloring, but that still wasn't an absolute rule.

"That is why I want a party to go out and investigate the castle again…"

"I see." I threw a glance at the rest of my party and saw them all — including Yumina — looking really uncomfortable.

Slimes weren't exactly popular among women. That was because of the nature of the little monsters. Though there were some flesh-melting Slimes, most Slimes weren't able to melt anything but clothes. And many required a lot of time and effort to do so.

Among such were those which, instead of liking meat, developed a taste for clothing.

Green Slimes were particularly infamous for this. They really loved clothing made from plant fiber and didn't hesitate to melt and feed on any sort of apparel. It had quite a strange diet, honestly. For example, even though they ate paper and cloth, they didn't have any taste for processed wood or actual plants.

When faced with a Green Slime, female adventurers often ended up with melted clothing, but weapons and armor intact. These were quite the wonderf— Er, humiliating situations. Of course, men faced the exact same risks…

No adventurer worth his salt would ever leave such troublesome Slimes to act as they wished.

"Very well! We will accept this task."

"Ugh…" The girls expressed their disapproval with a united groan. *I expected this!*

"Do you intend to let these villagers live under the iron fist of fear?! Is that what we adventurers do?! Nay! I say we do not!"

"But… someone else could do it, too…" Elze pouted as she talked back to me. *Won't take much to wear them down if I put on a little bravado…* Raising my hand, I adopted my most serious look.

"If one of the dangerous Slimes left the castle and attacked the village, we would regret it our whole lives. Don't you think so?"

"T-Touya-dono… that is true, it is… but…" Yae folded her arms and tilted her head with a pensive expression. Linze wasn't too perturbed by the situation, though. Slimes had an extremely strong resistance to slashing, piercing, and crushing attacks, but had next to no resistance to magic.

So, unlike Elze and Yae, who weren't casters, Linze had a way to fight back. Still, she wasn't too keen on the idea of going headfirst into a hive of the creatures.

The other caster in our team, Yumina, wasn't panicking either. However, she was piercing me with suspicious eyes.

"...Touya, are you thinking of something inappropriate?"

"Wh-What are you saying?! Are you stupid?! I have no such thoughts on my mind!" *I'm being mostly honest, at least! A part of me does have something else in mind, I'll admit it! But it's also true that we can't just leave the villagers like this.*

Yumina's gaze made a cold sweat drip down my head, but she eventually sighed and looked down in resignation.

"I suppose we have no choice. It's not something that we can ignore, and though unlikely, if Touya's nightmare 'Slimes destroy the village' scenario becomes reality, we would never be able to live this down. It would affect my father's reputation, too." If something like that actually happened, there might be people who'd begin spreading slander about a princess who ignored the pleas of the people and left a village to destruction just to protect her own skin.

Not like anyone around there besides the party knew that she was this country's princess, though. Then again, if they did somehow found it out, we wouldn't have any counter-arguments.

And even if the entire world forgave her, she would never forgive herself. That's the kind of girl Yumina was. Proud and sincere.

"H-Hmm... I suppose we have to do this, we do..."

"Bah... I really don't like this at all, y'know..." With Yumina — the youngest in the group — being willing to go, Yae and Elze couldn't let themselves bail on us. They reluctantly nodded, almost teary-eyed. *YES!* I celebrated internally.

"Did you say something, Touya?"

"I-I SAID NOT A THING!"

"Is that so...?" As Linze glared at me suspiciously, I forced myself to adopt my default facial expression.

Come to think of it, there might actually be really dangerous Slimes out there... I have to be on the lookout for Slimes I've never seen before.

...Green Slimes get a pass, though.

The castle was on a hill about half a day's walk away from the village.

Though small, it was just about good enough to function as a living space. However, with the walls ruined, it had no chance of being a proper fortress or anything.

We passed through the small gate and entered the courtyard.

To the right, I could see a bergfried-styled tower. It was connected to the residential building below. That was where people would've lived, while the tower was just a lookout. Anything below was for dungeons and the like... In normal castles like this, anyway.

"This place is super creepy..." Elze whispered while restlessly looking around.

Just as she said, it was damp and sodden. Clearly not the best place to live in. The courtyard, overrun with weeds, had several puddles here and there.

As we observed our surroundings, one of the puddles changed shape and began moving.

"Whoa!" My surprised voice made the puddle run away into the grass.

"The water moved, it did...!"

"That's no water. It's a Slime." *A Water Slime, to be precise.* They camouflaged themselves as water and captured any prey unfortunate enough to come close. Though dreadful, they were cowardly and never attacked creatures bigger than themselves. These Slimes always opted to flee, so they weren't much of a threat to humans.

"S-So there are Slimes here, then..."

"Let's be careful as we go. We don't know what else this place might have." I listened to Linze and Yumina as I walked on the damp ground and passed through the entrance arch.

We soon reached a large double door. I gently pushed it slightly open and created a small gap.

I looked inside to see daylight coming in through a window, lighting up what seemed to be an entrance hall. There was an old carpet on the floor, and on the sides, I could see sets of stairs that led to the second floor. It didn't seem like there were any Slimes there, at least not to my naked eye.

I cautiously walked inside.

"Seems like it's safe. You guys can come insi—" Before I could call them over, a shockwave rocked through my head and I heard a great sound reverberate through the hall.

"Damn it, that hurts!" It didn't hurt as much as the sound would make you expect, but pain is pain. Something fell from above and landed straight on my head.

The thing that fell on me bounced off and began to spin on the carpet at my feet.

A metal pot…?

An actual metal pot fell straight on my head just now? WHAT THE HELL IS THIS?! SOME KIND OF COMEDY ROUTINE?!

"A-Are you okay, Touya?"

"Yeah, I'm fine… It hurt a little bit, though." Linze got worried about me, so I just waved my hand to signal that I was okay. It hurt, but not all that much.

The people in old comedy skit shows had wigs with metal in them, the metal pots themselves were relatively soft, and the height was kinda low, so it was quite safe for them to have stuff dropped on them during the skits.

But modern metal basins were hard and dangerous, so many major performers warned people about trying to recreate such skits. I remember reading about it on the internet once. Even in an entirely different world, painful things were still painful.

I'm pretty sure fantasy worlds don't have any broadcast variety shows, so why would a metal pot from a popular Japanese skit of all things come down on my head...?

"Touya! The pot!"

"Huh...?" Yumina pointed at the metal basin, which changed shape into a lead-colored Slime and scuttled away from the entrance hall.

"That was a Slime, too...?"

"I've never seen or heard about a Slime like this. This may even be a new species..." *If Linze is right about that, did the wizard actually create it? Wait, what kind of use would a Slime that does that even have?*

There are wizards who had Slimes as familiars, so maybe this one works for him directly... I took out my smartphone, ran a search for "human" and didn't get any hits for anyone except us. It seemed the guy was no longer in the castle. I couldn't tell if he had just left or actually died, though.

We went through the door on the right side of the hall, split up and started examining every room connected to the corridor. Most of them were completely derelict.

"The only thing left of the books are the covers. I suppose the Slimes ate them." In one of the rooms — likely the study — Yumina picked up one of the dusty book covers. Paper was also made out of plant fiber, after all. There could've been some Green Slimes nearby.

"Th-This book isn't melted." Linze took out one of the books from the remains of the bookshelf. It looked more like a set of notes than an actual book. It seemed to be made from parchment and displayed some unintelligible symbols. I could only assume it was written in Ancient Magic Script.

"Do modern wizards still use Ancient Magic Script?"

"I-I hear they do it when they deal with research and results they wish to hide..." *Likely to prevent their secrets from being stolen, then. After all, these texts are useless to people that can't read them.*

Linze put her hand in her pouch and took out the pair of translation glasses I had given her a while ago. They were imbued with **[Reading],** a translation spell, and specified to enable the reading of Ancient Magic Script.

"This is... The log of his research results. Just as I had thought. It describes the natures of various Slimes... The Slime from before is here, as well."

"The thing that fell on me? What does it say?"

"Uhm... 'Metal Pot Slime. Takes on the shape of a metal pot and has a tendency to fall on people. This experiment was a complete failure.' That's all it says..." *Wow, I actually learned nothing from that! What an annoying Slime!* There were many more Slimes in those notes, so Linze continued to read with great curiosity. Every now and then, her expression turned sour, likely because of a particularly vile Slime.

"Let's take those notes with us. They could prove useful."

"You're right."

When we finished examining that room and began heading out to the corridor, we suddenly heard a thud from the other room.

The ones examining that room were Yae and Elze. We hastily ran to see that nothing bad had happened to them, but they walked out before we could enter. The two were rubbing their faces. Kohaku peeked out, too, looking slightly uncomfortable.

"O-Ouch… they caught me off guard, they did…"

"What happened?"

"One of those damn Slimes was camouflaged as the floor… And when we stepped on it…"

"It trapped us both like an adhesive and made us fall face first… We hit right onto the floor, we did…" Yae explained the details, rubbing her reddened nose all the while. *Again, eh? The Slimes here have some really annoying attack patterns.*

This is probably why the previous adventurers came back so battered.

"I've found it in the notes. It says 'Birdlime Slime. Can camouflage and has a high adhesiveness. Cannot be used effectively due to its inflated cgo. This experiment was a complete failure.' Another failure, then…" *Was the wizard failing on purpose or something?!*

There didn't seem to be anything else of interest on that side, so we decided to go back to the hall.

We opened the door to the hall, and when I took a step forward, a frustrating impact spread throughout my head and revived a recent pain.

"GOD. DAMN IT." I held my head and crouched down. The metal pot on the floor turned into a Slime and squirmed away from me again.

"Hold still, you little bastard!" At the limit of my patience, I took out my gunblade — Brunhild — and fired a few shots at the Metal Pot Slime. Unfortunately, the stupid thing smoothly evaded my bullets and escaped to the corridor on the other side.

Fast metal Slimes have no business existing out of video games!

"Are you okay, Touya? It sounded pretty bad."

"Ghh… It's… nothing I can't handle." The second hit hurt more, obviously. *I won't let you escape before this day is through, you little bastard.*

I stood up while rubbing my head.

Suddenly, at the end of the entrance hall, I saw a Green Slime.

I knew you'd be around here. After I saw those eaten-up book pages, I knew it'd only be a matter of time.

"There's a Slime over there. Watch out."

"Oh crap, that's a Green Slime, too. It won't kill us, but man, is it bad news…" Elze expressed her disapproval. Green Slimes only melted clothes, so dying to them was extremely improbable, but that didn't stop them from being a great threat to girls.

"Your coat can't be melted, right, Touya?"

"Yep. That's because it's imbued with magic resistance. The clothes under it would melt, though."

I have to make sure that doesn't happen. I don't want to be seen as some kind of pervert who only prances around in a coat.

Guess it's time to investigate the second floor.

"Uhm… the Green Slime…" While I was considering a few things internally, Linze suddenly tugged at my coat.

I looked over to the other side of the hall, where I saw a gathering of many Green Slimes.

"Whoa there… what the heck?!" One was fine, but several tens of Green Slimes made me a bit scared.

"Burst forth, Fire! Crimson Eruption: [Explo—]!"

"Linze, wait! Using explosive magic here is dangerous!" I stopped her from finishing the spell. *This is an old fortress, Linze…! The whole place could go down if you made even one big blast.*

Regardless of my reservations, the Green Slimes continued their slow, slimy crawl toward us.

"Come forth, Fire! Crimson Duet: [Fire Arrow]!" The fiery bolt she released hit a Green Slime and lit it on fire. However, the other Green Slimes merely avoided their burning brother and continued their slow march.

Yumina and I assisted with some shots, but normal bullets were ineffective. Elze and Yae couldn't help if they tried, and though our lives weren't in any danger, the situation was looking pretty bad.

"Kohaku!"

"Fret not." Kohaku transformed back into his true form and released a powerful shockwave from his maw. The Green Slimes were blown away, but the stony wall began to shake wildly. *Crap, this is too risky as well...*

To top it off, the Slimes seemed relatively unharmed. They regrouped and closed in on us like a green swamp.

"Hey! They're still coming closer!"

"Let's hide on the second floor for now!" We began running up the stairs to the side of the entrance hall. For some reason, the Green Slimes didn't try to come up after us. They just stopped and gently shook like jelly.

"...What is the meaning of this, Linze-dono?"

"Perhaps this fortress is split into many territories?"

"Doesn't matter. We're safe now, and that's all that matters." As we took a breather on the landing in the middle of the stairs, something was slowly closing in on us.

The realization hit me way too late. If the first floor was the territory of the Green Slimes, it was only natural for the stairs to be another Slime's territory, too.

"Let's just go up for now. We should get as far away from these gross things as possible and... eek!" As Elze tried to go up the stairs, she fell down on her behind. As we tried to figure out what was wrong, we noticed that the soft carpet on the stairs was somewhat damp.

"Hey! What the heck?! It's so slimy!" Elze accidentally touched the carpet and raised her hands to us. They were covered in a gooey, sticky liquid.

"Ah, it is over there, it is!" Yae pointed to the top of the stairs, where there was a semi-transparent Slime that looked like kuzumochi, one of those little chilled jelly desserts.

Its most noticeable characteristic was that it had leaked some fluid over the stairs. *Guess we know why the carpet's so damp.*

"Linze, what do the notes say about this one?"

"It says 'Lotion Slime. When in danger, it secretes a liquid similar to lubricant. Almost entirely harmless. This experiment was a complete failure...'" As she read it, Linze's tone turned sour... I could totally understand her.

"Kyah!!!"

"Ugh!" Elze tried to get up, slipped, and fell once again. But this time, she grabbed me by my coat and dragged me down along with her.

"A-Are you okay, Touya, ahh!"

"Hhawah!"

"Oh no!" Yumina tried to run over to me, and fell over, too. Moments later, Linze and Yae got caught up, as well. Heck, even Kohaku couldn't escape it. We all gained enough momentum to drop down to the bottom.

"Hyaaaaagh!!" We slid down the stairs, straight into a vile pool of green.

With a resounding splash, we were engulfed by Green Slime.

"Ghah!!"

"Kyah!"

"Auuugh!"

"This isn't happeningggg…!!"

"Noooooo!"

"Grr…!!" The first ones to escape the unpleasant sea of goo were Kohaku and I.

Kohaku grabbed me by the nape of my neck and took me back to the landing in the middle of the stairs with a single leap. But we slipped on the lotion again.

"Growlll…?!"

"Ow!" Kohaku let me go, and I fell flat on my back.

"Apologies, Master…"

"I-It's fine. I'm alright." I shook my aching head and I tried to stand up, only to almost fall once again. I probably looked really miserable as I did it, but I was able to stand up by supporting myself with the staircase's railing. *Damn it. They slimed me.*

"Nooo!! Help me!"

"T-Touya!"

"Don't worry, I'm coming!" *Think, Touya! Saying that's fine, but what can you do?! Wait… if the Green Slimes can't come up the stairs…*

"[Gate]!" I opened up a portal just beneath them. All of them — Slimes included — fell through it, exiting the corresponding portal I'd made in the open space one meter above the stair landing next to me.

The Slimes, forced onto the landing, backed away like a wave, slithering back down to the entrance hall.

Aha, so they are territorial creatures.

"Is everyone oka—" I was unable to finish my sentence.

Their clothes weren't in the best condition, to say the least. Seemed like the Green Slimes had gotten to chew on their fabric a little. Honestly, the girls all looked pretty unladylike.

I could see several spots of exposed skin here and there, shining bewitchingly thanks to the lotion on the stairs. The Green Slimes got busy enough to allow the girls' panties to peek out, too. It wouldn't have been far off to call them half-naked.

"Kyaaahhh! Don't look!"

"Ghuah?!" Elze punched me in the face with a gauntlet-clad fist. *Argh, that hurts!* She used her other arm to cover her chest. As my consciousness faded, I caught a glimpse of a light-red bra, but what I saw after that was nothing but stars. *Ah, the world is spinning.*

Why didn't their underwear melt…? Wait, silk… silk isn't a plant fiber, right? I think… I'll just leave it at that…

If only they'd bought cheaper garments… it could've melted too— No, no… don't think that… Even though my heart had secretly yearned for such an event, I had trouble deciding what to do after it had actually happened.

After I woke up, I faced away from the girls and glared at the Lotion Slime.

"Come forth, Fire! Crimson Duet: [Fire Arrow]!" The fiery bolt hit the gooey creature dead-on. The Slime burst and released a gas that resembled steam.

All that was left was to climb up to the second floor.

Slowly, making sure not to slip, we clambered up the stairs on all fours. We made sure to carefully calculate every movement. If we overdid it, we'd slip, but if we didn't move enough, we'd slip too.

Man, I had no idea [Slip] was such a cruel spell. Now that I'm on the receiving end, I don't like it one bit.

Calmly, cautiously, step by step, we traveled upward. We were in no rush. The tension was stronger than it had any right to be.

Soon enough, I began hearing some complaints behind me.

"Ah… I really liked that clothing too…"

"Awh… more than half of my skirt melted away…"

"Th-They wore away at my sarashi, they did! Th-This is terrible, it is!"

"This gross goo made my underwear see-through, I hate this so damn much!!"

"Wha—?!" I was too focused on the words behind me to realize that my footing was off, and I slipped down. *How can I focus on being safe if you're all talking about stuff like that, huh?! Show a little consideration!*

"Uwaaaaaah!!!" The momentum made me slip past the landing (the girls dodged me) and land straight on the first floor, where the Green Slimes awaited me. Thus, I paid another visit to the green swamp. *Holy shit, my life has actually turned into a comedy skit. I need to get out of here! I— Oh, wait.*

"[Gate]!" Just like before, I easily opened a portal. Except this time it was straight to the top, Slimes and all. *I should've done this from the start…*

Once again, the Green Slimes backed away like an ocean wave.

Thankfully — if that word was appropriate — I only ended up with my pants becoming shorts, and my shirt turning into the kind with an exposed midriff.

I opened a [Gate] on the landing, and another one just a few meters away on the second floor, letting the girls get up there with no problem. And that's how we escaped our sticky hell.

The four of them went straight into a nearby room. *They're probably gonna sort out their clothes.* I wasn't allowed in, of course. So I stood guard outside.

I could hear sounds of fabric being torn apart. I assumed they were shredding curtains or something to patch up their clothes. Getting back home and changing into new clothes wasn't a problem thanks to my [Gate] spell, but I just figured they didn't want to risk having their other outfits melted too.

While I waited, I killed time by using [Fire Arrow] to snipe some of the Green Slimes on the bottom floor. Something like [Fire Storm] would've been more effective, but I felt that using that kind of spell indoors wasn't wise.

The four finally left the room. Just as I had expected, they were covered in pieces of torn curtains — one for the upper and lower halves on all of them. They could actually move around, too, so that was a plus.

"...Any Green Slime we see next is getting crushed." The girls nodded in unison at Elze's proclamation. Well, I could see why they were so eager. A part of me was slightly disappointed, but I decided to keep that to myself.

And so we began exploring the second floor, only to find more of the same — a display of strange Slimes.

We found a bizarrely elastic Rubber Slime.

A spiky Needle Slime that didn't let anyone touch it.

A Light Slime that did nothing but glow.

And a slightly electric Shock Slime.

While they weren't too dangerous, they were still monsters that could cause trouble. There was no telling what kind of mutations they could create if they merged.

"So, the wizard wanted to create a very specific sort of Slime and made many failures on the way, right?"

"S-Seems that way, yes. He couldn't know the nature of the Slimes before they were born, so luck played a big part in it." Linze answered my question while looking at the research notes.

Slimes were magical creatures. One might even call them artificial, since they began as a species as a by-product of human magic.

That was exactly why there was no guarantee that they couldn't end up being dangerous. I had no idea how they multiplied, but I heard that Slimes could create new types of Slimes by consuming other Slimes.

This castle had the potential of creating dangerous, unknown creatures. For all we knew, the castle could already be housing Slime types that had evolved naturally, rather than by the wizard's will.

"I feel like we should just burn them all down, along with the castle itself... a purge, y'know?"

"I share the sentiment, I do. But is it really okay to do something like that?"

"The fortress is already abandoned, and I doubt my father would mind..." I could hear some dangerous talk behind me.

Well, with this level of Slime infestation, it wasn't exactly a place we could just leave alone. Even if we didn't do it, the country's knights or army would band up and eradicate everything here anyway.

We finished exploring the second floor. All that was left was the third one. We carefully made our way up. There could've easily been another Slime waiting with a trap, after all. Safety was the name of the game.

Once we reached the wide corridor of the third floor, we were greeted by a wall of plaster busts lined up on either side. All of them were in the shape of naked women. Not only that, but they all seemed to have strangely large breasts, too.

"What is this...?"

"Hey, why are you asking me?" As I listened to Yumina exhale a cold sigh at all the nude statues, I couldn't prevent my gaze from falling on to their breasts. Like all men, I was but a slave to my nature.

Most had pretty large ones, but one had a pair of bazookas so huge it bordered on enormous.

"Hm…?"

"What is wrong, Touya-dono?"

"Nothing… maybe. I think I saw one of the boobs move…" Everyone looked at me like I was a lunatic. I could even feel a hint of disgust at my wild imagination or something.

I'm not kidding! I totally saw those boobs sway!

In an attempt to confirm it, I reached for the voluptuous breast of the statue.

"Touya, that's…" Linze started saying, clearly disappointed in me.

"S-So you like them big…" Elze said, as if a sad fact had dawned on her.

"A-Are you frustrated in that regard, Touya-dono?"

"That's slightly disturbing…" Yumina muttered.

C'mon you guys, that stings. Well, I couldn't deny that I looked like a weirdo and a pervert to any third party.

I touched the left breast of the statue with my right hand.

It was squishy.

"It's soft?!"

The girls shrieked in disbelief. *Whoa, it's seriously squishy… squidgy… heh… squashy.*

What the heck?! This feels amazing! I got caught up in the moment and fondled the soft boob in my hand. Then the set of breasts fell to the ground.

"Hwah?!" I made a weird noise. *Holy crap that scared me!* The breasts suddenly lost their statue-like color and transformed into a skin-colored Slime. *Camouflage, huh…*

Without the Slime, the statue's breasts were slightly smaller than those of the other ones.

"'Bust Slime. It fixes itself to female chests and camouflages itself. Tends to aim for smaller chests. I'm getting close, but this experiment was still a failure.'" Linze's voice as she read the description was less "disgusted" and more "emotionless." That was only natural.

The Bust Slime slowly made its way toward Yumina. *Err... what should I do here...*

"**...Shred, o Wind. A Thousand Blades Born of the Gale: [Cyclone Edge].**" The windy blades Yumina unleashed tore the Slime into a thousand pieces. *Whoa...*

"...Growth period."

"Huh?"

"I'm still in my growth period."

"O-Oh, right..." Yumina's whisper caught me off guard. *Awkward...* Considering her age, it was only natural she'd be... small in that regard, so I hoped she wouldn't mind it too much.

I checked the other statues, and it seemed like there was only one Bust Slime.

We gathered our wits, walked through the third floor's corridor and entered the large room at the end.

It was extremely dim inside. The room seemed like the place where the master of the castle would come just to calm down. Before stepping in, I made sure to look up. *That Metal Pot Slime... isn't here. Good.*

The first thing I saw inside the stuffy room was a large couch with a skeleton on it.

There was a wizard-like robe on the floor as well. The Green Slimes hadn't come here to eat it, probably because it wasn't their territory. *So this is all that's left of the Slime-researching wizard, eh.*

Wait, why did he take off his pants and underwear? Was he getting ready for a bath or something? "Do you think this is the old wizard, then?"

"Probably." I couldn't help but wonder whether it was a natural death or if he had succumbed to Slimes.

If it was the latter, this castle might've already created a kind of Slime that melts humans.

…Not that they didn't exist already. Dungeons and other ruins had some of those here and there. They were often called "dungeon cleaners" because they ate just about everything.

On the table next to the couch, there was a logbook. It was almost identical to the one Linze had found earlier.

Sure enough, it was written in Ancient Magic Script, except for the very last bit.

"Uhm, let's see… 'It is done. My — no, every man's — dream became reality this day. My life is one without regrets. With this, I take off my robe and wizard hat. Ahh, I can see heaven…' What is this talking about…?"

"Touya, look!" Yumina pointed to the corner of the room, where I saw four squirming, skin-colored Slimes. They were pretty large, too. A single person could easily fit in them. *Are they the Slimes he was experimenting to create?!*

"They're transforming, they are!" *So, just like the Bust Slime, they can disguise themselves too? Wait, is this one of those generic scenarios where they all merge into one large Slime?* That didn't seem to be the case, however. The four Slimes changed shapes independently and slowly took up a humanoid form.

They're Slimes that can mimic humans?! That's seriously bad news! If they can become people, it'd be extremely easy for them to get their victims to lower their guards. Who knows what could happen if they left the castle and began to spread. We have to strike these vile things down here and n— Huh?! WHA—?!

"WHUH?!" "KYAAAAH!!!" The girls screamed in unison, louder than usual, too. As their screams rang out through the building, my eyes focused on the Slimes.

From the looks of it, these Slimes had the ability to change into what they encountered. Specifically, women.

The four Slimes took on the shapes of Yumina, Elze, Linze and Yae. They mimicked not just their skin, but even their hair and eye colors, as well.

They couldn't talk, obviously, so figuring out which was which was easy. However, if both sides were silent, it was extremely hard to tell the real from the fake. Even I didn't think I'd be able to.

… If the fakes weren't completely naked, that is.

"W-What are you looking at, Touya!"

"N-No! Stop!"

"T-Touya-dono! Look away!"

"STOP LOOKING RIGHT NOW!!" Red as tomatoes, the four screamed the same thing at me in different words. *W-Well, I can understand their feelings, but we have to defeat them and… ah shit, now my own face is turning red! How do I deal with this?! Okay, okay. They're only Slimes. They aren't the girls. Getting distracted by them is just wrong. Get it together, Touya… Wait, why the hell didn't they copy the clothes, anyway?!* I glanced at the girls and then gazed at the Slimes.

N-Naked… N-No, stop grinning! Stop grinning to yourself!

"Go to sleep."

"Augh!!" Yae hit the back of my neck with a knifehand strike. I was knocked out cold instantly.

So that was the "man's dream" the wizard wrote about. He wanted to be surrounded by naked ladies responding to his every whim and live the all-smiles harem life... For that sake alone, he spent years researching Slimes and finally made his dreams come true...

What a guy...

When I came to, the castle was burning. The raging blazes consumed it all, all the Slimes likely perished with it.

"It's a purge."

"Purge, yes..."

"A purge, it is."

"A purge." With expressions as devoid of life as porcelain masks, the four whispered as they watched the castle reduce itself to cinders.

And so ended the ambition of a certain wizard. Well, it wasn't really the end there. He had already made his desire into reality. He died at true peace with himself.

His cause of death might've actually been... no, there was no need to say it. I had to be honorable about it. Even if he *was* milked completely dry, that was likely exactly how he wanted to die.

Even though we successfully fulfilled the villagers' request, we were unable to look at each other's faces for a considerable while.

After all, it always came back to my mind... My face would turn red without fail.

And every time it happened. I said a little prayer. I sent my earnest thanks to that magnificent wizard.

Good day. It's me again, Patora Fuyuhara.

It's been only a short while since the first volume. And here you have the second one already. Isn't that amazing?

Well, it would be even better if I had anything I could write for this afterword. That's a bit of a problem here... Alright, what should I talk about...

In my mind, this work of mine is meant to be a simple, fun read with a slant toward the comedic, so there are a number of scenes made just to get a few laughs. One of the things I like to use for this purpose is [Slip]. It makes me remember something that happened to me once.

It happened when I first went to Yamagata city in the Yamagata prefecture. It was in the middle of winter. I walked down the station stairs, sentimental about finally being there. Then, when I took my first big step into the city, I slipped and fell as if I was in some kind of comedy skit.

The snowfall had made the ground icy. I was surprised by what happened to me, then I looked up and saw the people of Yamagata, walking around on the ice as if it was nothing. I honestly thought they were pretty amazing. Now that I think about it, that event might actually be what created [Slip].

Oh, damn. I was talking about something wintery, but this volume isn't coming out during the winter at all.

Anyway, here's my special thanks for this time. To Eiji Usatsuka. Thank you for the excellent dressing room scene you drew as the color illustration for this volume. I actually pumped my fist into the air when I saw the rough sketch.

To K, thank you so much for taking so many things into consideration for me.

To everyone at Hobby Japan's editorial department and everyone who took part in this and the previous book's publication, thank you all so much.

And to all those who read my work, regardless if it's this book or the web novel version, you have my deepest gratitude.

- Patora Fuyuhara

Patora Fuyuhara
illustration·Eiji Usatsuka

VOLUME 3
ON SALE
APRIL 2019!

In Another World With My Smartphone

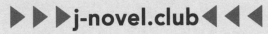

VOLUMES 1-2
ON SALE
FEBRUARY 2019!

How NOT to Summon a
Demon Lord

J-Novel Club Lineup

Ebook Releases Series List

Amagi Brilliant Park
An Archdemon's Dilemma: How to Love Your Elf Bride
Ao Oni
Arifureta Zero
Arifureta: From Commonplace to World's Strongest
Bluesteel Blasphemer
Brave Chronicle: The Ruinmaker
Clockwork Planet
Demon King Daimaou
Der Werwolf: The Annals of Veight
ECHO
From Truant to Anime Screenwriter: My Path to "Anohana" and "The Anthem of the Heart"
Gear Drive
Grimgar of Fantasy and Ash
How a Realist Hero Rebuilt the Kingdom
How NOT to Summon a Demon Lord
I Saved Too Many Girls and Caused the Apocalypse
If It's for My Daughter, I'd Even Defeat a Demon Lord
In Another World With My Smartphone
Infinite Dendrogram
Infinite Stratos
Invaders of the Rokujouma!?
JK Haru is a Sex Worker in Another World
Kokoro Connect
Last and First Idol
Lazy Dungeon Master
Me, a Genius? I Was Reborn into Another World and I Think They've Got the Wrong Idea!
Mixed Bathing in Another Dimension
My Big Sister Lives in a Fantasy World
My Little Sister Can Read Kanji
My Next Life as a Villainess: All Routes Lead to Doom!
Occultic;Nine
Outbreak Company
Paying to Win in a VRMMO
Seirei Gensouki: Spirit Chronicles
Sorcerous Stabber Orphen: The Wayward Journey
The Faraway Paladin
The Magic in this Other World is Too Far Behind!
The Master of Ragnarok & Blesser of Einherjar
The Unwanted Undead Adventurer
Walking My Second Path in Life
Yume Nikki: I Am Not in Your Dream